THE LOW ROAD

THE LOW ROAD

James Lear

CLEIS
PRESS

Published in the United States by Cleis Press Inc., P.O. Box 14697, San Francisco, California 94114.

Printed in the USA.
Cover design: Scott Idleman
Cover photograph: Louis LaSalle, www.louislasalle.com
Text design: Frank Wiedemann
Cleis logo art: Juana Alicia

ISBN-13: 978-1-61523-596-4

Chapter One

My father was a soldier, and his father before him. That's all I know about my family history, or all I am allowed to know. Since my mother and I returned to Gordon Hall a year ago, I have grown used to evasions, silences and lies on the subject.

For many years, since my late childhood, we lived out on the island of Rum, remote from the storms and alarms of the Jacobite uprising, protected by a few miles of water from the dangers of the mainland. My father, who I last saw when I was twelve, stayed at Gordon Hall, the family seat on the east bank of Loch Linnhe, where I believe he distinguished himself in the service of the Stuart cause. More than that I have been unable to discover. I know, from my mother's tearful silence on the subject, that my father is dead and that I will soon inherit Gordon Hall as head of the family. I am eighteen now, three years from my majority. Three years before I, Charles Edward Gordon, named after the rightful king now in exile, can take charge of family affairs and demand the truth.

We returned to the mainland in 1750, four years after the Battle of Culloden when my mother judged it safe to re-establish the family in its rightful home. Here we are comfortable and quiet, respected if distant members of the community, coming into contact with our neighbours at the weekly visit to the church at

Portnacroish, three miles from Gordon Hall. My only companions are my mother, my nurse Ethel – a grim-faced but good-hearted Highland woman who still treats me like a child – and a succession of female tutors, employed by my mother but regularly dismissed when, as inevitably happens, she suspects them of moral laxity. My mother fears that contact with these 'Hanoverian trollops' will corrupt me, and is constantly on the lookout for any sign of intimacy between us. I can assure her with a clear conscience that I have little interest in these girls beyond their slender grasp of Latin, algebra and, particularly, history. What I want more than anything is the company of men, but this is forbidden; my mother won't have my 'head filled with idle dreams of glory'. In this I have little choice but to obey her.

I am less able to obey my mother in other areas, however. Try as she might to stifle my curiosity, I am determined to know more about my father and his role in the glorious Revolution of 1745. I know that we were on the 'right' side, the Jacobite side, although you'd scarcely guess it from the house or its inhabitants. All trace of our historic allegiance to the Church of Rome has been purged from Gordon Hall – the exquisite little Lady Chapel gutted and converted into a grain barn, the ancestral portraits removed from the dining hall. We can't conceal our identity absolutely, and the locals know who we are – but, as my mother is at pains to point out, people forget the past quickly enough if nobody reminds them. She has even encouraged me to use my second name, Edward, in preference to the 'more inflammatory' Charles – the name my father gave me in recognition of his lord and master, Charles Edward Stuart. But even she is unsuccessful in effecting this ridiculous transformation.

Starved as I am of male company, I take pains to keep myself in readiness should the Glorious Cause claim my services. I ride daily, I run twice round the perimeter of the estate, I swim in the cold waters of Loch Linnhe, I practise my swordsmanship. This latter, I must admit, is a doomed enterprise without a proper fencing master, but my mother will allow no one even faintly resembling a soldier into the house. And so I stand before the great mirror in the hall attempting thrusts and parries with none to correct my flailings.

Fortunately I am strong by nature, happiest when outdoors, blessed with sturdy limbs and a healthy constitution. I inherited my father's looks and colouring: I have short, sandy-red hair, close-set blue eyes, a straight, rather leonine nose and a pale complexion that is prone to freckles, especially in the summer. Ethel says I still look like a schoolboy, but I am conscious of growing into manhood: my shoulders and chest are broad, my waist and hips still narrow. My backside, as I survey it in the mirror during my lonely fencing sessions, juts out like a shelf and forms a perfect hemisphere in profile.

I have said that I am surrounded entirely by women, but this is not strictly true. My sole contact with my own sex is Alexander, our groom, the only man I know who knew my father. Alexander kept the horses at Gordon Hall after Culloden, and remained in the family service ever since, tending the stables until our return from Rum. He's a quiet individual, maybe six years my senior – he must have been little more than a boy when he entered my father's service during the Uprising. Alexander greets me every morning when, shortly after dawn, I arrive at the stables to help him exercise the horses; our conversation is limited to curt exchanges on equestrian matters. I wonder sometimes whether Alexander is simple, so taciturn is he; but he alone holds a key to my past – and so I live in hope that one day he'll drop his guard. I can only assume that he's kept on at Gordon Hall under strict instructions from my mother to say nothing to me. With two ailing parents of his own, and any number of brothers and sisters to support, he's in no hurry to lose his position.

Like many of the local people, Alexander is tall and dark,

almost a different race from me. His thick black hair is cropped close to the skull; his skin is olive in colour, compared to the milky whiteness of my own. He has high cheekbones, deeply hooded eyes and a large, full mouth which, sadly for me, he keeps closed most of the time. But when he does choose to speak, he reveals a mouthful of extraordinarily white, regular teeth – a rarity in these parts, where most of the young men have lost theirs either in fights or under the tender ministrations of the dentist. Or lack thereof. His smile is as rare as sunshine on these misty lands, and just as welcome when it comes.

I have learned a good deal from Alexander. He's immensely strong, can spring on to a horse in a second, and can hold Starlight, our biggest stallion, at a rope's end. Occasionally, after a hard gallop and a quick wash at the horse trough, we've wrestled in the exercise yard; Alexander's not heavy, but he can pin me to the ground every time. The first time this happened I was fascinated by the black hair under his armpits, just inches from my face, and the patch of soft black fur on his stomach leading down into his coarse wool trousers. What little hair I have on my body – and it's all grown in the last six months – is just a shade redder than the golden hair on my head. Try as I might to initiate these enjoyable matches, Alexander usually shrugs me off with a quick twist of the arm and returns to rubbing down the sweating horses.

One morning in May, however, Alexander was in a fresh, mischievous mood – and this is where my story begins. It was a beautiful day, the mist hanging over the loch when I left the sleeping house in my suede riding breeches and white cotton shirt. The dew soaked my boots as I strode through the grass whisking the heads off a few early dandelions with my crop. I arrived at the stables just as the first shaft of lemon-yellow sunshine was breaking through, sparkling dimly on the waters and catching the steam as it spurted from the horses' nostrils. Alexander, as ever, was hard at work cleaning out the stables, humming to himself and talking to the animals as I crept silently up behind him.

'There's spring in the air, boys, and I should be out there running with you instead of shovelling shit for her ladyship,' he muttered, as I crept up the ladder that gave external access to the hayloft. Perched above the stable I watched Alexander from a new angle, occasionally seeing straight down the neck of his shirt to the firm, brown torso beneath, sometimes as far as the patch of black fur that so intrigued me. 'Where's Master Charlie?' he murmured in Starlight's ear, leaning himself against the stallion's thick grey neck. 'Still abed, the lazy little fucker, where I should like to be myself right now.' I wasn't offended; Alexander called me worse to my face when I made a blunder with the horses. But what did he mean about being in bed? Not in his own bed, surely; I knew that he shared that with two of his younger brothers. In mine, perhaps, enjoying the luxury of the big house. 'Wouldn't we have some fun, Starlight?' he said, leaning for a moment on his shovel. 'Me and Master Charlie...' He rubbed the stallion's spine where I had ridden bareback often enough. 'He's a fit little jockey, ain't he? Fit for service.'

It was the longest speech I'd ever heard Alexander utter, and I was so struck by the incongruity of the situation that, rather than betray my eavesdropping by laughter, I chose to launch myself with as much noise as possible from the loft door straight down into the soft, golden pile of hay beneath. Alexander should think I had simply run up the ladder for a prank, without knowing I had been spying before my sudden aerial entrance.

He yelled when I landed, then laughed, grabbed me by the ears and pulled me upright, hoiked me over his shoulder and ran out into the yard where he made to fling me into the trough. I could see the green, foamy water approaching at a frightening speed, and was just screwing up my eyes and mouth to endure the dunking when suddenly we stopped in our tracks. Alexander held me over his shoulder for a while then dropped me lightly on to my feet. We stood facing each other, both breathing hard. Somewhere overhead a lark was singing; the horses, excited by the burst of action and noise, were stamping in the stables. I braced myself for wrestling and made to grab Alexander by the waist, but he extended one lazy arm and kept me at bay while I swung and lunged impotently towards him. Finally he pushed a little harder and I landed hard on my arse on the damp earth, my legs splayed out straight in front of me. The shock of the landing took my breath away, and I sat for a moment gasping as Alexander stared down at me, smiling his rare, enigmatic smile.

'You're a cheeky wee fucker,' he said, his gaze boring down from beneath his heavy lids.

'And you're an insolent groom,' I said, returning the gaze and the smile. He extended a hand and pulled me to my feet. I watched the thick, corded muscles working in his forearm.

'Oh Charlie, look at the state of you. You're covered in filth.'

He was right; I'd landed straight in the mud that surrounded the horsetrough where the thirsty beasts were wont to shit and piss while they slaked their thirst. I tried to rub some of the muck off my backside, but this just made matters worse.

'Get the bloody things off, boy,' muttered Alexander. 'We'll hang them up to dry and brush them down later. I've an old pair of the master's you can borrow.'

Leaning on his strong, sinewy arm, I struggled out of my boots then, trying to avoid the stinking mud that coated the seat, primly pulled down the riding breeches until they bagged around my ankles. I must have looked ridiculous – my boots held up in one hand as I bent over, wriggling and squirming to protect myself from further soiling. From this ludicrous position I looked up to see Alexander laughing his head off. I was about to remonstrate with him (I could be a bossy little lord when I put my mind to it) when he charged me once again, threw an arm round my waist and heaved me into the air. There was little I could do; my breeches effectively bound my legs at the ankle, and my shirt had ridden up over my ears. I was conscious only of the fresh air on my bare bum, and of the heat from Alexander's arm where it encircled me.

He trotted me into the stable and dumped me face down over a bale of straw. 'Stay there, you dirty little bugger, and I'll get you cleaned up.' I freed my head from my shirt, and looked round over my shoulder. Thanks to my clumsy attempts to undress, I had smeared mud all over my buttocks and the back of my thighs. Alexander pulled off his own shirt, which I'd also managed to ruin in the process, and pulled a handful of clean, golden straw from the bale. 'Now then,' he said, 'let's see what we can do.' He started dabbing at my backside with the coarse straw; it tickled, and I squirmed. 'Stay still, will you? I can't send you back to your ma with a dirty arse.' He rubbed harder this time, removed the worst of the mud and discarded the dirty straw under the horses' feet.

'That's better. Now, let's try again.' He took a fresh handful and continued his job, rubbing my arse until it glowed with the scratching. 'Charlie, however did you get yourself into such a state?' he said. 'Look at yourself!' With one huge, calloused hand he spread my buttocks; the mud had worked its way down into the crevice between them. 'Get these off,' he said, pulling on the breeches that still constricted my ankles, 'and let the dog see the rabbit.' Between us we managed to divest me of the filthy garment; I remained kneeling over the straw bale. Alexander kicked my feet apart, spreading my legs as wide as they would go. Picking up his discarded shirt, he dunked it in a pail of water, wrung it out and dumped it on my arse. The shock of the cold water made me yell. 'Sorry, Charlie, but we'll soon have you cleaned up now.' He dabbed and scrubbed and rubbed with his soaking shirt, working it right down between my buttocks; the water ran down my thighs, over my balls and off the tip of my cock, which was pushed back between my legs and pressing against the straw. Goosepimples spread all across my arse and my legs; I felt my balls pulling up to escape another sluicing.

'Just rinse you off now, Charlie. Brace yourself.' I barely had time to look round before a pail full of cold water hit me full on. It went in my face, soaked my hair, my shirt, everything. 'There, that's better,' said Alexander as I spluttered in surprise. 'Now let's get you dry.' I was going to complain, but held my noise as he started to rub me down with a thin woollen blanket. He dried my eyes and my ears with the patience and tenderness I'd seen him lavish on the horses; he rubbed my hair a little more forcefully, pulled the soaking shirt off over my head and dried my neck, my back, my legs. Soon, thanks to the friction of the wool, I was as warm as I could wish.

Alexander seemed in no hurry to stop, and I had no desire to prevent him. His movements with the towel became slower, firmer as he dried my buttocks with extravagant care and attention. I have said that my arse formed a perfect hemisphere in profile; now, jutting up into the air with my legs spread a yard apart, it exerted some kind of fascination over Alexander. Every so often I felt the contact of his fingers as the blanket slipped aside, then, more and more, the full touch of his palm against my arse. I heard him hissing quietly, the way ostlers do when they groom a horse. Aside from that, the stable was quiet. Occasionally one of the horses stamped or snorted, a bird sang overhead. I could hear the blood thumping in my ears.

The warmth that Alexander's rubbing had imparted to my backside soon spread to my balls, which had come out of hiding and were now flopping down in their pouch. My cock, still pressed back between my legs, was responding to his ministrations by doubling in size and getting hard; pressing against the straw, I was now in a certain amount of discomfort, which I could only alleviate by pushing my backside further into the air. This freed my cock, which sprang up against my belly, making a slapping noise as it did so.

Alexander took this as a sign of encouragement, I suspect, and grabbed a buttock in each hand, kneading them roughly. New as I was to this kind of experience, I realised that a boundary had been crossed; we could no longer pretend that he was simply cleaning me up after a riding accident. Something altogether different was going on. Alexander stopped his mauling and stood bare chested, sweating slightly, rubbing a bulge in his coarse wool trousers, staring down at me with a dazed look in his eyes. I had no idea what to do, under the circumstances; half of me wanted to get up, laugh and wrestle him to the ground, to turn it all into a game. But I stayed where I was. I knew that there was further to go. My penis was throbbing so hard now that it was beating a tattoo against my stomach. Still looking at Alexander, I pushed it back between my legs so he could see that I was as hard as I could get.

'My God, Charlie, you're a big boy now,' said Alexander. I knew that my cock had grown considerably in the last few years; having nothing to compare it with, I thought little of it. So I just smiled over my shoulder and waved my hard cock around, slapping it against each thigh as I did so. My own solitary experiments in front of the mirror during fencing 'lessons' had taught me what happened if I played with my cock for long enough; now, however, I felt a new intensity as I displayed myself for Alexander's appreciative stare.

The feelings, in fact, were so powerful that I went into a kind of reverie, closing my eyes and resting my head on my left forearm, with the other hand continuing my exhibition. The smell of straw, the warmth of the sunshine that had just penetrated the stable's high ceiling and was belting down on to me, Alexander's heavy breathing and occasional muttered words, sent me into a dream.

I was awakened very suddenly by a new and totally unexpected sensation – something hot, wet and firm had made contact with my exposed arsehole. My body jerked as if a bolt of lightning had passed through it, and I whipped my head round to see Alexander's face disappearing between my parted buttocks. His tongue pressed and probed against my hole, now licking, now pushing, as his great hands pulled my cheeks farther apart. I could feel his stubble, as rough as the straw, as his chin butted against my balls. I let out one great, noisy sigh as Alexander burrowed into my arse like a starving man, coating me with his spit and rubbing his face into me. My arsehole, to which I had never paid the remotest attention before, seemed to be melting or burning, I didn't know which. Alexander pulled back only to renew his assault, this time pushing his firm tongue right into the centre of my arse, which yielded slightly and allowed half an inch of him inside me. I yelped – 'Oh my God!' – but that only encouraged him. Squirming up in my hole, he reached round with one hand and found my right nipple, pinching and pulling on it gently.

I was so overwhelmed by this barrage of new sensations that I had no real idea of what was happening to me, only that I was approaching something at breakneck speed. When Alexander rubbed his hand down my sweating stomach, through my wiry, golden pubic hair, and finally grasped my cock, my head stopped spinning and I had a moment of total clarity in which I seemed to see in sharp focus for the first time exactly what was happening to me. Then all hell broke loose. His tongue working up inside me, his hand gripping and rubbing my hard, swollen shaft – everything seemed to happen at once. My back arched up; I cried out and emptied myself in burst after burst. Alexander disengaged himself from my bum and watched me. When the feelings receded, and I lay spent and panting over the straw bale, he rubbed my back and arse with one hand, gently squeezing the last few tremors of sensation through my cock with the other.

'Charlie,' he whispered. I looked round.

His brow was furrowed; he looked worried. 'Are you... all right, boy?'

I turned over; he never let go of my cock. I sat in front of him as he squatted at my feet, and smiled. I couldn't find any words, but felt a great need to reassure him. He hung his head – at first in shame, I thought, until I realised that one hand had returned to the mighty bulge at the front of his trousers. His face was flushed, his lips swollen. He looked up at me. 'Please, let me...'

For answer, I knelt beside him, put an arm round his shoulder and eased him back until he was lying across my lap. I undid the tie at the top of his trousers and eased them down. His cock, now that he was lying back, extended as far as his belly button. Where mine was pale and thick, with a bright pink head when exposed, his was long and dark, lying on a bed of thick, soft black hair, the same as the fur on his stomach. I took it in my hand; it kicked appreciatively, and Alexander growled. 'Now, Charlie, wank me off,' he said, looking up into my eyes. I did as I was told. Slowly at first – my hand could barely encircle its girth – but then, as I got the feel of another man's cock in my grasp, I increased the speed of my strokes. Before long Alexander's narrow brown hips were bucking up and down as jets of white, sticky sperm splashed across his hard belly, matting the hair there, reaching as far as his neck and shoulders.

We lay for a while in silence as I weighed the softening cock in my hand. Alexander lay with his eyes closed, breathing regularly, the sun shining down on us both. I could have stayed there all day.

Suddenly we both leapt to our feet; a horn had sounded nearby. The mail coach was approaching. How long had we lain there? It must be nearly nine o'clock. I was due back at the house for breakfast, and Alexander was behindhand with his duties. Barely looking at each other, we struggled into our clothes; I brushed the now-dry mud from my breeches and ran out of the stable. I stopped, looked back, hoping to exchange one final smile with the groom, but he was bent over the saddle rack, furiously rearranging the bridles and bits that hung there in sorry neglect.

I ran back across the field and reached the house just as the wheels of the mail coach crunched across the courtyard. I hurried up to my room, planning a quick change of clothes and then to breeze down to breakfast as if I had been studying quietly upstairs, should anyone comment on my absence. I stripped and stood for a moment naked in front of the mirror. My buttocks were still pink from Alexander's ministrations, and there was a splash of dried sperm on my stomach. I picked at it idly, and my cock, although so recently drained, started stirring into life again. I felt the phantom of Alexander's hot, insistent tongue at my arsehole. No, there was no time for this. I struggled into my clothes, hoping that my erection would subside by the time I got downstairs.

When I descended into the hall with my excuses at the ready, I found that my absence had not even been noticed. My mother greeted me with a distracted frown and a dismissive gesture, and returned to reading the letter in front of her on the table. I enquired after her health, as was our morning custom, and she replied with an inarticulate 'Oh...'. After repeated attempts to get marmalade, butter or cream passed to me, I served myself. I had never seen her like this: dark-browed, troubled, almost tearful. But, selfish and hungry youth as I was, I soon forgot my mother's worries and concentrated on consuming a hearty breakfast, my appetite sharper than ever after the morning's exercise.

The rest of the day passed in an atmosphere of silence and melancholy. Mother closed herself away in her study; passing the window, I occasionally saw her pacing, praying and writing at her desk. Ethel shooed me out of the house, and I wandered around the grounds, enjoying the sunshine, dwelling, I'm afraid, more on my recent experiences with Alexander than on the troubles looming over the family. My lessons were suspended; the last of the Hanoverian trollops had been despatched to Edinburgh the previous week, and I was left to 'independent study' of my Latin and Greek texts. An eighteen-year-old boy, on a sunny day, his cock and arse still tingling from a thorough working-over by the groom, could not find it in his heart to return to the parsing of Menander. I roamed down by the lake, hoping to see Alexander exercising Starlight, as he sometimes did. I took a diversion from my afternoon run around the estate to drop in unexpectedly at the stables; there was no one there. I swam in the freezing waters of the loch, wishing it was Alexander's tongue, rather than the icy waves, lapping at my naked arse. Finally, after such a day of exercise, I retired to bed a little after ten and went straight into a deep sleep.

The last thing I heard was the sound of my mother's voice raised in anger somewhere in the lower part of the house far, far beneath me.

Chapter Two

The next day was Sunday, and so riding, alongside other frivolous pastimes, was forbidden. The stables were out of bounds, and besides I knew that Alexander would spend the day with his family in religious observance, leaving the feeding of the horses to MacFarlane, an elderly local busybody who had helped out on the estate since before I was born. I sat in church, the stiff collar chafing against my neck, my mind a million miles from the sing-song responses and the priest's uninspired homily. I greeted our neighbours, I shook hands with the fathers, bowed to the mothers and was agreeable to their daughters. In the carriage home my mother and I did not exchange a word, absorbed in our own meditations. My mother did not comment on my uncharacteristic silence. I imagine she welcomed it. Scowling out of the window, she fretted the fingers of one glove until they split at the seam. She tutted, suppressed a curse and shoved the offending article into her bag.

On Monday morning I awoke before dawn after a disturbed night in which I could think only of Alexander and the hours that would pass before I could see him again. I had rehearsed in my mind every detail of our last time together, had summoned up memories of each sensation – his hands on my buttocks, his tongue on my arse, the pinching of my nipples and the firm grasp as he milked the juice out of me. And I saw again and again Alexander's big, dark cock jumping and jerking in my hand. I suppose I should have felt shame or guilt – I'd been brought up strictly enough – but all I could feel was anticipation. I knew dimly that there was a great deal more that Alexander and I could do together. My cock was stiff all night. I woke up several times from dreams that, unchecked, would have ended with me spewing all over the sheets – an experience with which I was quite familiar. I resisted the temptation to take care of myself. I wanted to save it, to share it.

The moment the sky lightened over the woods at the east end of the estate, I was out of bed. I poured a little cold water from the jug and washed myself quickly, splashing face and neck to wake myself up. Not that I needed much rousing: my heart was beating so hard that I could barely keep still. I crept down the stairs to avoid waking the household, out of the double doors at the end of the great hall and into the grey morning. Where Saturday had been glorious and blue, Monday dawned dark and damp, the 'dreck' hanging thick over the loch, the kind of fog that wouldn't clear all day. I felt a chill in my bones, and ran across the fields to warm myself. Now that the moment was drawing near, I had misgivings. Would Alexander be there? Was this all wrong, dangerous even? I stopped short for a moment, thought of turning back. But where my mind misgave me, my loins forced me onwards. I felt again the heat, the squirming of his tongue inside me, and I picked up my pace.

When I reached the stables, Alexander was there as usual, measuring out the feed. He grunted a short greeting, turned his back and carried on working. The wind went out of my sails; I'd assumed that within seconds of meeting we'd be tearing each other's clothes off.

'How are you today, Alexander?' I asked, trying to catch his eye and smile.

'Ah, well,' he muttered, picking up a shovel and getting to work on the weekend's dirty straw.

'Did you have a pleasant Sunday?' This was ridiculous: I was trying to make small talk with a man who, only two days ago, had come in my hand.

'I'm busy, master,' he replied, turning to frown at me. I could think of nothing to say in reply. He carried on with his shovelling. I leaned against the saddle rack and watched his broad shoulders, the muscles of his neck and sides working inside his coarse linen shirt. Each time he bent over to take up a spadeful, I examined the curve of his arse. Each time he stood up to fling the dirt into the barrow, I caught the shape of his cock and balls outlined against the wool of his trousers. If he refused to catch my eye, he could surely feel my gaze burning into him. Within five minutes, I was stiff inside my breeches, a fact which the fine suede of the garment did little to conceal. A small dark patch appeared where the tip of my cock, impatient for release, was dribbling.

Still Alexander worked, ignoring my presence, scowling at the floor. Another five minutes passed; impatience made me bold.

'Look at me, Alexander,' I said, thrusting my hips forward.

He leaned for a moment on his shovel, wiped away the sweat from his brow and looked me up and down. I saw his eyes widen just for a second when he saw the obscene outline in my breeches, before his face stiffened once more into a mask.

'Yes, sir.'

'Don't you want...'

'Sir?'

'Don't call me sir.'

'No, sir. Is that all, sir?' Frowning again, he returned to his work. His buttocks rippled as he bent, his cock strained as he stood, and yet he would not relent. What prevented him? What had happened between Saturday and Monday to change him from lust-crazed hound to sullen, scowling servant? Ah, of course – Sunday. The low chapel at which many of the local estate workers worshipped was notorious for the extreme hell-fire severity of

its sermons. Where we were gently admonished to support the
king and give more money to the church, Alexander and his like
were shown the pit of hell, and returned to their cottages with the
whiff of sulphur in their nostrils, determined to renounce sin
henceforth. It was one of my mother's standing jokes that, if you
wanted a job done properly, you should get it started on Monday.
By Wednesday, she said, the men were backsliding into drink and
sloth; by Friday they were largely absent. Alexander was always
the shining exception to this rule, a man of 'singular energy', as
she said.

I should have respected his wishes now that I had divined
them. I should have knuckled down, helped him with his work
and removed from his reach the occasion of sin. I knew that perfectly well. But instead I thought only of my own pleasure. The
state of Alexander's immortal soul interested me a good deal less
than the very mortal flesh beneath his garments. In pursuit of my
appetites, I behaved like one of the sluts that my mother was
always warning me about.

I moved round to the other side of the stable, to stand in
Alexander's line of vision, and pressed the heel of my palm against
the base of my cock, making the head push even more blatantly
against the fabric of my breeches. He saw it, I know; he looked up,
his eyes widened, he turned his back on me. Undeterred, I moved
around to face him again, then, when I knew he could see me,
turned and wiggled my arse in his face. The breeches fit me like a
second skin, and I wore no underwear; I looked naked. He
coughed, turned and worked on.

By now the thrill of the chase was inflaming my blood, and I
was more than ever determined to capture the game. Circling
Alexander, I got him with his back to the corner of the stable and
started to move in. He could not turn without sticking his head
straight into the wooden wall; he had to face me. The distance
between us closed. Still he stared at the ground, but now he was

at bay, the shovel hanging useless in his hand, his breathing hard. I could see quite clearly that his lower self wanted me as badly as I wanted him.

'Alexander...' I whispered, and he looked up. As soon as I had his attention, I caught up the tails of my shirt and whipped it over my head. I licked my lips and pinched both my nipples. Alexander coughed and blinked, but he did not look away. I turned my back on him and lowered my breeches slowly over my arse, pulling the white cheeks apart to expose the soft, pink hole that he'd been inside so recently. I could hear him breathing hard, almost groaning.

I turned to face him again, and rolled the breeches down over my hard, thick cock. Lingering for a moment with the head still caught inside the fabric, I traced a finger down the thick, blueish vein that ran its length. Then I inched my breeches down and my cock, free at last, sprang up against my curved belly. Alexander, who seemed to hold his breath throughout the foregoing, let out a great sigh. Then there was silence. My cock stood rigid between us, pulsing a little with each beat of my heart, the skin pulled back just halfway over the head, the ridge of the helmet clearly visible through its smooth covering. Alexander was sweating.

I stepped forward. I could smell him. I could feel the heat belting off his body. I reached down and took his hand; it hung, heavy and limp, in my grasp. I moved it on to my cock, tightened his fingers round my stiffness, and let it go. It stayed there, at first motionless, then responding to my throbbing with a tentative squeeze, then another, firmer. We looked at each other for two seconds, five, ten. Then Alexander's countenance lifted, the furrows disappeared from his brow and he smiled.

'Oh Charlie...' he breathed, and passing a hand round the back of my head, drew me to him in a long kiss. His tongue, that dart of fire, parted my lips and slipped into my mouth as he gently rubbed my shaft and smeared the sticky fluid across the head.

I learned a good deal from Alexander that morning. After we'd kissed, he jumped across the stable and barred the door from the inside, bounded up the ladder in two leaps and locked the hayloft doors, and let down a rude sacking curtain across the window high in the wall. In the gloomy light, and the rising heat from the penned animals and our own bodies, we turned to face each other again. 'I want no interruptions,' he said.

Standing two yards away from me, Alexander stripped quickly, stepped out of his trousers and stretched his arms above his head. He smiled; his white, strong teeth flashed in the stable's gloom. 'It can't be wrong, can it?' he said, running one hand down his hard olive chest and scratching his pubic hair. 'It can't be wrong if we both want to do it.'

'Of course it's not wrong,' I said. 'Why did you think it was?'

'Because I thought I'd taken advantage of you. Because I'm older than you. Because I'm just the groom and you –' his cock jumped as he said this '– are the master.'

In answer to all of these points, to show my equal willingness and to remove any worries about our respective rank, I dropped to my knees and took his erection in my hand, holding it a few inches away from my face. At last, I had what I wanted. I played with it for a while, feeling its thickness, its heat, making the skin slide back and forth across his dark knob, watching his balls heaving inside him. Alexander stroked the back of my head, pulling me forward.

'Come on, Charlie, get your mouth on it.'

I gingerly kissed the tip, tasted the saltiness. He pulled my head in, down. 'Get your lips round it.' I opened my mouth into a little 'o' and encircled the head, running my tongue along the damp slit. Alexander grunted and pulled harder on my head, at the same time thrusting forwards with his hips. Another inch of him slipped into my mouth, and another. I looked up at him; my eyes were watering. His head was thrown back, his hands on his hips, his groin thrust forward. I took another inch; I wanted all of him inside me. But the contact of his cockhead with the back of my throat had an unexpected effect; I gagged and choked, my mouth filled with saliva. Immediately he pulled out.

'Charlie, are you all right?' I nodded, caught my breath, spat into the straw. 'Just take it easy. There's no need to rush. We're not going to be interrupted. Will you try again?'

Would I? I felt that I would never be content without Alexander's cock inside me. I spat into my hand, slicked up every side of his long, hard shaft before opening my mouth wider than before. This time his wet shaft slipped easier between my lips, and when I felt the familiar response as it hit my throat I stopped, breathed deeply through my nose and pulled back a little.

'That's it, Charlie.'

I went down again, back again. Alexander's cock seemed, if possible, to be growing in my mouth. After a dozen such intrusions my jaw was aching, my lips were stretched – and I could not bear to release him. I saw him looking down at me as the brown shaft disappeared between my pink lips; he caressed my neck, played with my ears, talking to me in the same soft, soothing undertone that he used with the horses.

'That's the way, my boy, a little bit faster now, hold on...' His hips were thrusting forward to meet my face with every downward stroke; his balls slapped against my chin. For balance I held on to his rock-hard buttocks, feeling them smooth and warm in my hands. My fingers crept into the crack, delving through soft black hair to find the tight nub of his hole. A louder grunt than usual told me that this was not unwelcome. As Alexander pulled back from my mouth, he seemed to be pushing against my fingers. Very slightly I increased the pressure on each thrust, remembering how good his tongue had felt inside me. As the pace quickened, his hole softened and opened to my finger and I was inside him to the first knuckle.

Now he was holding my head in place with both hands, fucking my mouth with rapid thrusts. I screwed my eyes tight shut, concentrated on loosening my throat and let him go, marvelling at the contrast between the hardness of the cock in my mouth and the silky softness that I was encountering at the back. Finally I felt his insides stir around my finger, he pushed himself all the way into my mouth and stayed there as my mouth filled with a hot, salty dose. I held on to him as long as I could, but finally had to pull back to breathe, and the volume of his come flooded my mouth, coating my tongue. I let the finger pop out of his arse, then let his cock flop out of my mouth. A string of sticky fluid connected the head to my lips as his shaft, still heavy, swung at half-mast before my face. At last I swallowed, unwilling to relinquish the taste of him.

Alexander stood, panting. I knelt before him, my hands resting behind me in the straw, my cock, straining for relief, jutting straight up at the gloomy rafters. He stared down at me for a while, gently tugging on his balls; his cock, after its first subsidence, seemed unready to go down just yet. I spread my knees apart and was about to take myself in hand, but Alexander prevented me, kicking my hand aside with his bare foot, and then pushing me backwards until I had no choice but to sprawl on the floor. He launched himself on top of me, stretching the full length of his body against mine, and gripped me in a powerful hug, the swell of his rock-hard biceps grinding into my chest and shoulders. All I wanted to do was come, and could have quite easily done so just by pressing myself against him, but he saw what I was about and pulled himself away.

'Not yet, Charlie. I've got a lot to teach you first.'

I relaxed, and stretched out in front of him, eager to. He kissed me on the mouth, then worked down my chin, my neck, on to each nipple, gently sucking and biting them. Each time I thought I could stand no more, and made to grip my cock for the half-dozen strokes it would take to bring me off, he intercepted me. His lips travelled down my stomach, nibbling the short, sandy hairs that grew there, traced the lines of my hips, skirted my groin and worked down to my legs. Lapping with his tongue he slicked up my thighs, then, with a hand under each knee, bent my legs up and over my body, lifting my bum from the floor. A few bits of straw and earth had stuck to my buttocks; he brushed them away with one hand, holding my crooked legs up with the other.

Then, with a wicked look in his eye, he spat on to his fingers and rubbed them against my hole. The familiar feeling of burning and melting started again as he pressed and probed, centring my whole being, all my sensations, around that tender little mound of flesh. Suddenly, to my dismay, he pulled away.

'Wait a minute there, Charlie. Let's make things a little easier for ourselves. Hold on.'

Grabbing me by the hips, he slid me over to the saddle rack, and placed each of my feet on the lower rung which stretched about a yard above the floor. I lay back with my head on a pillow of straw and relaxed; my legs, thus supported, could easily lift and part to display my hole to Alexander. He scooted around to the other side of the saddle rack and appeared beneath the cross bar. 'That's better, boy. Now, let me at it.'

I parted my legs as wide as I could and watched him at work. Spitting on his hand again he continued his teasing of my hole, which was now opening up and trying to kiss his fingertips, seemingly with a will of its own. He pushed a little harder against it, and one finger slid in – much further than I'd imagine it could, practically up to his third knuckle. I winced with pain and surprise at first, but then, after he'd kept it still inside me for a minute, relaxed around the sensation. Craning my neck, I could see to my delight that Alexander was once again as stiff as a pole.

Gently, slowly, he worked the finger around inside me, as if he was stirring a pot of porridge. Each new contact seemed to heat me further, and soon I wanted more. Sensing from the brazen shoving of my hips that I was ready for it, Alexander spat on to my arse-hole and introduced another finger. Again, the feeling of pain; again, the subsequent sensation of fullness and ecstasy. Now the gentle stirrings were replaced by a harder, cruder in-and-out thrusting as my arse became accustomed to his presence. A third finger joined the other two; I felt as if I must come soon or faint. My cock was spewing out its juice so much that I suspected, for a moment, that I had already come without knowing it; only the continued stiffness and eagerness persuaded me otherwise.

Carefully, one by one, Alexander removed his fingers and left my hole kissing the air. Then, prostrating himself between my legs, he grabbed my hips, pulled me towards him and buried his tongue inside me again. It was good, but it was not enough. 'I want your fingers back,' I said, sounding to my own ears like a spoilt brat. 'Please, Alex, stick them back in me.'

'No, Charlie, I've got something else to go in there,' he said, wiping his mouth after eating my arse. 'You're ready for it now. Just getting you nice and wet down there...' He returned to his job, pushing his spit inside me with his tongue.

'Now jump up here.' He motioned me to a saddle mounted on the end of a bench, an old, worn, glossy brown leather thing that we'd used dozens of times on Starlight. 'Let me see your bare white bum in that, my lad.' I was quick to obey, jumping up from the floor and leaping into position with indecent speed. I lay back, comfortably supported, and pulled my knees back to my chest, exposing my arsehole; I didn't need to be told what to do.

'That's a good boy,' he said, laughing at my eagerness. 'Now I'm going to ride you home.'

Reaching over to his workbench, he dipped his fingers in a large tin of dubbin and pulled out a glob of the yellow, sticky goo about the size of a walnut. Without ceremony he wiped it on to my arsehole, rubbing it around and inside me until the scent of warm flesh and warm dubbin filled the stable. He scooped up some of the excess, rubbed it between his palms and smeared it over his rock-hard cock until it glistened in the gloom. I knew what was coming. I feared it slightly, but I wanted it far more than I feared it. I spread my cheeks wider to signal my readiness.

He sat on the end of the bench, his cock directly in line with my hole, and pressed the head on its target. It was a familiar sensation; I'd grown accustomed to his tongue and his fingers inside me. Once I was open again he pushed harder, and the head was engulfed. I relaxed, breathed deeply, saw with joy the deep concentration on his face as he watched himself disappearing into me. Then, lifting himself slightly, keeping me glued to him, he pushed deeper. It hurt badly at first, as if I was being cut; this was not the gentle teasing of tongue and fingers. I bit my lip and tried not to cry out.

'Shall I stop, Charlie? Is it too much?'

I shook my head and held steady. The pain receded. 'Go on. All of it.' Gently, he eased in the last few inches.

'That's it. You've got all of me now.'

We lay like that for a couple of minutes, Alexander caressing my chest and stomach. I noticed with surprise that my erection had entirely subsided on the first blast of pain; my pleasure, however, had not. When I felt ready, I wriggled my hips in encouragement. Alexander needed no further permission. Grasping one of my ankles in each hand, he pulled his cock gently out of my bum, lingered with his head just inside me, then pushed in again, quicker and harder this time. I gasped but there was no pain, just a relief when I felt the fullness return. Buried inside me to the hilt, he pushed against me in short, deep stabs. Something deep within my guts seemed to open up, to flower – and almost instantly, my cock sprang to life again. He thrust again, pulled out, thrust again, increasing the tempo. I felt that I could not sustain much more. Alexander leant forward and placed my calves over his shoulders, pinning my arms down behind my head with his strong hands, and kissed me full on the mouth. His cock was hammering into me now, and my arse was moving in the same rhythm. My cock, trapped between our sweating stomachs, was almost painful. We kissed so hard I felt I must have bruised his lips.

Slowing his pace, he righted himself and grabbed hold of me with his right hand, gently wanking my cock which swelled up in gratitude and relief. He stayed rigid, immovable inside me as I writhed around, and just as I was about to come he thrust hard, fast and deep within my guts. My whole being seemed to be emptying out through the end of my penis, skewered and twisted as I was on the hard pole inside me. The sperm coated my stomach and splashed on the brown leather of the saddle.

With a business-like dexterity Alexander lowered my legs, pulled his cock out of my arse with a plop, wiped it on a handful of straw, then straddled my chest and sat down. One, two, three strokes of his powerful brown hand and he was spewing another load straight into my face. I shut my eyes and opened my mouth, desperate for one more taste. When he had spent himself, he leaned forward and kissed me hard. We lay, glued together by our drying spunk, until Alexander rose to dress. There was no running away this time, no turning of backs. As I prepared to go, we kissed again.

f

For some weeks the excitement of my regular liaisons with Alexander pushed from my mind all curiosity about the history of my family, the fate of my father or the growing preoccupation of my mother. I was glad to get out of the house; not just because I knew that further joys awaited me in the gloom of the stable, but also to escape from an atmosphere of misery and suppressed panic. I was lucky; never in my life had I had such freedom, such an absence of observation. Neither my mother nor Ethel seemed to care whether I completed my lessons or not. They spent their days closeted in the study, deep in conversation. No new tutor had arrived to replace the last one. My studies went neglected; instead I learned from my morning classes with Alexander.

Custom made us bold. Our regular sessions in the stable, extravagant as they were, were no longer enough; the simple, inexhaustible pleasures of the flesh had been joined by a desire for simple companionship. Our endearments did not disappear with our lust; we wanted to share everything. Where Alexander was the leader in the physical realm, I took the initiative in what I thought of as the spiritual dimension of our friendship, and insisted that we should continue on an equal and permanent footing. Alexander resisted – wisely, as I now see – but could not hold out for long. I invited him to the house for meals; a few stern words to my mother and there was no resistance. I arranged for him to move his belongings out of the family home and to lodge with us, despite the fact that his sickly parents relied on his help. So selfish was my interest that I chose to silence their protests with money.

Alexander lodged, officially, in the servants' quarters of Gordon Hall, where there had been an ample supply of empty rooms since our return. In practice, of course, he shared my bed on most nights – just as he had always longed to do. Sometimes we simply drifted into sleep together and woke in one another's arms to wash and run through the fields to the horses. But on most nights we fucked until we were exhausted, slept for a few hours, then fucked again until dawn. During that time I learned to give as well as to take, I fucked and was fucked in every conceivable position. I discovered – or so I thought at the time – every variation on the act of love between men. Experience would teach me that there were many, many things that Alexander and I had never even dreamed of during that happy summer.

As I grew accustomed to having Alexander in my bed, and the feverishness of our relationship was replaced by a warm affection, my old curiosity returned to me. I pestered him with questions, using every trick in the book to get him to talk about my father. I approached the subject obliquely, testing his knowledge of recent local history. I tried to surprise him with questions about the horses. 'When did Starlight last see action in battle?' He fell for none of them. He feigned ignorance where he could. When I challenged him, he simply smiled and said no more.

One night, however, I caught him out. It was a beautiful night, towards the end of August, the day of my nineteenth birthday. We had spent the day on a long hack along the loch and then inland to Glencoe, where we'd stopped and, observed only by a passing eagle, fucked in the heather and bracken. The midges had driven us back, biting us into a frenzy as we tried to cover our naked bodies and rush back to our horses who stood stamping, swishing their tails and their manes in angry impatience to move on. We galloped across country, over the heath and into the forest that abutted the Gordon estate. Finally, crossing into familiar ground, we tethered our mounts at pasture and bathed in the glen that winds through our land. We ran in the sunshine to dry ourselves, and stabled the horses just before sunset. My mother welcomed us both to supper – she was glad, I think, that I had formed a friendship with one whom she trusted so completely – and enjoyed a pleasant evening. My mother went early to bed, complaining of a headache; indeed, she looked pale and tense that night. Alexander and I sat and talked until the fire had died down, then repaired to my room.

I had Alexander exactly where I wanted him, spreadeagled on the bed as I lowered myself on to his perpendicular cock. I was enjoying the contrast of his olive skin against the clean white cotton sheets; I was also enjoying the relative comfort that the bed afforded us, accustomed as I was to the hard, dirty floors of the stable. I was just settling into a gentle bounce when I saw his face in the candlelight – such a strange, absorbed look, different from the usual expression of hunger that consumed him at such times.

I stopped my shameless riding, and returned his stare. He smiled, then frowned.

'What is it?'

'Nothing. It's nothing.'

'Something's wrong.'

'No. Come on.' He squeezed my cock and tried to use it as a handle to move me up and down. I grasped his wrist and stopped him.

'You're troubled.'

He looked away. I could feel his cock softening inside me. This was most unlike Alexander. I was frightened – frightened that he was going to tell me something that would end our idyll.

'Charlie, your mother...'

I did not expect to hear her mentioned at such a time. His cock slid out of me and I lay beside him.

'Yes?'

'Your mother is, you know, a very brave woman.'

'Why do you say that just now?'

'Did you not see her at supper? How she suffers?'

'She knows nothing about us. It's none of her business –'

'It's not about us, Charlie. There's more to heaven and earth than cock and arse.' I wished that were not true. I let my hand take hold of him, to tease him out of his pensive mood and back into stiffness.

'You know, don't you, what your mother has had to endure in the last few years?'

'No. She never talks to me.' I carried on squeezing him, noting with pleasure that he was responding to my care.

'Surely you can see... what is happening to this family? The changes, the secrets, the past that you've tried so hard to bury.'

'I've tried to bury! I've always tried to find out about the past and nobody will tell me. It's so unfair!'

Again I was the spoilt schoolboy; there was something about the subject that brought out the very worst in my character. I dropped Alexander's now-hard cock as if it had bitten me, sat up and folded my arms across my chest.

'I've got a right to know what's happened.'

'Oh, Charlie, it's best that you never know.' He was kneading my shoulders. I turned my back.

'No. It's no good. You can't just tease me with the truth and then tell me I mustn't know. I'm not a child, Alex. You should know that. I'm a man.'

'Yes, Charlie, you're a man in every respect, a good man, a worthy son to your father, but –'

'But you keep me in ignorance because it suits you.'

This time it was Alexander who tried to win me round with caresses.

'I only want to protect you and serve you, Charlie.' His finger had found my arsehole again. I wanted to carry on sulking, but I did nothing to stop him from sliding it inside me.

'Just tell me what happened to my father. Please.' I swivelled round on his finger and faced him. My cock was jumping back to attention. 'Please, Alex. That's all I want to know. I must know.'

He kissed me hard on the mouth with a kind of desperation. I knew that he was struggling against promises that bound him to silence. Devious as I was, I squeezed the muscles of my arse around his finger, rolled over on to my back and spread my legs in the air; that, I knew, was how he liked me best. I pushed my swollen cock towards him. 'Tell me, Alex. Just that. It can't hurt anyone.'

He looked down at me in defeat. 'All right, Charlie. You have to know one day. Your father was a general in the Prince's army. He led the defeat of the English at Arisaig. He was a great man, a great tactician and a fearless soldier. He died –'

'At Culloden?'

'No, Charlie, not at the battle.'

'Then when?'

'A few days before. He was betrayed by spies within his own camp and murdered. The Jacobite forces never recovered. The defeat came some hours later. Without your father at its head, the army was lost.'

'Who did it?'

'That I do not know. I swear, Charlie, that's the truth. That's all I can tell you. Nobody, not even your own mother, knows more.'

I lay there silent for a minute. But for the warm presence of Alexander beside me, I felt strangely alone. Stupid thoughts chased across my mind: revenge, suicide.

'It was a noble death, Charlie. There was no shame in it.'

'Then why such secrecy?'

'Your mother fears for you. As his son, you are suspect. We none of us want to return to the troubles.'

'Speak for yourself, I –'

'You, Charlie, are too young to know what it was like. Believe me. It was a bad time. Please, let's not talk about it any more.'

Again, I was quiet for a while. Perhaps Alexander was right. That was enough – at least for tonight. I would find out more. I had all the time in the world. Many more nights like this ahead when, as the trust between us grew, he would tell me all he knew. I felt again the gentle probing of his fingers, groped around until I felt his still-hard cock, and guided him into me.

Chapter Three

The following morning Alexander quitted my bed early, returned briefly to his appointed room to rumple the blankets (I doubt whether anyone was fooled by this ruse) and made his way to work. I remained where I was, enjoying the sunshine through the open windows, sprawling lasciviously on the stained sheets where, only a few hours before, Alexander and I had enjoyed our most ecstatic coupling to date.

I lay on my front, revelling in the slight soreness of arse and cock, both of which had been thoroughly abused the night before. The heat of the early morning sun made me drowsy; after all, I had not been sleeping much. My buttocks felt hot, as if they had been spanked. Pushing my groin into the mattress, I spread my legs and felt the sun on my tender little hole, so lately plugged with Alex's fat prick. Trying to revive the memory, I reached a finger round and teased it open. Within a few minutes I was happily fucking myself, and turned over on to my back to enjoy an easier ride.

My cock sprang up, the sun illuminated the golden fluff above it, and I was just ready to finger myself again, when I heard a noise at the open window. I froze. Nothing? My cock was demanding attention, and I pumped it. Again – a noise, a cough, just yards from where I lay. I grabbed the sheet, wrapped it around my waist and jumped out of bed. There, standing at the window, quite shamelessly looking in, was MacFarlane, the part-time labourer who helped out on the estate when we were short-handed.

'MacFarlane! What the hell are you doing?'

He said nothing, touched his cap, looked directly at the blatant pole concealed – but barely – by the cotton sheet. It was difficult, under the circumstances, to play the Squire.

'Are you spying on me?'

He coughed again, cleared his throat, continued staring. He wasn't much to look at: grey hair, a lined, weather-tanned faced, shabby clothes and big, calloused hands. I thought him ancient; I suppose he must have been about fifty.

'What do you want, MacFarlane?'

'Oh, nothing, sir... A beautiful morning, sir...'

'How long have you been standing there?'

'I'll trouble you no further, sir. Excuse me.'

Before I could stop him, he had scuttled across the lawn towards the house. MacFarlane had no business there; estate workers dealt only with the steward, a remote figure who ran the Gordon acres from an office in Portnacroish. The oddness of MacFarlane's behaviour, however, was of less immediate interest than the awkwardness of my position. At the very least, he had watched me wanking; well, good luck to him. The idea of being spied on, even by such an unattractive specimen, was not entirely without its charms. But even to my lust-addled brain, other, severer possibilities presented themselves. He had, perhaps, seen me with Alexander. That was a horse of a different colour.

I washed and dressed quickly and sat in my room in a dither. I wanted, of course, to run straight to the stables and tell Alexander what had happened. On the other hand, such a course might fuel any suspicions against us; if MacFarlane had been spying for anything other than his own pleasure, it was likely that others were watching too. My mother, for instance. It was her displeasure that I feared above all. Alexander had said how much she suffered; was this the cause of her misery? The drip-drip of sordid gossip, brought to her ears by paid informers like MacFarlane? And who was behind it? Ethel? Hardly; Ethel was such a prim soul that she could never contemplate anything so shocking. Then who? Enemies in the village? Enemies of my father?

An hour passed in dismal contemplation of my predicament, during which time I had almost decided to collar MacFarlane and force a confession from him. At any moment I expected to hear footsteps pounding down the passage, a hammering on my door, angry voices raised in denunciation. But the house was strangely quiet. I dimly heard a carriage crunch up the drive, heard the stamp and jingle of horses, the slamming of doors, and the sound of departing wheels; a delivery to the kitchens, most likely. Perhaps after all MacFarlane was a harmless old fool who had stumbled innocently on the sight of me with a finger up my arse-hole and had been unable to tear himself away. In my vanity, that seemed the most appealing explanation.

A little after nine, I strolled across the fields to the stable. Alexander would agree with me – MacFarlane was just a randy old goat, and if he enjoyed watching two fit young men fucking, good luck to him. We'd laugh, he might even be sufficiently piqued by the idea to initiate a quickie over the saddle-rack.

I was one hundred yards from the stable when I realised something was wrong. A strange horse was standing in the exercise yard, a beautiful black stallion that I had never seen before. One of the steward's horses, gone lame, perhaps, and waiting for the blacksmith? I walked on again, and stopped in my tracks. The strange horse was joined by a strange man – a tall, grey-haired character in a dusty blue livery who emerged into the yard and tossed a blanket over the black stallion's back and led him to the trough. Of Alexander there was no sign.

I broke into a run and reached the stable in seconds.

'You!'

The man looked up at me and raised his eyebrows.

'Who are you?'

He said nothing, shrugged, carried on ministering to the stallion. I pushed past him. Starlight and the others stood patiently in their stalls. Otherwise the stable was empty.

I emerged, blinking and alarmed, into the sunlight. 'Where is Alexander?'

Another shrug in answer.

'Damn you, I asked you a question! Where is Alexander?'

'Alexander...?' The man pointed vaguely towards the house, shrugged again and returned to the horse.

Alexander's family home was only a mile away; perhaps there was trouble, and he had returned to his parents. I ran there in ten minutes.

The cottage door was open, but I knew at once that there was nobody home. I shouted, I cried, I banged on the walls with my fists. The cottage echoed an answer. A few scattered goods, the signs of a hasty departure, were all that remained of Alexander and his family.

Panic was rising in my throat. What had happened? Who had betrayed us? I knew immediately that, somehow, this disaster was connected with MacFarlane's visit to the house. To my mother.

I ran back home and arrived panting in the hall. It was a moment before I could catch enough breath, but then, with an almighty bellow, I called my mother.

My voice broke foolishly. I felt near to tears.

Silence. I wiped my nose on my sleeve, smoothed down my hair and rubbed the sweat from my forehead. Exercising a little more control over my voice, I called again.

'Mother!'

The drawing room door opened slowly and my mother stepped out, her carriage unusually erect, the bearing she reserved for church appearances and admonishing the servants.

'Charles.'

'Mother, what is going on? Where is Alexander?'

'Everything is quite all right, my dear.'

'Where is he? What's happened?' I felt reckless. Confronted with the truth, I would not have denied it. Alexander at that moment meant more to me than anything.

'Charles, I want you to meet someone.'

'What? Did you not hear me? I want Alexander!'

'We have a... a visitor.'

I became conscious of a person standing just behind the drawing room door.

'Who?'

Mother quickly smoothed my hair and wiped a smut from my cheek. 'Charles, this is your new tutor, Monsieur Lebecque.'

The door glided open and, with a soft swoosh, a dark figure slid into the hall. My downcast eyes took in first the black leather pumps beneath a long, black garment that skimmed the floor. A row of buttons fastened it from the hem to the neck, as my eyes travelled up the otherwise unrelieved expanse of black serge. The hands were clasped behind the back. It was impossible to tell what kind of creature was concealed beneath: male, female, fat, thin, young, old. It was only when I finally, sulkily deigned to regard the face that I could tell, most emphatically, that this was a strong, strong-willed man of perhaps thirty.

He stood, quite motionless, and looked down at me, a good six inches my superior in height. Black hair was brushed back off a pale, square forehead. Thick black eyebrows met above brown eyes. A strong jawline; the only movement I could perceive was the rhythmic working of the jaw muscles, betraying a hint of uneasiness. A large, slightly curved nose of the aquiline type. A firm, full mouth, a cleft chin, a look of determination.

We beheld each other for a few long seconds. I was not disposed to be polite; somehow, I connected this interloper with

Alexander's disappearance. I must have been scowling; Mother made a nervous cough and tried hard to catch my eye. Lebecque, on the other hand, was unperturbed; if anything, he seemed to find me an object of amusement. His left eyebrow flickered up slightly; there was the hint of a curve at one side of his mouth, quickly suppressed. He extended a hand and waited for me to reciprocate. We shook; his grip was firm and very dry. My hands were sweating from my run – and perhaps from fear.

'Delighted to meet you, Monsieur Charles.'

He pronounced it 'Shaarl', in the French way – and it was obvious from the moment he opened his mouth that he was as French as his name suggested.

I mumbled a reply and pulled my hand away.

'Monsieur Lebecque will be taking up your, er... your interrupted education, Charles,' said my mother, crimson with embarrassment. 'He has come from Paris. Please, as the man of the house, my dear –' She checked herself. 'Please make him welcome.'

I was silent for a moment, surveying the foe.

'Are you a priest?'

'Yes, my son.' Again – I thought – that ghost of a smile. It was impossible to know what he was thinking. Insufferable Jesuit!

'Are you to teach me, then?'

'Indeed.'

'Very well. I must submit; I am not yet twenty-one. Now, if you will excuse me for a minute, I wish to speak to my mother.' Lebecque raised his eyebrows and caught my mother's eye. 'In private,' I added.

'Now, Charlie, there's no secrets in this household, are there? I think it would be better if you showed Monsieur Lebecque the library, and took him for a walk round the grounds, it's such a lovely day –'

'Very well, mother, if you wish it I shall ask my question in a stranger's presence.' I shot what I thought was a damning glance at Lebecque, who remained impassive, as motionless as granite.

'Not now, Charlie. Run along.'

'I am not a child, nor to be treated like a child. I am my father's son, mother.'

'Yes, dear boy, of course. But our guest –' She made to leave the hall, and I detained her with a hand – none too gentle, I fear – on her arm.

'Mother, speak to me. I demand an answer. Where is Alexander? What has happened?'

Quick as a snake, Lebecque grabbed my hand and wrested it from my mother's arm. The shock made me gasp, and I stood like a fool.

'Please excuse me, Monsieur,' said my mother, close to tears. 'I must attend to your rooms. Ethel will see to your man. Until dinner.'

She hurried out of the hallway, leaving me alone with the stranger. For a priest, I reflected, with a rueful rub of my sore wrist, he was remarkably strong.

'Come, Monsieur Charles, show me your home.' He extended a hand and pushed me none too gently out of the hall and into the courtyard. 'Your Scottish air is indeed very bracing after a long, tiring journey.'

I was in no mood to discuss the charms of the climate, delightful though the day was. 'Who are you, Monsieur?' I asked, aping his sarcastic politeness.

'Excuse me. I am Benoit Lebecque, theologian, from Paris, born in Rouen. I come with the highest recommendation of the Bishop of Paris, who has been gracious enough to find me a place in the household of one of the noblest of all Scottish families.'

'Why are you here?'

'Of course, to teach you. A tutor was required, was it not?'

'Yes...'

'And a tutor has been found. Perhaps we can discuss our

academic future when you have been kind enough to show me Gordon Hall.'

In the face of such stone-faced resistance, there was little I could do but oblige, although with bad grace. Conducting the tour at an uncomfortably fast pace, I whisked Lebecque through the ornamental garden, around the coppice and down to the shore of Loch Linnhe, where I had a good mind to push him in. I walked quicker and quicker; Lebecque was never behindhand, never out of breath. In a race, I felt sure, he could beat me. He met each of my offhand observations with an intelligent, sympathetic question to which I was obliged to reply. Within twenty minutes my hostile first impressions had crystallised into a most cordial hatred.

Finally we reached the west end of the estate and came into view of the stables. All of my misery returned; Alexander gone, our friendship betrayed. With the self-regarding logic of youth I blamed Lebecque for everything. I stopped in my tracks.

'Monsieur, I do not wish to be rude to a guest in my mother's house, but I am afraid that I must ask you a question.'

'Of course. You must always ask questions about that which you don't understand, my boy. And I, as tutor, will endeavour to answer them.'

'Very well. Where is Alexander?'

'Ah. Alexander…'

'Yes. You know where he is, I take it?'

'Alexander, I believe, has been obliged to leave the service of the Gordon family.'

'I saw him only this morning. He said nothing of it.' My bravery was being seriously undermined by the danger of crying.

'No. Sudden circumstances, I believe.'

'What have you done? Who are you?' I felt hot; I knew that my face had gone bright red.

'For myself, I have done nothing. I am here only as your tutor.

I advised your mother, perhaps, this morning over an issue that she found both painful and alarming.'

'You mean, you and she engaged spies.'

'Nothing so sinister, Charles, as espionage. Simply the discovery, easy to effect, that a member of the household had become... no longer dependable.'

'Alexander had done nothing wrong.'

'It is not his deeds that were dangerous, but his words. You will find from our study of history that it is always words that we fear more than actions. Now, please, show me to the library.'

Words! Then that was it. We had been overheard discussing my father. Perhaps 'they' – my mother, whoever else – had known about Alexander and me all along, and didn't care as long as it kept me quiet. But now that he had spoken for the first time of my father...

'I must beg you, sir, to tell me more.' Lebecque was striding ahead of me; I caught on to his gown and nearly tore it. He swung round on me in a fury.

'Enough questions! Stupid, foolish boy! You little know the danger to which you expose yourself and those you love! Silence in these times is the only defence! Your friend is safe and well. That is all you need to know.' His face, animated for the first time in my presence, now resumed its impassivity. 'Now please, the library. It is, I believe, a famous collection.'

f

The following weeks did little to improve my opinion of Lebecque. He was a fine tutor, certainly, a thoroughly learned man with the rare gift of communication. He breathed life into dead authors. He illuminated the dry polemics of history. He even indulged me with a few basic lessons in fencing. But the moment our conversation strayed beyond the appointed subject, his face closed like a trap and his eyes told me that I must ask no more. In his presence my mother was cowed and nervous, deferential in a way that did not become her, at least not towards a servant in the household. Ethel hated him openly, referred to him as 'that black crow' and swore he was in league with Satan. Lebecque glided through the household with infallible courtesy to us all. Outside lesson and meal times, he closeted himself in his room or took long rides on his black stallion, sometimes staying away for days at a time. His man-servant, Girolle, lay low somewhere in the village, attending Lebecque only on rare occasions.

My education was certainly improving, but in all other respects my life was miserable to me. I had become accustomed to Alexander's friendship, to his company both in and out of bed, and I missed him sorely. Every day I hoped that a letter would arrive, that an assignation could be made and that we could escape together to begin a new life somewhere in the Highlands, away from prying eyes. Every day brought nothing but disappointment. While my mind gradually resigned itself to his absence, my body was not so easily assuaged. My appetites, sharp enough before I had learned how to satisfy them, raged day and night with nothing but my hands to relieve them. A few relics of Alexander – the old saddle from the stable, a shirt he had left in my room, the pot of dubbin – I rescued and secreted for my lonely reveries, but even they could not satisfy me. I walked around the house and grounds in a daze of lust. Even Lebecque became attractive to me, much as I hated him. The man was, after all... a man. Sometimes, to my utter disgust, his face replaced that of Alexander in my dreams.

I took to swimming more frequently in the loch, hoping that the icy waters would give me some relief from the tormenting devils. The stretch of beach that skirted the estate was a favourite spot since childhood: fine, white sand, little dunes of coarse grass, bands of coarsely broken shells washed up by the tide. Jellyfish could be found on the wet sand after a storm; seals occasionally swam close to land and watched me through huge round eyes. Other than that, the only company on the beach were the seabirds that wheeled overhead, catching the last few flying ants of summer.

Lebecque had swum with me once or twice shortly after his arrival, more to ascertain that I was not making secret assignations than for any great pleasure in the exercise, I suspect. To my amusement he left his long cotton shirt on in the water; as a priest, I suppose, he felt the need to suppress the body at all times. I delighted in stripping off all my clothes and running stark naked into the shallows. Lebecque said nothing, ploughed through the water with amazing strength, ran out, stood for a moment with his wet shirt dripping around his knees, then jogged back to the house to dry and change.

But throughout August and September I had the loch to myself, and spent all my available time out there once the summer's midges had finally dropped from the skies. I swam and sunned myself, I studied my books, I studied nature and the beauty of my homeland. It was a sad time, melancholy rather, but the sharp misery of Alexander's departure had passed. Time had even dulled the edge of my curiosity. He had gone, I was alone, that was all that really mattered to me. Lebecque had told me Alexander was safe; there was nothing for me to worry about but that insistent devil in my loins.

So demented was I by the end of September that I was beginning to find erotic significance in Thucydides, Caesar and Cicero. It was impossible to study for long without some mention of a soldier or a slave tripping my mind into long, lurid reveries. I tried to cool myself in the loch, to diminish the number of times I made myself come, but too often I surrendered to the moment.

One warm afternoon in the dying days of the summer I was lying on my back in the sand, my head propped on a pillow of grass, allowing the sun to dry my naked body from a recent dip, trying to concentrate on the book in my hand but dreaming instead. My cock was half hard; these days, it was seldom any less. I stretched my legs, ground my arse into the sand and felt my cock twitch a little. I felt agreeably aroused, relaxed, happy.

A crunch of foot on gravel alerted me to the fact that there was somebody behind me. The sun was in my eyes, and so no shadows fell across me to betray another's presence, but the sound was unmistakable. Surely, I thought, it must be Lebecque. I pretended I had heard nothing, turned a page of my book and carried on reading. Silence for a minute or two, then, closer this time, another faint sound. The heat of the sun, and the interesting experience of being watched, worked together to bring my cock up to full stiffness. Well, if Lebecque would spy on me... knowing that I was a healthy nineteen-year-old boy... he would have to take his chances. I turned down the page in my book and lay it beside me, stretched my arms high above my head, ran my hands down my chest and stomach, and then gripped my cock and started to stroke it. I knew how to put on a show: Alexander had loved to watch me. I put those lessons to good use now, hoping to send a shamed Lebecque racing back to the house with a mess inside his black gown.

I was getting nicely into my stride, bucking my hips up and down, imagining Lebecque's face contorted with lust, wondering what was going on underneath his clothes, when a groan and a sudden shuffling movement made me turn round, as if to 'discover' and denounce my voyeur. But instead of Lebecque standing there I came eye to eye with none other than MacFarlane, staggering towards me holding his trousers up with one hand and gripping a big stiff erection with the other. I leapt to my feet in horror; MacFarlane, losing grip of his trousers, fell face first at my feet, his hairy backside wriggling as he tried to right himself. The initial shock wore off, and the absurdity of the situation took hold of me.

'Dear oh dear, MacFarlane, it seems that you make quite a habit of spying on me. What is it that you want?'

The old man groaned again and looked up at me, his face a burlesque of tragedy. 'Please, Master Charles, don't be angry. I didn't mean it. I didn't know you were here. I couldn't help what I saw.'

'You're a dirty wee bastard, aren't you, MacFarlane? Watching people's private moments.' I was standing right over him now. Despite the fact that I found him generally repulsive, my cock had not softened one iota. Its shadow stretched far out from my hips. I suppose I was enjoying my power over him – but, if I must be honest, I was also enjoying the opportunity to show myself off to another man – any man, however unattractive. It was a long time since my body had been appreciated. MacFarlane was an audience, if nothing else.

'Well, old man, take a good look.'

He peered up again, uncertain of what to do.

'Go on, I said look at me. I'm not going to hit you.'

'Yes, sir. Thank you, sir.'

He struggled into a kneeling position; in the sand where he had fallen there was a perfect impression of his cock and balls. The white sand clung still to him, as it did to my arse and back.

'Tell me, MacFarlane, what you were doing?'

'Watching you, sir.'

'Watching me what?'

'Watching you... playing with yourself, sir.'

He cleared his throat and licked his lips. Now that he knew there was no present danger, he relaxed a little. His cock, which had shrivelled before, lengthened and stiffened with an energy I found surprising in a man of his years. Years of outdoor work punctuated by too many hours at the bar had done their worst to his complexion, and he was certainly no beauty, but he was no monster either. His body, from what I could see, was sturdy enough. Not that it mattered; he could have been fat and scaly and covered in sores and I, blinded as I was by lust, would have persuaded myself to find him attractive.

'Do you like what you see, MacFarlane?'

'Oh yes, sir, very much.'

'Do you want to... touch it?'

He couldn't find words to reply, but instead shuffled forward on his knees and reached out a hand. Allowing him just to brush the tip (which left a sticky pearl on his fingers) I stepped back again.

'Not so quickly, MacFarlane. First of all I want you to tell me something.' I was devious.

'Yes, sir.'

'You must tell me the truth, you know, or...' I made my cock twitch.

'Yes, the truth, sir, anything.'

'Tell me, MacFarlane, what you saw in my room that morning.'

He gasped and bit his lip, hung his head in shame for a moment. Had I overplayed my hand? I thought not; his dick was harder than ever, like a steel rod against his belly.

'Look at me, MacFarlane. Look at me!' I spat on my fingers and rubbed them over the head of my cock, then put them back into my mouth, savouring the taste. 'You want to taste that, don't you? Want my hard young cock in your mouth?'

'Yes, sir.'

'Then tell me.'

'Do you promise, sir, not to say that I told you?'

'I promise nothing, old man.' He was transfixed by what he saw. I think he would have sold his soul to the devil.

'Very well. I had seen you and Alexander together a few times, in the stable, in your room...'

'You mean you spied on us?'

'Yes sir. I'm sorry. I couldn't help it. Once I knew what you were doing I spent all my time trying to catch you at it again. When you moved him into the house I knew that I could creep outside the window and watch you whenever I wanted. It was too much to resist.'

'All right. What's done is done. Is that all?'

'That's all, sir, I swear.'

'You're a liar.' I made as if to pick up my shirt and leave him.

'No sir, please, there's more. One day your mother called me into the house and asked me what I had been doing in the garden. She'd seen me, you see, crouched outside your window. I was so ashamed. I didn't know what she thought... whether she'd actually caught me...'

'Wanking.'

'Precisely, sir.' His hand went to his cock and jerked it two or three times. 'I was always greatly given to it.'

'So I see. Go on.'

'She asked me what I had heard. I didn't understand at first, but she asked again what conversations I had heard coming from your room. I said I thought you were alone, and so how could there be any conversation? But then she became angry, and said she knew that you kept Alexander in your room. I was going to defend you, sir, I swear it, to tell her that nothing happened between you, but she didn't seem to care. She only wanted to know what was said. Nothing, I told her, just idle conversation. It was the truth; all I had ever heard pass between you were words of friendship. She looked at me for a long time and then swallowed, as if there were a bitter taste in her mouth.'

'And then?'

'She told me to go back there night after night, to make my bed beneath your window no matter how cold the air, to listen to every word that I heard and to report them to her every morning.'

'And what did you hear?'

'You know, sir, that for many nights there was nothing but the... perfectly natural expression of... your friendship with the young man.'

'You listened to us fucking.'

'Yes, sir.'

'Until that last night.'

'Yes, sir.'

'And so you went and told my mother that Alexander had betrayed her trust and spoken to me of my father.'

'I'm sorry, sir.'

'What did she say?'

'Very little at the time, sir. That man was with her.'

'Lebecque.'

'Yes. Your tutor.'

'You needn't protect him, MacFarlane. He is no friend to this family.'

'I told your mother, in his hearing, what Alexander had said to you. She was alarmed; Lebecque was quite businesslike. "It has happened at last, then," he said. I was dismissed from the room and I heard no more.'

'You? A spy like you? Come on, MacFarlane, what did you hear at the keyhole, at the window?'

He looked up at me with genuine shame on his face. If he could have escaped from the trap now, I believe, he would have done – and relinquished the taste of my young cock once and for all.

'Tell me, MacFarlane, or I swear that on my majority I will have you clapped in prison.'

'I heard a few more words, just by mistake, sir. Lebecque told your mother that she must leave you entirely in his charge, that the safety of more than just the family was at stake if she attempted to interfere. She cried and begged him to leave. That was all I heard, sir, I swear on my mother's life.'

'Very well. I believe you.' With so much to contemplate, I had lost interest in the immediate prospect of MacFarlane's admiration. He, clearly, had not.

'Master Charles,' he said, after a few minutes of silence. I had almost forgotten his presence, but there he knelt, his cock still at full attention.

'All right, MacFarlane, do what you want. Remember, a word of this to anyone and you end your life in chains, do you understand?'

He looked up at me and smiled. At the first contact of his hand I closed my eyes, put my hands on my buttocks and tried to concentrate on the warmth of the sun, the image of Alexander. MacFarlane's touch was surprisingly adept, and within moments he had me erect in his hands. I opened my eyes just in time to see his mouth engulfing me; my shaft slid straight down to his throat in one slick movement. I gasped and tightened the grip on my buttocks. His right hand was working away at his own cock; his left was pulling and squeezing my balls. Shortly they tightened in their pouch and drew up to my body; I knew I was close. Slipping a finger inside my arse, I pulled out of MacFarlane's mouth and unleashed one, two, three, four huge spurts of come over his upturned face. He licked greedily as far as his tongue could reach, dived back down on to my still-twitching cock and sucked out the last few drops as he spent a great puddle in the sand.

I have never been able to share an orgasm with another man without a moment of tenderness in the aftermath. I cradled MacFarlane's head in my hands as he suckled for a while longer on my softening cock, which finally dropped out of his mouth shiny with spit and sperm. Then I turned, walked into the water and swam a few strokes out into the loch. When I turned to look back at the beach, MacFarlane had gone.

Chapter Four

The summer was over. Soon the daylight would stretch to only four or five hours. The waters of Loch Linnhe were cooling rapidly; I took my last swim one sunny October afternoon before the weather closed in for good.

The melancholy of autumn infected me badly. Where before my days had passed in a dream of sunshine, my dick my only distraction, now I spent the time brooding coldly on the mystery of my predicament. I mulled over every word that MacFarlane had told me. I tried to question him further, but he was as nervous as a hare and ran a mile if I approached. It was useless to ask my mother what was going on; as for Lebecque, he continued as he always was, a man of granite. Our lessons fared well; my competent schoolboy Greek and Latin gained fluency and subtlety, my grasp of mathematics and logic not far behind. Beyond that: nothing.

What was the nature of Lebecque's position in our household? What power did he hold over my mother, that she should tolerate his bullying? She had cried and begged him to leave, said MacFarlane, and yet he remained. He was a servant at Gordon Hall, and yet he kept a servant of his own at Portnacroish. He seemed to know more about me than anyone. 'It has happened at last,' he said to my mother when he heard of Alexander's confession. At last? What prior knowledge did he have? How could a poor priest, a tutor in a family far from his home, see so deeply into affairs that did not concern him?

My suspicions were growing to a head. Often I saw Lebecque creeping towards my mother's study, where they would stay cloistered for hours at a time. He sent and received letters with far greater frequency than I would have expected from a man in his humble position. When I braved him in lessons, tried to presume on my superior rank, I saw a flash of pride and anger, swiftly quelled, behind those dark brown eyes.

Starved of information but bursting with curiosity, I took the only course open to me: I jumped to conclusions. It dawned on me one day with a hideous clarity that Lebecque, far from being a servant in Gordon Hall, was preparing to be its master. Perhaps I had been reading too many novels (a practice Lebecque condemned as 'effeminate'), but I was quite sure that he was aiming for my mother's hand in marriage. Of course! She was still attractive, gracious, the mistress of extensive lands and considerable wealth. My father's name, I guessed, was a powerful influence in certain circles. Lebecque, as a Frenchman, a Jacobite sympathiser, entertained God knew what political ambitions – and a platform in the western Highlands, shored up with the Gordon fortune, was just what he needed. Yes: that would explain the hours of silent colloquy, the extensive correspondence (wedding invitations?), the barely-suppressed arrogance. One day soon I expected him to cast off his clerical robes and emerge in his true colours as my new Papa.

The idea disgusted me. Little as I remembered my own father, I had worked him up into a kind of idol, investing him with a romantic glow imparted, I suppose, by the secrecy that surrounded his legend. Something of the love I bore for Alexander had transferred itself to this ideal image of my father – and I worshipped him in private. I stole into my mother's room to unveil the tiny portrait she kept, wrapped in black velvet, in her dressing table. The resemblance between us was strong – the same sandy hair, the pale skin. He was leaner, sterner, perhaps – an ideal me. My idolatry contained a large measure of self love.

And to see him supplanted by Lebecque – this hawk-nosed, swarthy foreigner – this meddling priest – was unbearable! Insupportable! I should denounce my mother, like Hamlet in the play (another part of my reading of which Lebecque thoroughly disapproved; 'if you must read *modern* drama, read Racine'.) I should cast Lebecque out of the house. But what if he achieved his dastardly ends before two years were out, before I came into my majority? Then he could produce an heir, disinherit me, rule Gordon Hall alone. I would run away. Then they would be sorry.

So convinced was I of the truth of my conclusions that I interpreted Lebecque's every remark as confirmation of the impending disaster. We had spent an arduous afternoon struggling through the maze of Plato's Republic, Lebecque all patience, I being deliberately stupid just to antagonise him.

Laying down the book and moving the candle away from his tired eyes, he pushed the hair off his pale forehead and reclined in his chair.

'Ah, Charles, you take a very antagonistic approach to philosophy these days.'

'I don't. It's just… rubbish.'

'Well, that's one way of looking at it.' He closed Plato, rose and walked to the window. It was about six o'clock. Our lesson should have been over an hour ago. Outside it was dark; the moon was already up over the loch.

'Certainly, Plato would have found it hard to understand a great deal in modern life.'

'Like what?' I was always eager to turn the subject to recent history.

'Politics. Religion. The vengefulness of the ruling classes.'

'What are you talking about?'

Lebecque paused with his back to me.

'Charles.'

'Yes?'

'You love your mother, don't you?'

'Yes, of course.' I felt as if a confession was at hand.

'And you would trust her to make the right decision, wouldn't you, however strange it might seem to you?'

'I would wish to be informed of the reasons behind any decision,' I snapped.

'No doubt. But that is not always possible.' He paced across the room, more disturbed than I had ever seen him before. 'You know, do you not, the danger that is still at large in Scotland?'

'What do you mean?'

'That English troops scour the land hunting down any last traces of sedition and stamping them out most ruthlessly?'

I had been brought up to fear and despise English soldiers; I regarded them as nursery spooks meant to frighten naughty children, nothing more.

'Of course.'

'Then you must understand that your family stands in a very parlous position.'

'I don't see why. We are above any suspicion.'

'Yes, perhaps.' He looked at me, caught my foolish, sulky gaze. His face, for once animated and open, snapped shut again, and the light went out of his eyes.

'I think, Charles, that you must learn to respect the decisions of your elders.'

'I must understand them before I can respect them.'

I could see the familiar flash of anger behind his mask. 'That is not possible. Obedience is the first duty.'

'My position? And what is that, precisely? The heir to the Gordon estate, to my father's name. Soon to be the master of this house, able to choose what servants I like.'

Lebecque was thinking. He turned to the moon again.

'Charles, I have never insisted on the respect that my station should naturally command.'

'Your station? As a paid tutor?'

'As a priest, Charles.' He ran a finger round the tight collar of his black soutane. I saw for a moment a few strands of hair just below the neck line.

'You are not here as a priest.'

'And yet the fact remains.'

'I give you what respect I can.' I put as much contempt into the words as I dared.

'Charles...' He was frowning now. 'I have never asked you to call me "father", have I?'

Father? What did he mean? I jumped out of my chair.

'I will never call you father!'

Lebecque swung round, his mouth open. He was shocked to see me so angry. I was red in the face, clenching my fists.

'Never. Do you understand!'

I turned on my heel and slammed the door behind me, ran down the stairs and out on to the lawn. An owl skimmed a few feet above my head and swooped low over the grass, picked up a mouse and flapped silently over the loch. A dog barked somewhere over by the coppice.

The evening air cooled me quickly; I had to think. So, all my suspicions confirmed! Lebecque to be my father – my mother's husband! Casting off his vows of celibacy in order to clutch at power and wealth! So much for the priesthood. Perhaps the English were right all along; the Church of Rome was nothing but a mask for greed and perversion.

I ran down to the beach and sat for a while in thought. This was no time for hot-headedness. I had to fight my corner.

Over dinner I announced to my mother that I would no longer be taking lessons with Monsieur Lebecque, that my education would be better served by a period of private study. My mother was about to protest, but looked up at Lebecque's pale, pompous face and bit her tongue.

'That seems like an excellent idea, Madame Gordon,' he said, the smooth-tongued hypocrite. 'Charles is fast catching up with the limited abilities of his tutor. I would simply suggest that he avoids the temptation of fiction and other works of the imagination. Concentrate, Charles, on fact.'

The rest of the meal passed in silence. My mother obeyed him in everything. She even cleared his plate. When I saw her pouring his wine, like a servant – or a wife – I scraped back my chair and marched out of the hall.

†

For three weeks I avoided Lebecque. Our lessons had been suspended, and there was no natural point of contact save meals, which I insisted be served in my room. To my amazement, I met no resistance to this plan. Oh, they were happy enough to have each other to themselves! I was the unwanted son, the inconvenient memory of a dead man.

I took to habits of solitude, stalking around the house at night, sometimes not sleeping until the sun rose, then dawdling down to the stable to exercise Starlight, my only agreeable companion. My sexual appetites, so boundless in the summer, had dwindled to a few half-hearted memories of Alexander and the occasional quick, functional wank to clear my head. I was only interested in plotting. I devised a dozen ways of getting Lebecque out of the house: denouncing him to the soldiers, writing to his bishop in Paris, hiring MacFarlane or even Ethel to kill him. Of course, I pursued none of them.

On one of my nocturnal wanderings in November I had been surprised to see MacFarlane, that shadow that haunted the estate, skulking across the lawn towards the stables. Certain that he was up to no good, I followed him, took an alternative route through the coppice and, thanks to my youth and stealth, arrived before him. He came panting into the exercise yard and nearly screamed when I jumped out from behind the water trough.

'God in heaven, Master Charles, don't scare me to death!'

'What are you up to, MacFarlane? Who are you spying on now?'

'Nobody, sir. You know that. I'm a reformed character.'

'You're a sinner, MacFarlane, and you'll burn in hell no matter how much you repent. What were you doing near the house?'

'Nothing, sir.' He would not look me in the eye; I knew he was lying. 'How are you, sir? Have you been taking care of yourself?'

'I am very well, MacFarlane, as you see.'

'Yes, sir, very well indeed. I trust you have all the... help... that you need, as it were?' The old lecher was trying to distract me. I wanted to knock him down, but a sharp stirring in my balls implored me to let him in.

'Thank you, MacFarlane, if I ever require your services in that area I shall ask for them.'

'Perhaps you have someone else to do the job now, sir.'

'What do you mean?'

'Well, sir, I thought perhaps your tutor...'

'Lebecque? What are you talking about, you disgusting old fool?'

'He seems to be a man of... taste... I should say?'

He was mocking me. 'Watch your tongue, MacFarlane, or the proctor will cut it out of your dirty mouth.'

'You didn't complain about my dirty mouth before, Charlie.' He was openly playing with himself. I was determined not to repeat a mistake that had put me so much into his power.

'Good evening, MacFarlane.' I turned on my heel and walked away, hearing him laughing behind me.

Walking back to the house I saw a light in my tutor's room. What had MacFarlane meant, a man of taste? Had he spied on Lebecque the way he had spied on me – alone, aroused? But surely a man of the cloth was above such pollution. Yes, but he was a man for all that, a young, fit man. It was possible that Lebecque, like me, had ways of keeping a clear head.

As I neared the house I saw the shadow of not one but two figures against Lebecque's window. My heart leapt into my mouth; my mother in his room! That was too compromising, too indiscreet. Whatever their future plans, he was still a servant! I crept nearer. No, it was not my mother; it was a man's shape. I saw Lebecque, unmistakable in his long black garment, hand a package to the other. They kissed lightly on both cheeks in the French way. Of course, it was Girolle, the priest's servant. Their shadows disappeared from the window.

I was overcome by curiosity. What was Lebecque doing in the house? He was now, to all intents and purposes, unemployed. I had seen to that. And yet he stayed, he ordered his servants around, he acted like the master. I would find out.

An ancient vine clad the west wall of Gordon Hall, a huge sturdy plant that, according to my mother, held the house up. It never bore grapes, and was generally considered an eyesore, but now for the first time I blessed it. Years of poor husbandry had left it sprawling and woody; strong enough, I had long since discovered, to bear my weight. In happier times I had climbed as high as the first floor and ambushed Ethel as she sorted linen, swinging through the casement with a loud 'Tally-Ho!'. Lebecque's room was on the second floor, where the branches were undoubtedly thinner and weaker. It was a risk I was prepared to take.

I waited until I saw Lebecque again; he opened the window, took a few breaths of fresh air, pushed back his hair in a characteristic gesture and then shut out the night. Now, I assumed, he would turn to his books or his correspondence. His desk was at the wall opposite the window. He would be unlikely to see me; perhaps, however, I would see something to my advantage. What I expected I don't know; I told myself that I would catch him in some treasonable act, but in truth I was intrigued by MacFarlane's veiled remarks and wanted to know more.

And so I scaled the vine. It was surprisingly easy; I was agile and light, and the branches, although thin, were strong and supple. I waited for a moment with my head just below the window ledge, listening for sounds of movement; if Lebecque was pacing the room, he would catch me for certain. But all was silence.

I pulled myself up and peered into the room. There was only a single candle burning on the dresser, but it was enough; by now it was pitch dark outside, and I could make out every detail. The dresser, the desk, the open chest with Lebecque's clothes and books spilling out over the floor, the chair, two pairs of boots – but no Lebecque. I raised myself a little higher and caught sight of a mattress and a foot. The bed was directly under the window; Lebecque must have decided on an early night. A few more inches, and I could see the ankle, the shin, the knee, the thigh, expecting at every moment to see the nightshirt that protected his clerical modesty. But no: travelling up the thigh, the other foot braced against it, the right leg crooked, further, further...

A quick hitch up on the vine branch and I had the whole picture. Lebecque, directly beneath me, lay sprawled naked on his bed, illuminated only by the rays of a single candle. He was not asleep. His left hand was busy in his groin, pulling and coaxing his cock, while his right hand rubbed the matted black hair on his chest. I knew from our abortive swimming trips that Lebecque was a hairy man – that much had been revealed by his wet undershirt. Hair covered his torso like a thick rug.

I barely breathed. The left hand was shielding its cargo from my prying eyes, and I wasn't leaving until I saw it. He kept pushing it down, out of my sight. I could feast my eyes on the dense black pubic hair, the first pale inch of the root of his cock, but the thing itself remained hidden. Then, as I was about to give up hope, he let go and it sprang up hard and massive, wavered for a moment in the air and fell with a slap against his stomach. Lebecque gripped it again and held it straight; it cast a great shadow up his chest as far as his neck. He tugged on the foreskin, pulling it out an inch from the head, then moved it back to reveal a shiny, slightly pointed head. Back and forth it went, back and forth... I heard Lebecque sigh, he shifted his buttocks slightly and went to work.

God, I was as bad as MacFarlane. I hated Lebecque, wanted to undermine him, and yet I couldn't tear myself away. I justified my spying by the fact that any sudden movement on my part might have been dangerous, might have alerted Lebecque to the fact that his shameful practice was observed. And so I stayed rooted to the spot, my own cock dribbling shamelessly inside my trousers. I could do nothing to relieve myself; both hands were fully occupied gripping on to the windowsill.

It didn't take long. Lebecque masturbated with a businesslike air. When he came, he didn't yell or groan. He simply sighed, threw his head back with his eyes tight shut (thank God – otherwise he would have looked straight into my face) and emptied what looked like half a pint of spunk over himself. He was still for a while then stood up and padded towards the dresser for a cloth. I removed myself from his field of vision just before he turned to the window.

Swiftly and silently I descended the vine, ran round to the front of the house and gained my room within two minutes. A quick tug at the buttons and my still-stiff cock bounced free, more eager than it had been for months. Very few strokes brought me off. I came, to my satisfaction, as copiously as my tutor.

Disgust set in soon afterwards. This was the man, I reminded myself, who was plotting to marry my mother and disinherit me.

This was a priest who soiled himself, who was unfit to live under the same roof as a Gordon. Yes, such were the foolish thoughts of a gloomy youth who was already half in love with a man he professed to despise.

I consoled myself with the thought that this new information gave me power over Lebecque, that I could use it to oust him from my mother's affections and rid us of him once and for all. To that end I turned up at breakfast the next morning and cheerfully announced that I required tuition today. 'I have reached a particularly sticky passage in Plato,' I said to Lebecque, looking into his brown eyes that had so recently been closed in ecstasy. 'I need a helping hand, Monsieur Lebecque. Perhaps we could work on it together?'

'Of course, Charles. The Republic, or...'

'The Symposium. I need you to show me what it means.'

My mother, unversed in the classics, was delighted. 'Oh yes, Charlie, that's excellent! You are coming along so well.'

'I feel I could come a lot quicker with a hand from Monsieur.'

'Of course,' he said, folding his napkin. 'Shall we...?'

I held the door open for him in what I thought was a crushingly sarcastic display of politeness, and followed him up the stairs to the library, where we used to take our lessons. On the way I taunted him with questions.

'Have I misconstrued the genders in Plato, Father? I mean, it seems to me that Socrates is advocating something that simply doesn't make sense.'

'No, Charles, I doubt that.'

'You see, Father' – oh, what irony I packed into the word, how pleased I was with myself – 'a child like me cannot be expected to understand something as illogical as love between men. Is that what it means? You must explain it to me.'

We had reached the library. This time he held the door open and ushered me inside, then closed the door firmly behind us.

'Your reading of the Greeks is, as you know, exactly correct, Charles. There can be little doubt in your mind. You have experience, I believe, of the love that can exist between... comrades.'

This took the wind out of my sails.

'I told you once before, Charles, that actions are rarely dangerous. What we do, certainly in the field of human relations, is nothing compared to what we think. Or the most dangerous thing of all – what others think of us. Especially when they are ill-informed and prejudiced.'

'I see.' He had fallen into my trap. 'So the vows that you made as a priest are more serious than the things that you might choose to do while bound by those vows.'

'Perhaps.' For the first time, Lebecque seemed uncertain of his ground.

'Priests of the Roman church are celibate, are they not?' I was the great orator, the prosecutor. I was Cicero, Alcibiades.

'They are.'

'And should not pursue wives.'

'Indeed.'

'And should renounce impurity, I imagine.'

There was silence between us.

'What are you getting at, Charles?'

'Are you intending to marry my mother?'

'Your mother? Oh for God's sake –'

'What about profanity? Where does the church of Rome stand on that?'

'Have a care, young man.'

'And what about pollution of the body?'

Again, he was speechless. I pressed home my advantage.

'Last night I watched you. I was outside your window and I watched you.'

'You watched me.'

'I did.'

'I see.'

Now he would hang his head, admit he was a fraud, pack his bags and leave Gordon Hall for good. I was magnificent.

'Well, Charles, you have seen things that... I suppose it is unfit for you to see.'

'I should say so. *Au revoir*, Monsieur Lebecque.'

'No. You must understand certain things.'

His hand was beating a tattoo against his thigh. It was impossible for me to look at him now without a vision of his hands milking a quantity of sperm across his hairy stomach. And he knew it.

'There are things that happen in a man's life, Charles...'

'As I know. Remember? I had a friend once.'

'Yes, of course, poor Alexander. Most regrettable.'

'You destroyed his family.'

'Ah, no, Charles. I saved him and his family. And you for that matter.'

'You... what?'

'I would like to address you as a man.'

'Go ahead.'

'As a man of understanding, I hope.'

'What little understanding I have, sir, you taught me.'

'Charles, for one moment come down off your high horse and listen to reason. I have tried to tell you that there is danger for you and your family. I stand between you and that danger. If not as tutor, then as comrade.'

'You are not worthy to live under the same roof as my mother.'

'Why? Because, as you so nicely put it, I pollute myself? Come, Charles, I am flesh and blood, as you saw.'

Yes indeed, that I had seen very clearly. I knew what was beneath the robe. I could picture it now.

'I cannot be a saint, not in this life. I would be happier if you would accept that. We are... equals in this house.'

'No, sir. We are not.'

'Charles...' There was a look of imprecation in his eyes. I thought for a moment he was going to cry. With his left hand he took me by the arm. Again I saw the picture from last night, felt the heat of his grasp burning right through me. 'I want you to know –'

A loud smash from the lower part of the house interrupted him. Ethel's voice raised in a scream. I heard my mother crying 'Lebecque! Lebecque!' and loud male voices coming from the hall.

Lebecque grasped me tightly for a second, looked me in the eyes and ran from the room.

He reached the bottom of the stairs a few seconds before me. The hall was full of people: my mother, Ethel, MacFarlane and half a dozen English redcoats – those devils of my childhood imagination. They were a dirty, ill-disciplined crew, leaning against the banisters, plastering their filthy hands over the walls. The leader was a little smarter than the others – a sneering, arrogant young man who stood smiling and motionless while Ethel battered on his chest with her fists.

'Get out, English devils!' she cried. 'There is nothing for you here. Nothing!'

Lebecque took command of the situation at once. He put a gentle arm round Ethel's shoulders and steered her out of harm's way, interposed himself between the soldiers and my mother.

'Gentlemen,' he said, 'what is your business?'

'Search and confiscate,' drawled the sergeant. 'Stand aside.'

Lebecque stood his ground. 'Which regiment?'

'You're French.' It was not a question; it was an accusation.

'Yes.'

'Stand aside.' The sergeant squared up to Lebecque; in a fight, they would be evenly matched. The soldier was shorter but looked strong and pugnacious, clearly used to fighting; on the side of his face, from one curly brown sideburn down to his jaw, there was a fresh scar. His eyes betrayed the bully beneath the uniform.

Lebecque, however, was no puny cleric. I knew well enough the strength in the limbs beneath his robes. But instead of pushing the sergeant back and clearing the insolent soldiers out of the house, he meekly stepped aside.

'What are you doing, Lebecque?' I hissed. 'Let's throw them out!'

'For God's sake, Charles, keep a cool head.'

The sergeant seemed to notice me for the first time, and looked me up and down with a wolfish grin. 'This is the child of the house, I presume?'

He knew exactly how to anger me; he was not many years my senior, and only a little taller than me, but his uniform gave him authority.

'Be careful who you are addressing, sir,' I said, trying to look haughty. 'This is the home of a Scottish family. You are not welcome.'

'Charles, please go upstairs,' said Lebecque. The soldiers were laughing openly. 'Let me deal with this.'

'You? Why you? I am the man of the house!' The sergeant guffawed.

'Charles, I beg you –'

'Go on, boy,' said the sergeant, 'let Mummy tuck you up in bed. There's nothing for you to play with here.'

'I will not be told –'

'Charlie...' It was my mother this time, white-faced, wringing her hands. I stood my ground.

The sergeant relished my discomfiture. 'Snot-nosed kids should obey their mothers. Even the child of a Jacobite whore.'

Silence fell with a thud. Lebecque clenched his fists. The sergeant stood there, insolently chewing. His soldiers sniggered and wiped their noses. All eyes were on me.

'Nobody insults my mother in front of me, sir!'

'Go to the playroom, Scottish brat.'

'Charles...'

'Nobody! Get out of my house!' I jumped down the stairs and launched myself on the sergeant, grabbing for his throat. He was too quick for me, stepped backwards and left me sprawling at his feet. He stuck the muddy boot of his toe in my face and rubbed it around my mouth.

'You don't want us to take you as well, do you, pretty boy? You know what happens to babes like you in the army, don't you?'

'Don't touch him.' Lebecque's voice sounded commanding. The sergeant stiffened, as if in the presence of a commanding officer.

'Take what you want and leave.'

'Well, that's very kind of you,' drawled the sergeant, relaxing again. 'Gibson. Bright. Arrest him.'

Two of the brutish soldiers stepped forward. My mother screamed in fright, but they didn't touch me; they went straight for Lebecque and held him by the arms. A third soldier bound his hands with a rope. Lebecque offered no resistance.

'There,' said the sergeant with mock kindness, 'we needn't go through the motions of searching the house now. Prisoner gave himself up, didn't he? We'll trouble you no further, sir.' This last with grating sarcasm to me. 'Good day. Men! Fall in! About turn! Quick march!'

The soldiers ambled out of the house, talking and laughing. Lebecque, bound at a rope's end, was pulled after them. My mother and I were rooted to the spot.

The last thing I saw was Lebecque's head turned to face us one last time, an imploring look in his eyes.

The soldiers pulled him through the door and were gone.

Chapter Five

Three weeks passed and we heard nothing. We lived in daily dread of a return visit from the redcoats, but Gordon Hall remained silent. I begged my mother to tell me all she knew about Monsieur Lebecque, but she dismissed me, took to her bed and refused to see anyone except Ethel. I sought Girolle in the village but he, said the landlord at the inn, had disappeared, leaving a purse of silver to cover his lodging. Lebecque had passed out of our lives as suddenly, as mysteriously, as he had arrived.

Well, I had achieved my ends. The threat to our family was gone. Lebecque's humiliation was complete. I could not have planned it better myself. So why was I nagged by a sense of guilty and misery? For all that I tried to gloat, I felt that I had betrayed a man, that my arrogance and stupidity had endangered a life. Lebecque may have been a bad priest, a hypocrite – but I could not forget the look in his eyes as he was dragged out of Gordon Hall to face God only knew what tortures at the hands of his captors. And just before, he had tried to tell me something. He had paved the way to an understanding between us and I, in my pride and ignorance, had rebuffed him.

Finally one day the mail coach brought an envelope addressed to my mother in an unknown hand. Within was a brief, scrawled note from Lebecque.

Most honoured Madame Gordon

Fate has been kind to me, and I am comfortable enough in captivity. Do not attempt to find me. Further communication is impossible. I beg you to forgive the imposition on your family and the danger and discomfort in which I placed you. I would wish Master Charles to keep up his studies, and enclose directions to that end.

Your servant
Benoit Lebecque

Wrapped in the note was a thick, sealed package bearing the inscription 'CEG' – my initials in Greek characters. Poor, honest Lebecque had found the time to worry about my education. I had misjudged him.

How far I had misjudged him I was about to find out. Dawdling up to the library, I anticipated nothing more than a series of dry grammatical exercises, a translation from Aristotle, perhaps. I sat down, carefully broke the seal and unwrapped the package. Inside were four sheets of thin, dirty paper, closely hatched with Greek script. I sighed and prepared to start work. Within two minutes my eyes were starting out of my head.

φιλοσ Χαρολοσ

This salutation, in perfect Attic Greek, was followed by Lebecque's confession. Sweating and impatient with my own imperfect powers of translation, I worked my way through the letter. By the end I was in tears. 'Dearest Charles,' it began.

I pray that this letter, written at great danger to myself, finds you and your mother safe and well. I know you will wish, both of you, never to see me again, and if God is just you never will. I must ask you to perform one final task for me, and then forget me. But first, to understand the importance of this favour that I ask you, you must know who and what I am. Charles, you always wished to understand. I tried to protect you, but now you have your wish.

I am not a priest but an ordinary sinner; an extraordinary sinner, perhaps I should say. You will judge for yourself, I am sure. Remember, though, that all I did was in service of my King and to protect you, your family and many, many others like you.

My name is truly Benoit Lebecque, and I am by vocation a scholar and theologian. I might have made a good priest, but God chose a different course for me. Perhaps, as you told me, my carnal appetites would have made a hypocrite of me had I worn the habits of a man of God while polluting myself within. But that is a charge of which I exonerate myself.

I was forced from my studies by the demands of the Stuart cause. My family has ancient links with yours; our fathers were sworn supporters of Prince Charles, who now lives in exile near my home in Argiers. In the aftermath of our defeat at Culloden, and the shameful murder of your father, I swore to serve those few powerful and prominent Jacobites still living in Scotland, who wished to escape the dangers of General Wade's avenging army and join their Lord in France. To that end I was despatched north to live with you in the guise of a humble priest and tutor. In fact I directed a small army of spies through Girolle and others, who made contact with our targets and, when the time was right, put them to ship from the west coast, to temporary havens in Ireland and finally on the long voyage to safety in France.

All went well, and we rescued perhaps a dozen from certain death. Then, alas, we were betrayed. By whom? I am not sure. I only know that information given to the soldiers led them directly to Gordon Hall, where they were under orders to force me into open resistance and then arrest me on whatever pretext they could. To spare you and your mother the pain of further violence I allowed them to take me, suspecting rightly that I was their only target.

Your mother resisted my presence in the house from the start, but was loyal to the memory of her husband and sacrificed her own peace of mind for the good of our glorious cause. Please, Charles, comfort her now and reassure her. I wish I could give better news, but I fear her trials are not over. Your family will never be free from suspicion. I will say nothing to incriminate you, even on pain of death. But while you remain at Gordon Hall, you are in danger.

Now, Charles, to my final commission. In my trunk, among my few humble possessions, there is an encrypted list of all the families to whom I was to bring assistance. It is concealed under a false panel at the bottom of the chest. You must find it and destroy it immediately. Girolle held all the day-to-day papers, and has returned with them to France. Only this document remains and must be destroyed. Please, Charles, obey me in this. As long as the list survives, the danger to you and your family is acute.

Finally, to me. I am held in solitary confinement in a castle near Fort William. My journey here was arduous but I avoided any real brutality. The soldiers, as all redcoats, were a degenerate rabble and taunted me endlessly with their vileness, but laid not a finger on me, perhaps out of respect for the cloth. They know nothing of the truth, only that I am a spy. They believe me to be a priest.

Although Fort William is not far from Gordon Hall, it took us three days to reach it. We stopped at every inn and every house along the way. The drunken soldiers, when they could not find a woman willing to entertain them, had their own amusements which I was forced to witness. I shall not describe them to you, Charles. You know I have no grounds for moralising. I know much of the world, and have experienced much. I know about the love that exists between men. What I have witnessed among this rabble is a grotesque travesty of that love.

Finally we reached Fort William, and none too soon; the soldiers were tiring of my silent presence, and preparing to amuse themselves with me. I was delivered to the captain of the garrison and put straight into a tiny cell which has now been my home for three weeks. I was provided with bread and water through a tiny hatch in the door. Nobody spoke to me. I had one blanket, filthy and lousy, to protect myself against the cold nights. A bucket in the corner of the cell serves all my other needs.

The silence was the worst thing; after a few days I started talking to myself just for the company of a human voice. I feared madness, Charles, in that terrible time. But God was merciful and sent a kind young soldier to tend me. The rope burns on my wrists were still open and dirty; my head was scabbed and scarred from the vicious attention of the prison barber who shaved it when I arrived.

This soldier, a pale, blond English boy only a little older than you, came to my cell at dawn, not daring to speak above a whisper for fear of detection. All the guards were under strict instructions to leave me entirely alone until General Wade himself should arrive at the castle to question me; perhaps they hoped I would die in the meantime. My soldier, however, took pity on me.

First of all he brought me meat and drink from his own rations, took away the stinking slop bucket and returned with clean cloths and a bowl of hot water. He sat patiently beside me while I wolfed the food, watching me through dark, troubled eyes, nervously wringing his hands. When I had eaten he took the plate from me and whispered in my ear.

'Don't make a noise. Let me help you.'

Carefully, gently he tore away the bandages I had improvised from a few torn strips of my shirt and dabbed at my wounds with clean water. Then he slid the ruined garment over my head and attended to the weals on my back where the soldiers had beaten me with sticks. He cleaned my neck, my ears, my scalp. The water, and the touch of kindness, felt so good that I revived and, for the first time in weeks, seemed to breathe freely.

The soldier lifted me carefully to my feet and pulled away the foul rags that were all that remained of my undergarments. After all this time in solitary confinement I was disgracefully dirty, and thoroughly ashamed of myself; the soldier did not seem to mind, and pushed my hand away when I tried to stop him. He wrung out his cloth and dabbed away at my hindquarters, rubbing gently until I was once more presentable. Then he transferred his attentions to the front. I must have smelled terrible. He didn't seem to mind.

Soon I was clean once more, and I felt the strength and self-respect returning. My guardian angel, still kneeling before me with the cloth in his hand, seemed in no hurry to finish his job; perhaps he was as lonely as me, and relished this sympathetic human contact. He was drying me now with a clean towel, slowly, carefully. I noticed that his hands were shaking.

God forgive me, I realised at once that I had him in my power. I am not a cruel man, Charles, but I know that a man in desperate straits must clutch at every opportunity that presents itself. When I saw him lick his lips, I seized the advantage. I grasped him by the wrist – his arms were thick, white and hairless – and held on to his hand, staring straight down into his imploring eyes. He was terrified, I could see. What punishments, I wondered, would await him? He had compromised himself quite enough by helping me... but now?

The tenderness with which he had ministered to me had awakened my lower self, and I was half erect. I will spare you descriptions, Charles; I know that you have seen it all for yourself, that night through my chamber window.

My soldier, however, had never seen it before and was transfixed. I let go his hand and swayed my hips slowly before him. It was all a ruse, I suppose, but I was not immune to the charm of the situation. When he took hold of my fully hard cock, I was as pleased as he was.

At first he was too scared to do much, and needed reassurance, so I knelt down beside him (his hand never left me), took him gently by the chin and kissed him. Oh Charles! After denying myself the pleasure of human contact for so long in my guise as a priest, I cannot tell you how sweet it was to kiss another – even in these degraded circumstances! The soldier's breath was fresh; unlike his *confrères*, he did not drink beer or smoke tobacco. He returned my kiss with ardour, and we sank to the cell floor in a passionate embrace. I tore myself away and barked out an order: 'Strip!' My soldier recognised the voice of command, jumped to his feet and divested himself quickly and efficiently of his uniform.

What I saw astonished me. The whiteness of his skin, and the athletic development of his body, resembled exactly the marble statues of ancient Greek athletes that we see in the great collections of Paris. There was only one difference: where the Greek ideal is minutely endowed, this living statue was blessed with a huge, hard rod curving up between his legs. It was my turn to stare. The soldier blushed and tried to cover himself with his hands, as if he was ashamed of his arousal. I stood beside him, put an arm round his shoulders and took it in my hand. I thought he would faint.

'Nobody has ever touched it before, sir.'

'Not even your wife?'

'I have no wife. Oh please, sir...'

His knees were buckling; I had only handled him for a few seconds and great white bullets were arcing out across the cell floor.

I thought now that he would dress and hurry away, but far from it. With the last drop hanging from his still-hard cock, he fell to his knees and took me in his mouth. God, it was good! I was ready to come in his mouth, but he had other plans. Kneeling on all fours, he presented his hard, white arse to me. I needed no further bidding. Hawking into my hand, I smeared spit over the end of my cock and placed it against his hole. One rude shove and I was inside him. He wanted to cry out in pain, I know, but could not. The bestiality of the situation inflamed me, and I was merciless. Reaching round to feel him, I found that he was still as hard as wood. When I pumped myself dry inside his tight arse, I held him in a fierce embrace and watched as he coaxed another load to splatter against the damp stone.

We held each other for a while until my soldier, awakening at last to the dangers of our situation, dressed and left me – not, however, before I had extracted from him a promise to visit me again with pen and paper.

So now, Charles, you know all. You know what sort of man I am, and you will perhaps guess how hard it was for me to play the tutor-priest in Gordon Hall. You will understand the sorrow with which I destroyed your friendship with Alexander. You will also understand the lengths to which I will go to furnish myself with the means to write you this warning. I hope, Charles, that to understand all is to forgive... not all, perhaps, but some.

It is only the thought of your safety that has kept me hopeful during this terrible time. I may never be able to communicate with you again. Forgive me for imposing my experiences on you. Now I wish I could erase it all and start again, but my soldier is waiting at the door to take this message away and smuggle it out of the prison. I enclose it in a letter to your mother.

Charles, your image is with me always.

Enough. I must close now.

Do my bidding and then find safety.

Pray for me

In haste

BL

What had I done? God, what had I done? In an agony of soul-searching I fled from the library and ran along the corridor, half blinded by tears. I found the door to Lebecque's old room, mercifully unlocked. Nobody had been inside since his arrest; my mother must have believed that he would one day return.

He had left it tidy. The trunk was neatly packed, the bed made, the few books and papers in perfect order on his desk. I dived into the trunk and started flinging the contents about the room: his riding boots, a Bible, a small framed portrait of a woman, a few garments, his shaving kit. It was all here, and poor Lebecque was in prison facing certain death.

The trunk was a cunning piece of workmanship with a false bottom that it took me several minutes, and three broken nails, to unfasten. There was the list wrapped in purple silk – just two pages of meaningless symbols, numbers and letters. For this Lebecque had been willing to sacrifice his life. I cast around me for the means of destruction, but there was nothing to be found. There would be a fire downstairs. That would have to do. For a moment I held one of his shirts to my face and breathed deeply, hoping to catch a trace of him, then leapt to my feet and ran as if the whole English army were at my back. My mother, disturbed by the racket, appeared at her bedroom door like a ghost, calling after me. I ignored her and bounded down the stairs, into the hall and flung the papers into the flames. I barely breathed until they were consumed in ashes then, grabbing the poker, I smashed the few curled black remnants into powder.

Panting, sweating and with tears smudging my face, I sat on the floor in a daze. My mother glided into the room and clung to the door frame.

'Charles! What is the matter?'

'Nothing... nothing...'

'I insist that you tell me what you are doing.'

'I cannot.'

'Is it Lebecque?'

I nodded, and wiped my face. I had to take control of myself. I was truly the man of the house now, without Lebecque's protection.

'Mother, I think we must leave Gordon Hall.'

'What? But I thought –'

'I do not consider our position here to be safe. Please make preparations for our departure. We will close the house down.'

'But Charles –'

'Please, mother. There may be no time to lose.'

I don't know what I feared exactly; I did not fully understand what Lebecque feared. It was enough that he had trusted me with this final commission and had counselled retreat. He would find me now, after the event, obedient. Now that it was too late to make a difference. Too late to save him.

My mother, recovering miraculously from the ailment that had kept her to her room for so long, bustled around the kitchen with Ethel, directing the packing-up of crates and trunks for our removal to the island of Rum. Within eight hours, the house was put to sleep: dust covers on the furniture, bags on the chandeliers, the shutters barred and locked over every door and window.

I had done my share of the work; as the only man on the estate, I had no choice. MacFarlane, whose services we would usually have called on under such circumstances, was nowhere to be found. I had little doubt in my mind that he was the spy who had sold Lebecque to the English.

A coach and horses was hired at vast expense from Portnacroish, our goods loaded on board by the surly driver, and all was ready for our departure. I was proud of the haste with which I had obeyed Lebecque's orders – and yet, for all that my mind was occupied with details, I was troubled in my soul. I was running away.

It was what he had told me to do. If he had been here, he would have pushed me into the coach himself and slammed the door on me, ready to face any dangers on his own. Why? Was I not a man as well as he, able to stand up and fight? Did he truly believe in his heart that I would abandon Gordon Hall – and, more to the point, that I would abandon him to the tender mercies of the English? He had said things in his letter which I'd had no leisure to consider – certain phrases – 'Your image is with me always' – a note of tenderness and regret running through the fevered confessional. I could not interpret it now, I was confused, tired and afraid. My mind jumped back to our last conversation, the imploring look as he was led away like a dog. Duty told him to send me away, to forget me. But something within – behind that trap-door face, that granite exterior – wanted me to do otherwise.

I climbed into the coach beside my mother and we rumbled down the drive, leaving Gordon Hall and all its memories behind us. We rounded the coppice, we passed the stables, drove through the gates and out on to the road, headed north-east to cross the loch at Ballachulish Bridge. My head was spinning.

Delayed at Ballachulish by a queue at the tollgate, we waited motionless for ten minutes. My mother, wrapped in her shawl, was shrinking back into a corner of the carriage. Ethel, exhausted by the day's alarms, had fallen asleep. Finally the traffic ahead of us inched forward, stopped, inched forward again, and we were moving.

Just before the horses stepped on to the bridge, I eased the door open and dropped quietly to the ground. The carriage picked up speed; I heard my mother's cry and caught sight of the white flash of her bonnet as I jumped over the fence and slid, unnoticed by any but her, down the slope to the river bank.

ƒ

I rested quietly by the water until dusk, watching the rats playing on the bank and hearing the rumble of wheels above my head.

Finally the tollgate was closed and all was silent.

It was a three-hour walk back to Gordon Hall, but I knew the road like the back of my hand, and gained my home without incident. I was not so foolish as to stay there; when trouble came, I was not intending to face it alone. But I needed supplies for my journey, and I could think of nowhere else to get them.

My journey? Of course, I had decided to go to Fort William and rescue Lebecque. How? I wasn't sure, yet. Perhaps I would recruit a small private army on the road and storm the castle. Perhaps I would present myself to the captain of the garrison and win him over with the sheer force of my oratory. Or perhaps they would clap me in irons with Lebecque. Anything was better than the thought that he would simply forget me, would believe that I had slipped away to safety on the islands and left him to rot.

The strength of my feelings surprised me; it was not so long ago, after all, that I loathed and despised the man. How easily that had changed.

In Gordon Hall I equipped myself with a sword, money, some warm clothes and all the food I could find (it was little enough) packed up in a leather knapsack. From Lebecque's trunk I took his cotton shirt and the small framed portrait of a woman; tokens of him, I now suppose, to bring good fortune to my journey; that was how I thought of it at the time. Perhaps the woman was his wife. I preferred to believe it was a sister.

I needed to sleep, but would not allow myself the luxury. How could I think of warm beds with clean sheets when Lebecque was shivering in the misery of a filthy cell? Determined to punish myself, I set out from the house a little after midnight. This was my first mistake. Well rested, with a clear head, I might have fallen into trouble a little less easily.

The way to Fort William took me back along the shore of the loch to Ballachulish, through the Glenduror Forest, a scrubby collection of trees and heath barely worthy of the name; I planned to stop at the village of Auchindarroch to exchange a few coins for provisions; the rest of my little horde I would need for bribes.

The inn at Auchindarroch was busy even in the small hours of the morning. As I emerged, cold and tired, from the last few trees of the forest, I could see the windows blazing with light; a few more paces and I could hear the welcome sound of human voices. With a lighter heart, I trotted the last few yards and opened the door to feel the heat from the fire.

A tired-looking barmaid pushed past me with a tray full of pewter tankards. There was a powerful stink of beer and tobacco in the air. Sprawling around the fire was a company of five men, all, I would say, in their thirties or forties, a rough and ready group but, I thought, honest-looking Scotsmen each and every one of them. When I entered the inn they had been joining in a chorus of Loch Lomond – a crypto-Jacobite hymn, as every young Scot knew well. My immediate fears that these were the dreaded red-coats were swiftly allayed. I felt, for the time being, safe.

The barmaid, her cargo delivered, appeared at my side. 'We're full. You should run along, lad.'

'I don't need a bed,' I said. 'I have a long journey to make. I only want provisions.'

'You don't want them here, my dear,' she whispered, but the men had heard her.

'What's that, Molly? Let the young man in! He looks exhausted. Here, young 'un, come and sit by the fire and give us a song.'

I declined, and repeated my request to the barmaid for food and drink. With a defeated look, she trudged off to the kitchen and left me.

I sat myself on a stool at the end of the bar, well apart from the circle of jolly companions but close enough to the hearth to feel some benefit of the fire. Like all true Scots, they were an amicable crew and could not bear to see a countryman alone and melancholy

– not when there was good cheer at hand.

'Come on, lad, join us! We'll not bite you!'

'We're not the bloody English vermin,' said another, spitting into the hearth. 'God send confusion to them all!'

Cheered by this crude confession, and by the sight of the forbidden tartan here and there about their persons, I gained confidence and joined them. No sooner had I sat down than a tankard of ale was in my hand, a friendly arm round my shoulders and a gabble of voices asked for my story.

I looked around the circle of faces. They were a tough-looking bunch. Three of them I took to be brothers: each shared the same brown, wavy hair, the full mouth and a generally simian cast of features. One of the brothers was tall, with huge, long arms that hung out of his side, magnificent against the fur and leather of his sleeveless tunic. The second was shorter, thicker set, a little less apelike than his big brother, less prone to laugh and joke. The third and youngest of the brothers was darker and finer than his elders and wore a white shirt unlaced to the stomach, revealing a smooth brown chest. He had taken off his muddy trousers and was hanging them over the back of his chair to dry by the fire; his legs, unlike the rest of his body, were thick with hair. Their two companions were older and less striking. One was a beetle-browed giant of a man, his head covered only by a quarter-inch of cropped steel-grey hair, his eyebrows jet black in contrast. The other had Viking looks: straight flaxen hair, pale eyebrows, invisible eyelashes and tattoos of strange, curling devices up his arms and around his throat. Both his ears were pierced with gold hoops.

Had I been less full of bravado, I would have considered a little before falling in with such unusual company. However, with the excitement of my quest before me, and the warmth of the fire without and the beer within, I was all too ready to join the gang. They were interested in me. They treated me like a man; a novel experience for me. When they asked what I was doing, I was happy to tell them.

'I'm travelling to Fort William to rescue a friend of mine.'

'Oh yes,' said the middle brother, 'and where is he, pray?'

'In a castle.'

'Ah. The castle.'

'Held by the English.'

'The English!' He looked at the company and smiled. 'God send confusion to them all!' They spat in unison and laughed. I tried to follow suit, made a mistake with a mouthful of beer and ended up coughing until the tears were running down my cheeks.

'Hey, there, Molly,' shouted the tallest brother, 'bring some whisky for this young man!'

A bottle and glass were set in front of me; from that point on, the glass was never empty, no matter how much I drank.

'And who are you, brave hero?' asked the youngest brother, replenishing my draught. 'What is your name, that we might toast you?'

'Charles Edward Gordon.'

'The Gordons of Gordon Hall! The King's blessing on you!'

'The King!' They all stood and lifted their glasses. We sat and drank again. By now I was ecstatic thanks to whisky and self-regard. I thought they were a jolly crew.

'Perhaps, my lads, you will join me on the road and help defeat the English devils at Fort William!'

'God send confusion to them all!' they chorused again, and we spat together, a little more successfully this time.

'Well, that's a generous offer,' said the middle brother, clearly the brightest of the gang, its leader. 'It would certainly be an honour to serve a noble young man such as yourself, wouldn't it lads?' The others mumbled agreements and laughed. I laughed with them.

'Are you with me, then?' I cried, leaping to my feet with what I hoped was a heroic flourish.

'Now,' said the middle brother, 'that depends. We are fighting men, you see, loyal to the King in exile, and we could not lend our arms to one who was in any way less than our equal. It is a question of honour.'

'I'm the equal of any man here,' I said, putting a hand on the hilt of my sword.

'Of course, Charlie, of course. A very able swordsman, I'm sure. Come on, now, give us a taste of your skills. Let's see a few passes there, lad.'

I needed no second bidding. Like a child with an audience of grown-ups, I drew my sword and attempted my best lunges and parries. They were pitiful, I suppose, but the gang cheered and clapped however badly I stumbled.

'Excellent! Excellent!' shouted the oldest brother, and stood up. He was over a foot taller than me. 'Now, let us see if you can drink like a man!' He picked up a foaming tankard and downed it in one, his thick throat working in great waves as he guzzled the ale. He slammed the vessel down on the table, smacked his lips and put his hands on his hips. The youngest brother handed me a tankard. The rest of them sat and watched me. I was aware that the crop-headed man and the Viking, who had not addressed a word to me, were smiling and whispering to each other.

I took the tankard, raised it to my lips, drew a deep breath and swallowed. One, two, three, four gulps and it was gone – a substantial amount of it down my front, soaking my shirt. They cheered and handed me a glass of whisky, banging their fists on the table to encourage me. I tossed the whisky off in one go, gasped and sat down. My head was spinning, my knees weak.

'Ah, he's a bold lad,' said the middle brother, gripping my thigh, 'and it's cruel of us to torment a child such as he.'

'I'm no child,' I slurred. 'I'm as much a man as any of you.'

'Well, let's see about that. Davie, you show him.'

Davie, the youngest brother who was still warming his bare legs at the fire, lifted up his shirt and pulled aside his undergarment. A large, soft cock flopped out into the open. In the firelight, and to my fuddled senses, it appeared to be golden.

'Are you as much of a man as Davie, now?'

'Yes, and more!' I would have risen to any challenge, no matter how dangerous or humiliating. I stood up, untied the drawstring at my waist and let my trousers drop to the floor. I was wearing nothing underneath them. My cock was, perhaps, a little longer than his; certainly, it was thicker.

'Well, that's a man's piece for sure, Charlie,' said the middle brother, 'but you can never tell what a man's really got until he's up and ready for action, if you know what I mean.'

While he was speaking, Davie had already started manipulating his organ until it was sticking out straight in front of him; it had grown considerably. I was still convinced that I was the winner, and in order to show myself off at my full capacity I closed my eyes, thought of Alexander's cock up my arse and started tugging on my balls. Within a few moments, I was as stiff as a post, my foreskin pulling back halfway over my shiny red knob.

'It's a close-run thing, but I think Davie's got the edge,' said the middle brother. I was outraged.

'No, I'm bigger than he is.' I stuck my hips out to emphasise my point.

'We'll just have to measure you up. Stand face to face.'

Davie and I did as we were told.

'Right you are, Jamie,' said Davie to his brother, 'you're the judge.'

Jamie, the middle brother, took our two hard cocks in his hand and held them side by side, pressed together. The heat from Davie's weapon was helping me to get even bigger.

'It's a close thing…' said Jamie, rubbing his hand appreciatively up our shafts, which excited me further, 'but I think I have to say that young Charlie-Boy is the winner.'

God, I was so pleased with myself! I shook Davie's hand as if I had just won a prize. I clasped my hands above my head in jubilation. Out of the corner of my eye I noticed the two silent members of the group glaring at me, massaging sinister-looking bulges in their groins; it only heightened my sense of victory.

'But still, I don't think you're the overall winner just yet. You've got to match up to Johnnie.'

Johnnie, of course, was the tallest brother. If everything was in proportion, I was licked. But I wouldn't give up.

'Come on then, Johnnie,' I said, 'let's see what you've got.' I waved my hips around, making my cock swing in challenge.

Johnnie smiled – not altogether a friendly smile – and pulled off his shirt. His body was powerful: great long muscles, a stomach like a cobbled street. Staring me straight in the eye, he undid the thick leather belt round his waist and threw it aside. His trousers did not drop to the floor; they were held up by a hefty pole in the fork of his legs.

'Come on, then. See what you're up against.' He grabbed my hand and placed it on his cock. Even without seeing it, I could tell it was massive; my hand went barely halfway round it.

'Pull it out into the open, Charlie,' said Jamie. 'Have a good look.'

I did as I was told. I was not disappointed. It was a monstrous piece of meat, a good few inches longer than my own, of awesome girth.

'Now,' said Jamie, 'there's a rule to this game. The winner takes all. That's fair, isn't it?' I couldn't concentrate on what he was saying; I was still staring in disbelief at Johnnie's horse-cock.

'Take it in your hands. Come on, get both hands on it.'

I took it in a double grip; there was plenty left over. I moved my hands up and down. Johnnie leaned against the back of a chair, thrust his hips forward and enjoyed himself.

'Now, Charlie,' continued Jamie, 'let's see if you can get all of that in your mouth.'

I knew for certain that I couldn't, but I wasn't going to be accused of not trying. I bent forward, licked the tip of Johnnie's cock, opened my mouth as far as it would go and took maybe the first three inches. It was not the length that prevented me from going any further, but the girth. My eyes were watering.

'Is that as good as you can do?' taunted Jamie. 'Well, it's got to go somewhere. Once you've got Johnnie all roused up like that, he has to put that thing somewhere or he goes off the rails. We don't want that, lad. So what shall we do?'

I felt fingers at my backside; the Viking and the shaven-headed man had finally joined the party, and with thick, dirty fingers were probing my hole. Instead of turning on my heel and running, naked as I was, out into the freezing night, I spread my legs a little wider to improve their access. It was a long time since anything other than my own finger had touched me there, and it felt good. The alcohol had numbed me to anything other than physical sensation. Somehow, the idea of being used by this group of big, brawny men appealed hugely. We would be an army of lovers – like the Spartans, I thought.

Davie took his brother's place in my mouth; his cock I could comfortably accommodate, and I practised on him all the skills that I had learned on Alexander. Rough hands were holding my buttocks apart; Johnnie had disappeared from my line of vision. I knew what was coming, and I was too stupid to avoid it.

The pain of his entry made me black out for a moment. When I came to, I was scarcely aware of my surroundings; the buzzing in my head was so confusing. Gradually I became aware of two things: the cock moving in my mouth, and the other, bigger, cock moving in my arse. I looked up and saw Davie taking a long swig from the whisky bottle; he dribbled a good deal down his lean brown stomach, and it mingled in my mouth with the taste of his cock. Johnnie was ploughing slowly, steadily away inside my arse; thank God I had been thoroughly fucked by Alexander, otherwise

I think I would have died from the pain. I knew better, though; instead of tensing, trying to force him out of me, I concentrated wholeheartedly on relaxing. The pain didn't go, but it levelled off into a bearable discomfort.

Davie pulled out of my mouth and, pulling my head back by the hair, shot a big, salty load of come into my face. His place was taken by the shaven-headed man, whose hard cock slipped straight down my throat and continued to pump me from that end. Johnnie, meanwhile, had picked up the pace of his fucking; I reached round and felt his huge balls pulled up tight against his body and I knew that he would come soon. In order to speed up the process and rid me of that giant intruder, I started wiggling my arse, tensing the muscles inside me to increase his pleasure.

'Look at the little fucker, lads,' said Johnnie, 'he's got a hot tail on him, that's for sure. Look at him wriggling that little pussy around my cock. Oh, Christ...' He thrust harder, harder – and then, when I could take no more, buried himself deep inside me and shot his load. The shaven-headed man, inspired by his friend's efforts, came copiously in my mouth, then pulled out, held my mouth shut, pinched my nose and forced me to swallow. At last, I was free, but not for long. Another cock – the huge, pale weapon of the Viking, rising straight from a bald, shaven crotch – loomed into my face. Without resisting, I let my mouth drop open. He didn't even care whether I sucked him or not, he simply fucked my mouth as if he was masturbating into me. Jamie, the ringleader, had stripped himself naked and was biding his time, fingering my sore arse until the Viking had finished off. It didn't take long. Now there was only one to go. I opened my mouth to take Jamie's prick – not as big as his brother's, I noticed with some relief, but a handsome piece nonetheless. But he had other ideas.

Pulling me upright, he cleared one of the tables with a sweep of his hand, lay down on top of it and motioned to his brother. Johnnie picked me up as if I weighed nothing, pulled my legs apart and lowered me on to Jamie's dick, which he was holding erect in readiness. I sat down and it was buried inside me.

In this position, at least, I had some control over the fucking. Davie took another swig of whisky and handed me the bottle; I was glad of it. Kneeling, and resting back on my heels, I started to move myself up and down on Jamie's cock. To my eternal shame, I began to enjoy myself. The sight of the four spent men, lying in attitudes of abandon around us, filled me with a certain pride; I had satisfied them. Jamie's cock felt good stirring around in my guts. I had remained flaccid throughout my previous ordeal, but now, as the head of his prick battered the sensitive spots inside me, my cock was hard and drooling like a baby.

Shifting my position slightly, I changed my movement from up-and-down to backwards-and-forwards, shunting myself around on my knees. Jamie reached forward and gripped my cock, scooped up the sticky fluid that was spilling out of it and brought his fingers to his mouth. The other men, lazily watching my whorish antics, were already becoming hard again, ready to take advantage of my eagerness. Finally, when I felt that Jamie was ready to come, I hoisted myself up off my knees, rested my weight on the balls of my feet and rode him as hard as I could. As he squirted another load inside my arsehole, I came all over his hairy belly.

I was sweating, drunk as a lord, and very pleased with myself. I was ready to take them all on again. Jamie was looking up at me and laughing. The other brothers were stiff and ready for me.

I felt a hand slip round me from the back and catch me by the waist, another clamped over my mouth. There was a whoosh, a cracking noise in my head, and I knew no more.

Chapter Six
Fort William, 2 November 1750

Dearest Charles

Unexpectedly I find myself able once again to write to you. For the blessing of pen and paper, and the unspeakable relief of unburdening my heart in a letter, I have to thank my only friend in this foul prison, the young guard of whom I told you. Do not judge him (or me) too harshly. We have used each other for our own ends, and come to an understanding in the process.

I send this to Gordon House uncertain whether it will ever reach you. If you have taken my advice, you and your mother will by now be far beyond harm's reach. Perhaps a loyal servant or friend will find this letter and forward it to you. Perhaps it will never reach you; that, after all, might be for the best. I cannot help hoping in my weaker moments that you stayed at Gordon House to face the danger, only so that I could picture you there reading my letter and – dare I hope? – thinking more kindly of me than was your habit.

The cell which has been my home these last weeks is approximately eight feet by eight feet, enough for me to lie down on the straw mattress. The ceiling is six feet high, the only place where I can stand upright. And yet, despite my cramped circumstances, I contrive to keep myself fit and well.

The bars on the small, square window serve as a rudimentary gymnasium, and I force myself every hour to exercise my arm and leg muscles by hanging from them. I exercise as well on the cell floor, raising and lowering the weight of my own body by the strength of my arms and my abdominal muscles, and run on the spot for half-hours at a time in order to prevent myself from falling into lethargy and despair. That is my greatest terror. I hear the cries of some of the poor souls elsewhere in the prison, those who have lost hope and reason. God preserve me from that fate.

I do not know what end awaits me. The fact that I have been here for so long gives me hope; an immediate execution is what I expected, and the passing of every day seems to take me further and further from a sudden end. But I do not entertain vain hopes; I know too well that politics can turn on a sixpence. My life could end tomorrow.

I would not, however, die altogether unhappy. I have found a kind of peace here in my cell; a resignation and an understanding. Charles, many times we read the works of the ancient philosophers together. Now, perhaps, I begin to understand their meaning.

The single light in my darkness is the regard I bear for you. Perhaps I did not make it clear to you; I know that your mind was closed against me from the start, as well it might have been. I sent your friend away; I seemed to alienate your mother. I was of necessity hard and cold to you. You could not know that during my short time at Gordon House I came first to like you as an intelligent, personable and spirited young man, then to admire your courage and integrity, and finally to love you. I bit my tongue, preferring duty to happiness. I do not regret it. I would not have burdened you with the additional, unwanted responsibility of my love. You have enough on your plate. But now I regard my feelings for you as the one pure thing in a life that has been otherwise sullied by compromise and dishonesty. I hope you will not despise its memory.

Throughout my youth I fought against impulses towards my fellow man. My many friends – students at the university, mostly – never guessed that I harboured physical desires towards them. I rejoiced in the Platonic, fooling myself that a healthy friendship with these athletes and scholars was all I desired. Only once did I let myself go further, with the brother of a friend during one long, hot summer party at their family home outside Paris. He was a little older than me; I was perhaps your age at the time. He took me on a long walk through the woods and fields that bordered the estate, and, in the shade of an oak grove, introduced me to the physical side of life. We never discussed it afterwards, and I swore it would never happen again.

It was only when I came to Gordon Hall that I realised the error of my ways. A marriage had been arranged for me at home; if ever I returned a hero, I was quickly to become a husband. The girl was the daughter of a neighbour, of good family, a friend since childhood. I am thankful now that I spared her the heartbreak of a marriage contracted under false pretences. When I met you, Charles, and discovered the nature of your friendship with Alexander, I realised that I was fighting my own true nature for nothing. I swear that I did not send him away out of spite; he would undoubtedly have been captured and punished if the redcoats had found him. MacFarlane, who betrayed him to me, would have betrayed him to them for the same coin.

MacFarlane spared me no detail of what he had seen and heard through your bedroom window. He was a wise man in his way, and I have no doubt that he detected in me an interest over and above the purely professional. He as good as told me so, and offered to arrange things between you and me for a further consideration. I, of course, pretended not to understand him. But I could not rid myself of the image of you naked in Alexander's arms. When we swam together in the loch, I was shaking with fear and anxiety as much as from the cold water. I could not trust myself. I had to give up swimming in order not to betray myself.

But I could not stop my imagination, try as I might. I started to dream about you. Our lessons became torture to me. I was glad when you put an end to them; the effort it took not to reach out and touch your hand was exhausting to me. But separation made things worse, and I was haunted by my feelings for you. While I should have been concentrating on my mission in Scotland, assisting your countrymen in their escape to France, I was wandering around the countryside in a daze. As the summer wore on, I was no longer able to sleep. I could gain a few hours' respite by masturbating, holding your image before me at every stroke. When I suspected that you had witnessed one of these episodes, I was ashamed. Now I am glad. It is the nearest we will ever come to the complete union that I so desperately long for.

There is little else to say. I hope, Charles, to be able to let you know what happens to me, but I promise I will never press an unwanted suit on you. My friend, the prison guard, has promised to supply me with paper and pen for as long as he can. I saw him one day spying on me through the bars on my door, pressing his face against them as I completed my exercises. I was sweating, and consequently stripped naked, trying to keep my clothes as dry as possible. He beckoned to me, and I went to the door, expecting him to come in and resume our relations on the cell floor. He said, however, that he was scared to open the door, and finally persuaded me to hoist myself up on some broken brickwork and stick myself through the bars. The sound of his lips slurping and smacking around my stiff cock echoed off the cell walls. It did not take long for me to come; something in the novelty of the situation, degrading as it was, pricked me to a state of extreme arousal. The muscles in my arms were bulging and straining as I held on to the bars and pushed myself as far forward as I could. I tried not to cry out when I came. The guard held me in his mouth and swallowed every drop. I climbed down and rested my sweating forehead against the cool bars, and watched as he pulled his cock out of his uniform trousers and splashed his boots with hot, white sperm.

And so I manage to keep myself provided with pen and paper, as well as rations slightly superior to those I might otherwise expect. Forgive me, Charles, for putting them to so ignoble a use. I do so only in the belief that you will understand me. The desire to unburden myself to a fellow man, suppressed in me for so long, has burst out now that it is too late for me to enjoy it. Take warning from my example.

God protect you
BL

Chapter Seven

I have no idea for how long I was unconscious. When I finally came to I was conscious at first of an unpleasant pitching motion which I attributed to the blow I had received on the head. Gradually I became aware of my other senses: a foul taste in my mouth, a mixture of sour whisky and male flesh; a pain in my head and my arse, both of which had been assaulted by blunt instruments; a peculiar smell in my nostrils, of tar and sweat and something earthy. There was a faint sound of knocking and splashing. Only my eyes could make out nothing. I was surrounded by darkness.

I must have fallen asleep again; when I awoke, a dim grey light enabled me to make out a little of my surroundings. I was lying on a rude cot knocked together from a few planks of wood. A rough blanket covered me. I could discern a few pale squares high above me, through which the light was filtering. I guessed that it was very early in the morning; the light had that weak, smoky quality of a Scottish dawn. By straining my ears, I could make out the sound of breathing or snoring. The gentle rocking continued. My head, by now, was clear. I assumed that I must be on board a ship. I was dreadfully thirsty.

I established by a few cautious movements of my limbs that I was neither injured nor bound. Once the light had increased to such an extent that I was in no immediate danger of braining myself or falling down a hole, I crept out of the cot and made my way towards a dark shape which seemed to be the source of the breathing. I was right; lying against a thick wooden pillar, his head thrown back and his mouth open, was a sleeping man. In his right hand he held a small bladed instrument; beside him was a large pile of brown root vegetables, smaller than a turnip, of a sort that I had never seen before. Evidently he had been in the process of peeling them when he had fallen asleep. A dispiritingly small mound of peel lay on his left.

The vessel was silent, and I had leisure to observe my companion. He was a young man, a few years my senior, dark haired, bearing the marks on his face of a recent fight. His right eye was blackened; his nose, evidently broken long before, was recently bloodied. It struck me, as the light increased, that he looked a little like Lebecque – a coarser, uglier version, but the same basic type. His dirty white shirt, which was torn to the waist and stained with blood, revealed a strong, hairy torso not unlike my tutor's. His face bore a resemblance too – Lebecque without the intelligence.

But my interest in him was nothing compared to the real object of my desires – a bucket of water that lay just beyond. To reach it I had to crawl right up to him and reach over his arm. My hand slipped on some of the wet peelings and I fell heavily into his lap. The man woke with a yell and a curse. I righted myself, and for a few moments we stared at each other, our faces a few inches apart in the gloom. Then, remembering that he carried a blade, I righted myself and stepped out of his reach.

'You're the boy.' His voice was thick, slightly slurred. I was not sure if this was the result of his recent battles, or his normal means of expression.

'Where am I?'

He laughed, then gripped his jaw in pain. 'You're in the hold.'

'What vessel?'

'The *Florida*.'

'Where bound?'

'Liverpool. We're moored at Oban.'

'How did I get here?'

He laughed again, and regretted it just as quickly. 'Don't ask me, boy. You were lying there when they threw me down last night. I'm on punishment detail. Peeling spuds.'

'Spuds?'

'Potatoes!' He laughed and set about one of the roots with his knife. 'Haven't you ever seen one before?'

'Who's the captain?'

'Moore.'

'English?'

'Yes. Not a bad bastard.'

'What happened to you?'

'Drunk and disorderly. Insulting an officer. Usual thing. Fighting over a... well, let's not go into that. I've taken my punishment.' He rubbed his nose and sneezed.

'What do they want with me?'

'Aren't you full of questions? How should I know. What are you? Jacobite? Moore picks up prisoners from the redcoats, ships them down to Liverpool for "questioning", at least that's what they call it.'

'But I've done nothing...' Then I remembered my foolish bragging to the mercenaries at the inn. Oh yes, I had been brave enough then. Telling them how I was the son of a great Jacobite hero, on my way to Fort William to rescue a French spy from the English devils – God send confusion to them all! Well, a long way my fine talk had got me. Fucked at both ends, sold to the redcoats (I hope they got a good price for me) and on my way to an uncertain fate in England.

'Are you hurt?' My companion, at least, had a glimmer of compassion.

'No,' I said, 'just my head.' A big clot of blood had dried in my hair. Otherwise I felt well enough.

'Let's have a look at you.' He got up; he was shorter than Lebecque, closer to my height, much thicker set. 'Come on over to the light.' He led me closer to one of the portholes, where a faint ray of sunshine permeated the stygian bowels of the ship. Carefully, gently, he looked me over.

'Pretty little mug,' he said, holding me under the chin. 'Where are you from?'

'Loch Linnhe.'

'Highlander. I thought so. You've the Highland colouring, sandy red hair, white skin. What age are you?'

'Nineteen.'

He thought for a moment. 'Are you brave?'

'In a fight? Yes, I think so.'

'In other ways?'

I did not understand what he was getting at. 'What do you mean?

He changed his tack. 'Been at sea before?'

'No.'

'You'll not know, then, the ways of seafaring men.' A faint light was dawning in my mind.

'I suppose you mean men who go without a woman for many months.'

He grinned awkwardly. 'Different customs at sea. I don't say one's good, one's bad. It's just the way things are. It'll take us a few days to reach Liverpool. Be careful, that's all I'm saying.'

'Thanks for the warning, but I can look after myself.' Nothing, of course, could have been further from the truth. Thinking back to the usage I'd received at the hands of my friends in the inn, I absent-mindedly rubbed my still-sore backside. A dull twinge of pain shot up inside me and brought back a tangible memory of the huge battery of cocks that had stretched my arsehole to its limits.

The sailor sat down and carried on with his peeling. Above us, on the deck, the crew were beginning to stir. The ship rocked as we prepared to sail. I sat down, dipped a tin cup into the bucket and drank, wondering all the more about the maritime customs to which he had referred. I idly watched him at work, the starch from the potatoes drying in splashes on his powerful arms and legs.

'Shall I help you?'

'No, lad. Thank you for the offer. There's only one peeler.'

'Let me do a few for you.'

'It's all right. Rest yourself.'

'Let me clear away the peels, then.' I started to scoop up handfuls of the cold, wet, slimy things that surrounded him, piling them neatly beside me. In my eagerness to be of assistance, I inevitably slipped again and landed face down in the potatoes, which rolled all over the floor. I spent the next ten minutes chasing them around the dark corners of the hold until I had retrieved them all. Occasionally I heard the sailor laughing. What a fool he must have thought me.

Thinking that my assistance had done more harm than good, I decided that a companionable silence might be of more use and so I sat beside him and drank another cup of water.

'There's still a spud rolling around on the floor somewhere.'

'Where?'

'Can't you see it?' He hitched up the tails of his filthy white shirt and there, between his legs, was a large, peeled potato which I must have missed during my attempts to tidy the hold.

'I'm sorry.'

'Well come on, boy, pick it up and put it on the pile.'

I reached down to grasp it, but my hand slipped on the wet surface. It seemed somehow to be attached to the floor. I gripped it again, more firmly this time, and lifted it an inch or two off the ground, but further than that it would not go. Finally I heaved harder, the potato came free in my hand and I sat down hard. The sailor was looking at me and grinning, holding up his shirt tails and pointing a big, hard, wet cock at me. I examined the potato in my hand. While my back had been turned he had bored a hole in it just big enough to slide his prick into. When he saw the look of astonishment on my face, he burst out laughing.

'Bet you've never seen a spud like that before, boy!' His cock shook and bounced as he laughed. The white starch from the potato coated it, running down his balls and gathering in the wiry hairs on his scrotum.

Crawling forward on my hands and knees, with the hollow potato held in front of me, I positioned the hole over the head of his cock again and pushed it down with a rude squelching sound. The sailor sighed and stretched out his legs. I pulled the potato back until I could see the edge of his knob popping out of it, then pushed it down again. Up and down, up and down it went, until his cock had swollen so much that that potato barely fitted around it.

Finally I threw the vegetable to one side and replaced it with my mouth. I lay on my belly in front of him, burying my face in his groin, sliding my lips up and down his cock, feeling each thick vein with my tongue, tasting the strange starchy taste of the potato mingling with the more familiar savours of sweat and piss. Resting his weight on the palms of his hands, the sailor hoisted his hips in the air in order to allow me easier access. I increased the speed of my sucking and fondled his balls, which were big and heavy. Moving down, I took them one at a time in my mouth, rolling them around, running my tongue all around them while the sailor moaned and bucked his hips.

At length he kneeled upright, I got on all fours and allowed him to fuck my mouth while he held on to my ears. Reaching over, he ran a hand over my arse, finding the sore spot where it had been so recently abused. Again, I felt a twinge – of pleasure this time rather than pain. I wriggled my arse responsively.

Pulling himself out of my mouth, he pushed me down until

my face was pressed against the floor of the hold, and then undid my trousers. I expected, then, to feel the heat of fingers or cock pressing against my arsehole, and was bracing myself for the pleasure to come; all through the sucking, I had been thinking how much I wanted this thick, hard piece of meat inside my bowels. But instead something cold and wet slapped against my arse: he had scooped up a huge handful of potato peelings and shoved them between my buttocks, rubbing them around until I was covered in starch. A few peelings clung to me as he picked up more, mashing them against the firm white flesh of my backside, rubbing them over my balls and then grasping my prick in a cold, slippery grasp that only made it hotter. Only then, when I was thoroughly plastered with the thick white fluid, did I feel at last the sudden hard prodding of his cock head against my slimy hole. I breathed deeply, opened up and felt him slide into me. A few short, hard thrusts and he was spewing his own load deep inside me.

With his prick still buried in my arse, the sailor flipped me over on to my back, spat on my cock and took me in his hand. I was desperate to come, and squirmed around on his still-hard pole, forcing it into the most sensitive corners of my arse while he wanked me gently at first, picking up pace until he was lifting me off the ground with each stroke. When I came, it splattered up his stomach and chest. He ran his fingers through it and brought them to his mouth, then leaned forward and kissed me. His cock slid out of my arse with a wet plop just as we heard footsteps approaching the trap door above our heads.

Quickly, silently, the sailor crushed his mouth against mine in a bruising kiss, pulled me down to lick the last few drops of come from his dirty, sweaty chest, then motioned me back to the cot. I scuttled across the floor; he hefted his cock back into his trousers and started work on another potato. The trap door above our heads creaked open and slammed down on to the deck; the sudden influx

of light caused me to wince. Boots appeared at the top of the ladder, then a pair of legs encased in thick blue cotton, a big, rounded
bum, a heavy leather belt, and a bare back.

'Time to wake up, sleeping beauties!' The new arrival jumped
the last three feet to the ground, landing deftly on the slippery
floor. When he turned to face us I saw a powerful, deeply-tanned
torso, perfectly smooth in contrast to the hairiness of the other.
Slabs of muscle slid and twitched under the toffee-coloured skin.
White teeth gleamed out of a mocking smile. Black eyebrows and
eyelashes framed pale blue eyes, forced into brilliance by a mop of
hair the colour of dirty straw. Evidently this was a man of some
authority on the ship; possibly the captain.

He strode over to where my sailor was hunched on the ground,
and made as if to kick him in the face. The sailor flinched in fear,
then, when he realised he had been tricked, scowled sulkily and
returned to his work.

'Fuck you, Déssert.'

'That's Mister Midshipman Déssert to you, shithead.' He had a
French drawl to his voice. Clearly this was not a regular naval vessel. What band of pirates had I fallen among? My sailor grumbled
and turned away.

'Where's the new pussy? Have you fucked him yet, shithead?'
There was no reply. I thought it best to feign ignorance, and pretended to wake out of a deep sleep. Déssert strode over to the cot
and stood with his feet a yard apart and his hands on his hips,
every inch a pirate out of a tale told to frighten children.

'Time to get up, pussy.' He prodded me none too delicately
with the toe of his boot. I rubbed my eyes and sat up. Déssert's
groin was hovering a few feet from my face. I had a distinct pre-
monition that it would be closer still before we reached Liverpool.

'You're wanted up on deck. We don't carry passengers, you
know. There's work to be done. Oh yes! Do we have work for you!'
He laughed – not kindly. I cast around me for the clothes I had

been wearing when I left Gordon Hall. Of course they were nowhere to be found.

'Where is my coat?'

Déssert laughed again. 'Your coat? You're wearing all the clothes that you arrived in. You want to be more careful about the company that you keep, Mister Gordon.' He knew my name, then. 'There are some dangerous characters at large in the Highlands. A nice little piece of arse like you isn't safe to roam around at night. Who knows what they might take from you?' With that he threw a bundle into my lap and jumped back on to the ladder. 'Change into your uniform and report to me up on deck in five minutes.' He was gone.

I untied the bundle and extracted two garments, neither of which I could identify at first. One was clearly intended for the upper body, one for the lower, but they were of a design hitherto unknown to me. The shirt, if I could call it that, was little more than a sleeveless singlet which, when I pulled it on, stopped short around my midriff. The trousers were unfathomable: there seemed to be a part missing. They were loose around the hips, and depending on which way I wore them they left either my cock or my arse exposed to the elements. I assumed they were some kind of over-garment, to be worn with the proper underwear, but there was nothing else in the bundle. I turned to the sailor for help, but he just shrugged and carried on with his work. I would have complained, but there was something about Déssert's tone of voice that quelled my disobedience. Adjusting the trousers so that the gap was at the rear (my theory being that I could more easily hide myself by keeping my back to the wall) I climbed the ladder. I caught my sailor friend casting one last fond look at my arse as I ascended, and then emerged, blinking, into the daylight.

Strong hands gripped the waistband of the trousers and hauled me up on to the deck; several voices raised an ironic cheer.

'Here's our new recruit! Make him welcome, boys!' Déssert held me up for inspection, then dropped me and shoved a scrubbing brush into my hands. He motioned with his foot to a wooden bucket of filthy suds.

'That's your work for the morning, my lad. Get down on all fours and scrub the deck.'

I was not used to this kind of address, and something in my expression must have betrayed my contempt for his orders. Seizing my ear, Déssert dragged me down to the ground and forced me to kneel at his feet. 'Come now, Mister Gordon, is this mutiny?' I hung my head and said nothing. Resistance was futile. I dipped my brush in the pail and began to scrub.

It was then that I realised that my decision to wear the trousers with the hole at the back had been a foolish one. Forced as I was to work on hands and knees, my arse was open to inspection by the entire crew, none of whom seemed to have anything better to do than stand around watching me work and passing comments on my performance. I tried to ignore their comments, but certain words – particularly the oft-repeated syllable 'fuck' – kept jumping out from the babble.

After a solo performance of perhaps five minutes, during which I had kept my head down and looked at nobody (partly to hide the shame burning in my cheeks), I heard Déssert blow a whistle, and the crew jumped into action. Bales were loaded into the hold, ropes wound and unwound, the sails hoisted into position. For all that they were a ragged-looking crew, they lacked nothing in discipline when it came to work, and within half an hour the ship was ready to sail.

I tried to keep out of the way, hoping that they would forget my presence in the business of embarkation, but no. Every time one of the crew crossed my path he would either pass comment on my arse, or make some lewd suggestion as to what I should do to his prick. Some of them were not content with words alone, and aimed sharp swipes of foot or hand at my bare bum. One of the sailors, a huge black man – the first I had ever seen – inserted one thick, dark finger a few inches into my hole. The shock made me gasp and sit up, flushed with embarrassment. He wiggled his finger around inside me, whispered a few obscenities in my ear and let me go.

After that I was spared no indignity. Déssert, finding fault with my work, subjected me to six strokes of his thick leather belt while the crew looked on and counted, cheering when he showed them the red marks that shone out on my lily-white arse. Then, with the assistance of the black man and another brutish-looking creature, I was hauled to my feet and bent over a barrel. Déssert pulled my cock and balls down so that they hung between my legs, and invited the sailors to take turns pulling and yanking on them, promising an extra tot of rum to the man who could give me an erection. There was little to excite me in the situation, and I remained obdurately limp until the black sailor, who seemed to enjoy a privileged position on the ship, knelt between my legs and started lapping at my arsehole with his tongue. The sensation was so soothing on my poor, abused posterior that I sprung a stiff rod immediately. The black sailor stood back to show the results of his handiwork, and I was just beginning to feel a little happier about my position when I was doused with the filthy contents of the pail I had been using to clean the deck. The sailors roared with laughter.

'That's enough now, men! Back to work!' Déssert lifted me off the barrel with surprising gentleness. My legs almost gave way; he held me up with an arm around the shoulders.

'Don't be afraid, little one,' he said. 'We won't really hurt you. We have to deliver you in one piece, after all. The men must have their entertainment – and on this voyage, it is you.' His large golden hands pulled the vest over my head, then tore the trousers off me; both garments were dripping and foul from my drenching. We stood face to face, his powerful torso with its ridged stomach and prominent nipples opposite my own smooth white flesh, streaked with muck and covered in goosepimples. Looking over Déssert's shoulder I saw a face watching us through the cabin window – the face of an older man, smiling. This, I assumed, must be the captain.

I had little time for reflection. Déssert took a length of rope, made a loop in one end and passed it over my hands, tightening it at the wrists. The other end he tied around my ankles. Thus hobbled I was led to the foot of the mast and tethered like a goat. Beside me were three rough-hewn wooden troughs with outlets leading into a runnel cut into the deck that directed their contents over the side. I could tell from the pervading smell that these were the 'heads' – the ship's latrines. My degradation was complete.

We set sail as the sun was rising in the sky, and by the time we'd cleared the mainland it must have been full noon. A misty morning had given way to an unseasonably warm day, and the heat was beating down on my naked body with some force. I was warm and comfortable enough at first, but soon I became aware that my pale flesh was burning.

The black sailor was the first to visit me.

'All right, pretty boy? Comfortable?'

'I'm too hot,' I said, and immediately regretted it. He hauled out his cock – even blacker than the rest of him – and weighed it for a moment in his palm. Bending his knees, he let loose a thick jet of piss into the nearest trough and then, when it had gathered its full momentum, directed it straight on to my chest and stomach.

'There you go, boy, better now?' I was drenched from chest to legs again; the smell of his piss on my hot flesh was overpowering. Choking back my anger and disgust, I had to admit that it was, indeed, very soothing.

The next visitor was a wiry Highlander, a handsome-looking redhead with a gold tooth and a great quantity of red fur visible at the neck of his shirt. Without preamble he dropped his trousers and exposed a pair of massive thighs and a big, white cock dangling down from its red wiry bush. This time there was no pretence of aiming for the trough; he simply stationed himself in front of me, pulled my head back by the hair and pissed straight in my face. I closed my eyes tight shut and tried to close my mouth. There seemed to be an inexhaustible supply of piss in the man; finally, however, he flicked the last drops in my face and I opened my eyes. Instead of walking away, however, he stayed where he was, pulling on his foreskin until his cock had fattened and lengthened. Taking me again by my wet hair he pulled my face towards him. I did not need to be told what to do. I opened my mouth and let him in. I thought that he would simply use me as a convenient hole in which to dump his sperm, but he wanted more than that. I was obliged to do all the work, sucking and slurping on his now rigid tool until he was almost ready to come. I had always been accustomed, when pleasuring a man's cock in my mouth, to use my hands for extra stimulation; now, however, with my wrists bound behind my back, I was obliged to do everything with lips and tongue.

At length he pulled out of my mouth and sprayed my face with his sperm. It ran over my lips and down my chin; there was nothing I could do to wipe it away. I cleaned myself as best I could with my tongue.

My cock, of course, was painfully stiff by now, and there was nothing I could do to relieve it. I could only hope that one of the sailors would take pity on me and help me out as one by one they soaked me with their hot, yellow piss, dumped a load of come on me or in my mouth, occasionally stuck a couple of fingers up my twitching arsehole. But not one of them would touch my cock.

This ordeal lasted the best part of the day. Mercifully, as the ship turned south I was spared the full glare of the sun and was able to doze in between 'entertaining' the crew. They were an insatiable rabble; there could not have been more than fifteen of them, but I must have received double that number of visits during the course of the day. The black sailor, whose name was

George, returned and pissed out another hefty load. Déssert came by every couple of hours to give me water and bread, but he too relieved himself on me. By the time the sun was sinking on the starboard side of the vessel, the decks around me were awash with piss.

To my surprise, we dropped anchor at sunset. We can't have been far from the English coast; it seemed that we had found a good soft mooring for the night. The crew furled the sails and placed lamps in the rigging. Déssert came and cut my ties with a knife, tossed me a cloth and allowed me to clean myself up a little. Then I was led to the prow of the ship where the crew were lounging in readiness – for what?

'Now, Mister Gordon,' said Déssert, 'you've acquitted yourself honourably today, I think we'd all agree. Any complaints, gentlemen?' There was a good-natured cheer. 'You see? A happy crew, thanks to you. And as a token of our gratitude we will allow you to serve the evening tot of rum.' He pointed to a stone bottle with a little tin cup attached to the neck by a chain. 'Come on, Mister. Let's see if you can do it without spilling a drop.'

Still naked, I took the bottle and poured out a measure with a steady hand and passed it to Déssert. He tossed it off, smacked his lips and motioned me to continue. Thus I served all the crew – and at each stop I was subjected to more coarse physical familiarities until my cock was once again straining out in front of me.

'Double rations!' shouted Déssert, to the delight of the assembled sailors. I passed around again; this time, the liberties taken with my person were even greater, as the alcohol emboldened the already shameless crew. When I reached the end of my round, all hell broke loose. George grabbed me, held my arms and sat me on his lap; I could feel his huge black cock, still mercifully inside his clothes, pressing against my buttocks. Déssert dropped to his knees in front of me and took my cock in his mouth; another of the sailors joined him, chewing on my balls. George's fingers penetrated my arse; a throng of cocks were waving around in my face

as one, then another, was pushed towards my lips. Déssert, dropping his trousers, knelt down and turned his arse towards me;
George took my penis (now slick from its recent sucking) and
guided it into the Midshipman's anus, while the rest of the crew
cheered. I gripped his hips and fucked him as hard as I could. It
was too much; I gritted my teeth and came inside him. Stars burst
before my eyes.

Nothing seemed to satisfy the sailors, however, who were now
passing the rum bottle freely between them. As I lay on the floor,
I saw George standing over me, coaxing his massive cock to its
maximum hardness. Another of the sailors was licking my arse,
evidently in readiness for a fresh assault. I squirmed and wriggled
with pleasure, and hands pinned me down on all sides. My knees
were lifted into the air, and George positioned the head of his cock
at my hole. I held my breath and waited for the pain.

Suddenly, from somewhere above my head, came the blast of a
whistle. George's prick, which had just started to ease into my
complaining sphincter, twitched once and pulled out, leaving my
hole gaping in the air. The hands that had held suddenly let go,
and I was dropped on to the deck like a rag doll. The sailors, as a
man, stood to attention. Many of them, including Déssert and
George, had erect cocks standing to attention as well. Silence fell.

'At ease.' A cultured voice. From my position on the deck I
could see the captain closing his cabin door behind him and
standing on the bridge, looking down on the orgy beneath him.

'Déssert.'

'Yes, sir.'

'Your men appear to be getting a little rowdy.'

'Sir.'

'What's going on down there, Déssert?'

'We're fucking the boy, sir.'

The captain sighed. 'I can see that, Déssert.' There was silence;
I wondered whether the crew was about to be disciplined. Instead

the captain came a few steps down from the bridge and leaned an elbow on George's massive black shoulder.

'And what's he like, George?'

The black sailor grinned. 'Very nice, sir.'

'So I see. Bring him up to the cabin, please. I don't want him split in two on that thing.' He indicated George's still-stiff prick with his cane; it bounced and throbbed, a sticky thread hanging from the head.

The Highlander picked me up off the floor and threw me over his shoulder; my bare feet made contact with his burning cock, and I was unable to resist grasping it between my soles and wanking it that way a few times. He laughed and whispered a few crude endearments in my ear before ducking down and delivering me to the captain's cabin. I could hear from the deck that the orgy was in full swing. One last glimpse over my shoulder and I saw Déssert in my place, the rum bottle being held to his lips, ready to take George's prick up his arse.

f

I lay for a moment unable to feel anything but relief. I had been dumped on the captain's bed; the softness of the mattress was a blessing to my bruised, aching limbs. I knew, dimly, that my filthy body was soiling his clean cotton sheets, but for the moment that didn't concern me. I cared only that the assault had stopped, and I had a chance to recover.

Captain Moore stood with his back to the cabin door, looking down at me. He was smart enough, sporting the uniform of a British naval officer, although I suspected that he no longer had the right to wear it. He was older than the rest of the crew, about forty, with a lined but still handsome face. His light brown hair was receding slightly, and cropped short to his skull. He had the full figure of a man accustomed to dining and drinking well, but the physical exertions of life on ship kept it in proportion. He opened a box on the table, took out a cigar and lit it. I noticed that his hands, in comparison with the rest of the crew's, were clean and well kept.

He stood for a while in silence, smoking his cigar and surveying me through half-closed eyes. I had no doubt that he had rescued me from the crew only in order to enjoy me for himself; my experiences to date had taught me that any able-bodied man would take sexual pleasure at every opportunity. If I could only rest for a while, I would be able to oblige. I was grateful for each passing minute of peace.

'I apologise for the rough handling you've received,' he said at length, speaking through a cloud of smoke. 'The men get their spirits up, and there's only one way of controlling them.' From the deck I could just make out noises of shouting and banging; the orgy was continuing without me.

'I trust you have not sustained any serious injury.'

'No. Thank you.'

'You certainly proved popular with the crew.'

'Yes, sir.' I looked down at my chest and stomach, which was still covered with sperm and dirt from the deck.

'You needn't worry about the rest of the voyage. You'll stay here until we get to Liverpool.'

He seemed kind, even polite. This gave me courage. 'Sir,' I said, 'what awaits me in Liverpool?'

'Interrogation by General Wade, young man. Your reputation precedes you.'

'My reputation?'

'A Jacobite rebel. The son of a notorious rebel. The leader of a plot to rescue a French spy from Fort William. Oh yes, your plans are known, I'm afraid. You were indiscreet, Mister Gordon.'

'I was foolish and boastful.'

'Did you tell the truth?'

'Of course not.'

The captain smoked in silence for a little longer. The cabin was warm and quiet, and I was comfortable at last. A large copper was heating by the fire, and the fragrant smoke of his cigar made me drowsy. The captain never took his eyes off me. I was unconcerned. Let him look. I'd had time to rest now. My body was coming to life again. My cock felt warm and heavy.

'You are filthy.' He said this not as an accusation, merely an observation.

'Yes, sir.'

'I am about to take my bath. Come and assist me.'

He held out a hand and pulled me to my feet. He was fully uniformed; I, of course, was naked. I expected to feel his hands on my body, but instead he indicated a hip bath hanging from a nail above his bed.

'Fill it from the copper.'

The captain retired behind a screen while I set the bath on the ground by the fire and filled it from the copper. Soon there was a foot's depth of hot, steaming water in the tub.

The captain emerged from behind the screen with a towel wrapped round his waist. His torso was a little on the heavy side, but the girth of his arms and shoulders suggested that he was still strong and virile enough. Dropping the towel to the floor, he stepped into the bath. I caught a glimpse of a fat cock and balls before they disappeared beneath the surface of the water. He handed me a cloth.

'Wash me.'

I poured a dipper of water over his head and rubbed his neck and shoulders with the cloth. He grunted in satisfaction and leaned forward, offering the expanse of his back to my ministrations. Wetting my cloth again, I washed and scrubbed my way down to the base of his spine. He sat up and held out each arm in turn. I washed each limb as far as the armpits, then, standing behind him, rubbed the cloth over his chest and stomach. He leaned back to give me easier access; I was not surprised to see that his cock was now breaking the surface of the water, not yet fully erect but agreeably distended.

I rubbed further down his abdomen, then, moving round the side of the tub, attended to his legs and feet.

'Now my face, Mister Gordon.'

He closed his eyes and waited. I could easily have picked up a knife and murdered him in his bath – but to what end? His death would only have delivered me again to the tender mercies of the crew. The captain knew he had nothing to fear.

Squeezing the cloth out, I rubbed it gently over his forehead, his eyes, nose and mouth, around his ears and over his cropped head. Finally I scooped up another dipper of warm water and emptied it over him to rinse the dirt away. He spluttered, wiped his eyes and sat up.

'Thank you. Now, let's have you.'

He stepped out of the bath, wrapped the towel around his waist (not before I'd had a good look at his cock hanging half stiff between his thighs) and stood beside me. He opened a little brass bottle that stood on the washstand, emptied a teaspoonful of perfumed liquid into the palm of his hand and started to rub it all over my chest, neck, shoulders and back in smooth movements. The stuff foamed up and shifted the dirt with it. Taking the cloth, he washed down my legs, between my buttocks, round my groin, under my armpits, until I was covered from head to foot in white suds. He tossed the cloth into the bath, splashing water over the floor, then positioned himself behind me and started rubbing my chest and stomach, my hips and, increasingly, my groin. I'd been sporting an erection ever since he got into the bath; now I felt that I might come again.

To my astonishment, the captain started to kiss the back of my neck, the lobes of my ears, licking and gently biting me as his hands worked me over at the front. Soon he was concentrating exclusively on my cock; the slipperiness of his hand in the suds was almost unbearable. I could feel his cock grinding into me through the towel; I slipped a hand round his waist and it fell to the ground. Now there was nothing between us. He positioned his cock along the cleft between my buttocks and let it rest there while I squirmed in his grasp. I could feel his great heavy balls beating a tattoo against the top of my thighs.

Picking up his cane, the captain reached out and pulled open one of the great mahogany presses that lined one wall of his cabin. The door swung open, revealing a row of clean white shirts and dress uniforms – but my attention was caught by something much more interesting. There, on the inside of the door, was a full-length glass which, as it came to rest against the table, reflected the captain and me in a soapy embrace. I saw my own pale skin, the roundness of my muscles, my legs braced, bent at the knee, as the captain's strong arms embraced me, one hand running over my stomach, occasionally pinching a tit, the other gripping my cock. His mouth was at work on my ears, his cock was rubbing up and down my arse.

The captain had an expert touch; he knew from the tightness of my balls, and the hardness of my prick, that I would come at any moment. And so he relinquished his grip, stood me in the tub and emptied the rest of the copper over my head until the suds were all washed away. The water ran off the end of my cock like rain out of a blocked gutter. Dabbing himself with the towel, he sat down in one of the handsome brown leather armchairs that furnished his cabin.

'Come here, boy.'

I stood in front of him, my cock throbbing with every beat of my heart. I badly wanted him to fuck me, and he knew it.

'I have another job for you.'

'Yes, sir.' My voice was shaking. God forgive me, however precarious my position, I felt that I was already in love with the man.

'You must shave me.' He indicated a straight razor, brush and soap that stood on the washstand.

'Shave you?'

'Yes. And no accidents.'

In silence, I lathered up the brush and covered his chin in thick white foam. The razor was clean and sharp; I steadied my hand and set to work. It was hard to concentrate, but soon I had him as smooth and clean as any professional barber.

'And down below, please.'

I stood like an imbecile.

'Mister Gordon. That is an order.'

He shifted forward in the chair, pushing his hips forward. His cock, still engorged, was lying over his thigh.

I lathered up again and applied the foam around his groin, over his balls, then, holding his cock out of harm's way with one hand, made my first tentative stroke with the razor. It glided across his groin leaving clean, bare skin in its wake.

How easily I could have unmanned him! Just one swift motion of the razor...

Two strokes, three, four, and his bush had gone completely. His cock had now come fully to life in my hand. I let it drop against his stomach and moved down on to his balls. Pulling them down slightly so they were tight in their sac gave me the best results, and soon they too were clean as a whistle. I picked up the cloth and rinsed him down with clean water.

The sight of his bare crotch was extraordinary. Of course, his cock looked bigger; there was also something incongruous about the smooth hairless groin and the powerful, masculine physique. The contrast was dizzying.

I dropped to my knees and started to lick all around where I had just shaved. I took each egg-like ball in my mouth and marvelled at the smoothness of the skin. I licked up and down the captain's cock until it was covered in my spit, then rubbed my face around it until I was just as wet. The captain shifted forward a little more and spread his legs, directing me further down. His arse was still hairy, and I lost no time in letting my tongue burrow through the damp fur until it reached his hole. It opened up to my eager caresses and I delved up into the soft, salty centre of the man.

When I came up for breath the captain was sweating, his cock drooling. He hoisted his knees in the air and spread his buttocks, looking at me with an expression that said more clearly than any words that he wanted me to fuck him. I was disappointed at first; I had been so inflamed by the feeling of his cock pressing into my arse, and the fact that he was the captain, the man in charge, so much older and more experienced than me, that I had wanted nothing more than for him to fuck me for the rest of the voyage. Now, however, I was struck by the reversal of our stations: there he lay, a man of forty or so, a leader of men, with a crotch shaved as smooth as a baby's, holding open his hole and begging me to fill it.

I took a handful of the fragrant liquid from the bottle, smeared it over my cock and knelt before him. He rested his calves on my shoulders and steered himself on to me. At first he was too tight, and I couldn't get in. I pushed harder, and half my cock slipped inside him. His face was contorted with pain, but he didn't cry out. I pulled out again, gave him time to recover, then renewed my assault. This time I encountered no resistance, and I slid into his hot, smooth tunnel until my hips were pressing into the back of his thighs.

I kept the pace slow; I wanted to prolong the moment. The captain never took his eyes from mine. With one hand he toyed with my balls, felt my cock as it slid in and out of him; with the other he supported his head. His prick bounced and throbbed between us.

We fucked for five, ten minutes. Every time I felt I was about to come I stopped, pulled out and allowed myself to cool down; the captain's eyes implored me to come back. Finally, however, it was too much. I picked up the pace and began to fuck him with a will. He threw his head back and started wanking, pulling on my balls all the while. Just as I started to squirt my load inside him, he sprayed his chest and stomach with a great volume of come, some of which ran down his shaven groin. I pulled out of his arse and licked every drop of semen from his body. I fell asleep with my head in his lap.

Chapter Eight
Fort William, 1 December 1750

Dearest Charles

My circumstances have changed radically since last I wrote. I have come through the valley of the shadow of death, and I find myself unexpectedly alive and, what is more, able once again to write to you. Whether you receive these outpourings I will never know; it is enough for me that, on some plane, I can communicate with you.

My solitary incarceration here in the castle lasted for another week or so after last I wrote; I lost track of the days, to tell you the truth. My friend the guard never visited me after that last time; I do not know whether he has been moved from the prison, or simply found another to amuse him. I feel certain that he did not abandon me by choice, but that may simply be a reflection of my own need to believe in some spark of human goodness in the misery that has surrounded me for so long.

Bread and water were delivered to me daily, and the slops passed out, but I grew painfully thin despite my best efforts to keep myself fit. I have always been lean, but now the flesh had dropped away from my bones, leaving every muscle and tendon in sharp relief. It was no longer comfortable to sit on the cell floor; my poor backside had dwindled away, and my bones were grinding into the stone. I spent more and more time lying inert on my mattress, daydreaming.

I suppose the worst part of my ordeal lasted for another week. I will not trouble you with the mental torments that I went through; suffice to say that it was the image of you, the one bright thing in my life, that kept me sane. Finally one morning I heard the keys in my cell door and prepared to slop out; instead two guards stepped into the room and, pulling me to my feet, marched me down the corridor. It was the first time I had stepped outside my cell, and my legs could barely walk along the passage. They half carried me, half dragged me to the governor's room.

I was left outside with one of the guards standing over me; the other passed through the door, and before long I could hear two or more voices raised in argument. The door flew open, and there stood a man I took to be the governor: a fat, red-faced, white-haired creature who looked me up and down with utter contempt, turned to cover his nose and walked away. Another came out: a tall, lean, sunken-faced man who surveyed me through a pair of green spectacles as if I were a curiosity at the zoological gardens. A third – younger than the others, with a pale shiny face and abundant carbuncles – took his place, spat on the ground beside me, and retired. The door was slammed again, but the debate continued. Two of them – the younger one and the thin one, I assumed from their voices – were in favour of taking me straight down to the courtyard and cutting off my head. The other counselled caution; I may be a spy, but I was a priest. If the French heard that they had murdered a priest...

The door opened again and the guard pushed me into the room. I stood, swaying with fatigue, barely able to focus on the faces of my interrogators, who sat with their backs to the window.

'Monsieur Lebecque.' It was the thin one who spoke.

'Yes, sir.'

'You are a man of God, are you not?'

'Yes, sir.'

'A priest?'

'Yes, sir.' God forgive me for lying.

The young man butted in. 'You were sent here to perform an act of treason against the King, weren't you, Lebecque?'

'No, sir.'

'Then why are you here?' His voice raised to a scream. The veins in his neck bulged, and I thought that a boil on his neck was about to burst.

'I came as a tutor to the Gordon family of Loch Linnhe, sir.'

'You lie!' He choked on his own spittle and gasped for breath for some minutes.

The fat governor took over. 'Who are your contacts in Scotland, Monsieur? That is all we need to know.'

'Contacts, sir? I have no friends. Only the good lady my employer and her son.'

'Hmm. Mrs Gordon.'

'The widow of a notorious rebel, sir,' supplied the thin one, with a voice like paper.

'A woman of spotless reputation,' I added.

'Silence!' boomed the governor. 'Do you understand where you are, Lebecque?'

'Yes sir, I believe so.'

'Then you must know that your life is in question.'

'I accept my fate.'

'Damn you, priest!' squealed the young one, finding his voice again.

'You alone have the power to save yourself,' resumed the governor, joining his fingertips to form a cage. 'Name your contacts. That is all I ask. You will be returned to your own people.' I caught a sidelong glance between the other two; he was lying, of course. I am a seasoned enough politician to know that.

'I have told you, sir, that I know nobody. As a priest of the Roman church –'

'A filthy Jesuit spy!'

I ignored the interruption. 'As a priest, I lead a greatly restricted life. I am not, like you gentlemen, a man of affairs.' My knees were trembling, due only to the unaccustomed effort of standing. They interpreted it as fear, to my disgust. It was, however, a happy accident.

'Look at him,' said the young one, 'he's fit to soil himself.'

'So this is your soldier, your spy,' said the governor. 'A cowering priest who's so weak he can barely hold his head up. Oh yes, a great danger to His Majesty, I'm sure.'

'We have papers from London –' began the thin one, but he was silenced.

'Enough!' roared the governor, his jowls shaking like the wattles of a turkey. 'This is the result of your intelligence! For this I have expended the resources of my meagre staff. God help me! Never again will I listen to the council of fools. Guards! Take him down to the main prison.'

'With respect, sir,' said the young one in tones of false obsequiousness, 'I maintain that he should be kept in solitary confinement –' The governor's look was enough to silence him.

'Take him out of my sight!'

The guards took me by the arms and marched me out of the office. My neck, for the time being, was safe.

From the frying pan, however, I was delivered into the fire, or so I thought. The main part of the prison was a huge dungeon in which some two dozen poor souls languished, chained to the walls, sharing one disgusting pail into which all were forced to relieve themselves. The guards had me secured in a moment and walked away jangling their keys.

As soon as they were out of earshot, the voices began.

'Oh ho, who's this?'

'It's the priest.'

'A Frenchman, they say.'

'A dirty foreigner.'

'A frog.'

'Hey, Frenchie, I'm going to cut you.'

'You're going to get it tonight, you dirty bastard.'

I could not tell where the words were coming from; I sat on my haunches and buried my face in my hands. I tried to pray. I tried to remember the light and air of the Gordon Hall estates, the sight of you running naked into the clean waters of the loch, laughing at me as I waded around in my shirt tails. All I could hear was the hissing of hate, which filled my ears as the stench of the bucket filled my nostrils.

The hours passed. Every so often the guards would roam through the dungeon, rattling their keys and laughing. A meagre meal of broken meats and water was served, upon which the convicts fell like a pack of dogs. I didn't have the heart to fight, and went hungry. As soon as the guards had gone, the threats began again.

'It was priests who betrayed Scotland,' said one.

'The French let us down, the traitorous bastards.'

'You die tonight, priest.'

Fortunately for me, there was little that they could do to hurt me, chained as they were to the walls. I suffered what blows from feet and hands could reach me. The night wore on, but the voices never rested.

'I've got a blade, priest.'

'We're going to cut your balls off.'

'Hey priest, start praying...'

I felt hands on my legs, holding them down. Two of the prisoners had crawled to the furthest extent of their chains and were leading a concerted attack on me. I shrank back to the wall and felt their hands clawing at me in the darkness. They found me again, and a sharp jab ripped into the flesh of my calf. I cried out as the cruel blade was twisted in the wound. Again they stabbed and slashed, cutting my feet. If only I could move further against the wall. Sleep would be impossible; I might at best survive the night without further injury.

More hands were laid on me; I could not see where they were coming from. Perhaps their eyes were more accustomed to the darkness than mine. Again, the jabbing pain, the twisting, the wetness of blood on my legs.

I had given up all hope of my life, when from right beside me I heard a sudden snoring, a spluttering and a curse. One of my assailants had missed his mark; the blade had ended up embedded in the thigh of my neighbour who, miraculously, had slept through the foregoing. Now, however, he sat up and bellowed. I didn't need to see him to realise that he was a very large and powerful man.

'Who the fuck did that?'

The other prisoners were silent.

'I asked a question.'

There was a faint moaning and gibbering from the four corners of the cell. My fellow prisoners were clearly terrified of this giant. Finally one of them piped up in a weaselly voice.

'It was the priest. He done it.'

The others joined in. 'That's right, Morgan, it was the Frenchie.'

Morgan growled. I felt certain that what the authorities had failed to achieve, Morgan would now do for them. But he said nothing as they made their cringing accusations. I heard him move beside me, expecting at any moment to feel hands around my throat. Instead I heard two words, not loud, in a voice that demanded obedience.

'Leave him.'

The others were instantly silent. Morgan shifted and lay down again. When peace seemed at last to have been restored to the cell, I relaxed sufficiently to stretch out on the ground. My protector shifted a little closer to me, threw one massive arm across my upper body and thus, huddled together for warmth (and for my protection) we spent the rest of the night.

Morning brought light into the cell; not God's light, but a few dismal tapers that were stuck into holes in the wall by the guards, who threw us our breakfast and removed the slops. Again, the jackals fell on the food and I went without; starvation, rather than violence, now seemed my greatest enemy. Morgan, however, had other ideas. He sat aside during the ugly scramble for meat and bread, a huge ape of a man with a shaven head, beetling brows and a long, livid scar down the left side of his face. His arms, in which I had spent the night, looked so powerful that I could understand why none dared disobey him. The manacles and chains that held him to the wall, though, were stronger.

Sitting on his haunches, he reached out one massive hand, swatted one of the prisoners around the head and waited. The prisoner, nursing his ringing ear, reluctantly handed over a sizeable piece of cold mutton and a thick crust of bread, into which sunk his teeth. He must have seen my eyes bulging out of my skull with hunger, and with another blow to a cellmate's head he furnished me with the best meal I had enjoyed in weeks. I bolted the food like a starving dog, and immediately felt sick. Morgan handed me a cup of water – not the cleanest, but to me it tasted like the fresh mountain burn that runs down into Loch Linnhe. I guzzled it in one draught, choked and spluttered and sat wet-eyed and gasping for breath. Morgan saw my predicament, laughed and clapped me on the back so vigorously that it would have sent me sprawling across the cell floor had it not been for my chains.

With food inside me I felt human again, and began to hope that the governor's indecision had won for me a reprieve. Hope, I have always found, is much easier on a full belly. My situation was also greatly improved by the protection I had won from Morgan – although God only knows why he decided to champion me. He was not, I assumed, a religious man. Perhaps it was some spark of fair play that would not allow him to see one man destroyed by the mob. Whatever the reason, the rest of the prisoners gave me a wide berth, and I spent the day in peace and relative happiness beside my giant guardian.

He was not a talkative man. I tried on a few occasions to engage him in conversation, but got nothing back other than a few grunts and guffaws. It was only when I asked about his home life that he seemed to take an interest.

'I've a wife at home.'

'What's her name?'

'Margaret.'

'And children?'

'A little girl of five years old.'

'When did you last see them?'

'A year ago.'

'Why are you here?'

That was the wrong question to ask. He clammed up again, rubbed the scar on his face and turned his back on me. Some of the other prisoners had been listening to our conversation, and now they rolled their eyes and stuck out their tongues as if they would tell me if they could – and then I would find out what a fine fellow my new friend was! I didn't care what he had done – after all, how many of us were there for 'crimes' no more serious than mine? – it was enough for me that he had obeyed the law of

Christ, and shared with one less fortunate than himself.

The day wore on in a foetid silence. The guards brought lunch, a foul slop that, I suppose, was meant to be soup, which we drank from dirty wooden bowls. It was disgusting, but it was better than nothing. We took it in turns to relieve ourselves, then many settled down to sleep. The cell was silent apart from the buzzing of flies, the groaning and farting of the sleeping prisoners. I lay wide awake, curled up against the huge bulk of Morgan's stomach and chest. I guessed, from the regularity of his breathing, that he too was asleep. I was wrong.

'Father...'

'Yes?' Now was no time to tell him that I wasn't really a priest.

'Can you write?'

'Of course... er... my son.'

'Will you write a letter to my Margaret?'

'With a good will, Morgan. But I have no paper and no pen.'

He smiled, showing teeth that looked more like the fangs of a dog, and pulled back his mattress. There, pressed flat by his weight, were two sheets of folded paper and a battered old pen. He took them carefully out and handed them to me with a look of pride and delight on his face.

'And ink?'

He held up a finger, spat on to it and started rubbing it against the crumbling brick of the wall behind us. Soon he had worked up enough reddish-black paste to make a small blob the size of a penny piece in the bottom of the one of the wooden bowls. He diluted it with a small draught from his drinking cup and handed it to me.

'Ink.'

I had to admire his resourcefulness. Seeing my surprise, he laughed softly and rubbed my head, then took my hand, thrust the pen into it and waited for me to prepare my pen. The ink was lumpy and full of grit, but astonishingly it worked. I made a few exploratory marks on the paper, then waited for his dictation.

He seemed lost in thought. 'I want to tell her that I love her and miss her,' he said, 'but I want it to sound nice. You write it, Father.'

'Dear Margaret,' I began, and paused. What words would a man use to his wife? I had no idea. Morgan scowled and looked impatient, motioning me to carry on. I would have to use my imagination.

'It is many months now since last I saw you, but you are ever-present in my mind,' I wrote, drawing on my own innermost feelings for inspiration. 'Although I live in darkness, I have a light that shines in my heart: the light of our love. I pray that you are safe and well, and that you have not forgotten me. One day, in this world or the next, we will be together again.' I need not tell you, Charles, that these words might just as well have been addressed from me to you.

'That's good, Father. But –'

'Yes?'

'I want to tell her that I miss her in another way as well.'

'Yes?'

'You know...' He pointed awkwardly down to his groin. 'That way.'

'I see.' This was a harder commission. I thought for a while, and started to write. 'I think about the good times we had together, and I hope you do too. My body is...' I scratched the last words out. I couldn't think of what to say. My experience of love, as you know, has been somewhat limited. Morgan, in deep thought, scratched his head. I scratched my chin. We looked for all the world like two unlikely scholars bent over a book of Latin verse. Finally his face lit up with inspiration.

'Turn the paper over,' he said. I did as I was told. Stretching out his legs, he unbuttoned the horizontal fly on his trousers and released a member that was as big as the rest of him. It flopped out and rested on the floor.

Grasping my hand, he positioned the sheet of paper underneath his cock, so that I was holding it. It was growing rapidly; within a minute or so it was too big to fit on the sheet of paper, and the head was rubbing against my forearm. I shifted back a little to fit it on, and, discerning his intentions, traced its outline with my pen. My artwork completed, I held it up for his inspection. He seemed delighted. I inscribed the words 'Thinking of you always,' folded the letter up and addressed it according to his instructions. He hid the letter under the mattress to be smuggled out later, and emptied the ink over the sleeping form of one of the inmates.

His prick, however, he was in no hurry to put away. 'Once it's up,' he said, 'it stays up until I make it go down.' He started absent-mindedly pulling on it, closing his eyes and, presumably, summoning up images of Margaret to help him on his way. I couldn't tear my eyes away. The sight of his huge, calloused hand working on that long, fat cock, the foreskin sliding over the head as the chains that bound his wrists jangled quietly, held me in a spell. I was so engrossed in the spectacle I did not notice that Morgan had opened his eyes and was looking down at me. His hand came to a rest. I looked up and caught his quizzical scowl. Was he going to chastise me for my imprudence? No: instead he moved his hand away and, still scowling, as if uncertain of what to do next, let his cock jump and twitch in the air. Looking around to check that we were not observed, I reached out and took it in my grip. Morgan closed his eyes again and allowed me to do whatever I wanted.

I caressed every inch of his cock and balls, admiring the weight and thickness, marvelling at the smoothness of the skin and the roughness of the hair surrounding it. I worked the tip of my finger into the little hole, and heard a satisfied grunt from somewhere above. I slapped the shaft against the flat of my palm, and was gratified to see that it bounced back even stiffer than before. Drips of fluid were appearing at the head, and I bent down to lick them off. At the first contact of my tongue, Morgan opened his eyes again. Perhaps he was about to object, I don't know; I didn't wait to find out. Instead I slid my mouth as far down his cock as it would go. I had only ever done this once before, with the brother of my friend long, long ago in France, and I made a fumbling, inexpert job of it. I think it must have been uncomfortable for Morgan; maybe it was the scraping of my teeth, or the scratching of my stubble against his balls, but he pulled out of my mouth and sat for a while in thought. Then inspiration seemed to strike.

He pulled me to him, parted my thighs and tore open the seam at the back of my trousers, making a rent just wide enough to expose my arse to the air. I knew full well what was coming, and I was frightened. I had never taken the passive part before, but I knew from my few experiences of this kind of thing that it can be painful for the 'female' partner. My guard had taken my rude batterings without complaint, and seemed to find pleasure in them. But I knew there would be pain first.

Still sitting with his back against the wall and his legs stretched out in front of him, Morgan lifted me on to his lap; my chains were just long enough to allow it. A little more tearing and my own cock was free, springing up against his, their undersides glued together. He spat on his fingers and spread the saliva against my arsehole, working first one, then two fingers into me. It was uncomfortable, no more, and after a while I grew accustomed to the feeling and began to enjoy it. Another finger, and I was soon riding up and down in earnest. He pulled them out, and I knew that the biggest test was about to come.

I raised myself as high as I could to allow the head of his cock to make contact with my opening then, holding my cheeks open with my hands, lowered myself slowly on to him. It hurt, of course, but I was past caring. My cock was still entirely rigid, translating each sensation of pain into one of pleasure. Morgan grunted and buried himself inside me. I put my arms around his neck and he buried his face against my chest as he began to fuck me. When we broke apart after a few minutes, the hair on his stomach was plastered down by the juices that had been flowing out of my cock.

Morgan half stood up; I clung round his neck and kept my arse clamped tight around his cock. Now that I had it, I was in no hurry to relinquish it. Laying me gently on to his mattress, so that I was lying on my back, he picked up my legs, pulled a little way out of my arse and began his battery in earnest. My feet were weighed down with the chains that jangled with every thrust, but I could do nothing; my whole being was focused below. My head was thrown back, and I could see quite clearly that two or three of the other prisoners were watching the show, some of them masturbating openly. I didn't care; if anything, it added to my pleasure. Strive as we might, Charles, we are all animals. I was no better than any of them. How could I be, lying on my back in a filthy prison cell taking the cock of some great shaven-headed brute up my backside?

I spread my legs as wide as they would go, took hold of my penis and stroked it back into a full erection; it had subsided somewhat during the battering of my hole. Morgan shifted his weight on to his hands, braced his feet against the wall and pistoned into me. Something in this new position found a spot inside me that I never knew existed and, before I could prevent it, I was squirting all over my hand, my stomach, on to the floor, even on to the wall behind Morgan, where a glob of sperm ran down the damp stone and puddled on the floor. The stirring in my guts must have worked some magic on Morgan, who glued his mouth to mine, stuck his tongue down my throat and fucked me harder, harder, until by his grunting and thrusting I knew that he was coming inside me. The other prisoners, inspired by the sight, added their own contributions. The cell was heavy with the odour of male sexual pleasure.

I let my legs, stiff with pain, fall down at last; Morgan pulled out and wiped his cock on his blanket, then stretched out on the mattress. He held out his arm and signalled for me to join him. And so we slept again, our limbs, and our chains, entwined.

†

The rest of my sojourn at Fort William has been a holiday compared to the preceding weeks. As Morgan's 'wife' I am ignored, if not respected, by the rest of the prison. At least there have been no more attempts to hurt me. The guards, all of them corrupt, smuggle letters for Morgan and, at his request, for me; it is him you have to thank for this, Charles, if you ever receive it. I spend the days chained to the wall, but well fed and watered, telling stories to Morgan and any other prisoners who care to listen. I draw pictures to entertain them – mostly what you might call 'erotic' sketches, although I fear that my limited artistic abilities render nothing more than crude diagrams. At Morgan's request, I attempted a portrait of Margaret, using our usual reddish brown ink for the outline, and a special blue tint worked up from the dye in his trousers to represent her eyes. Morgan even asked me to draw a picture of my 'loved ones'; I executed, very badly, a portrait of you, Charles, with which he seemed pleased enough. I secreted it inside my clothes, where it remains.

At night I am Morgan's property exclusively. Some of the other prisoners have attempted to 'borrow' me while he is asleep, but fortunately for me the limitations of our chains, and their fear of the big man's displeasure, have protected me from anything worse than visual offence. My protector is a man of prodigious appetites, and fucks me every night before we sleep, every morning when we wake, and sometimes in between times. He is always affectionate, and considerate of my satisfaction as well as his own.

I have grown accustomed to the experience, and am learning how to give more pleasure to both of us. If this is the worst I have to fear, I am well content. It is not how I would have imagined my life turning out, but it is not such a bad fate. My chief regret is that I may never share my new-found expertise with the one I would most dearly wish to.

When we lie together in the dark, as the rest of the prison sleeps around us, he tells me often of his plans to escape from Fort William and return to Margaret and his child. One of the guards, he believes, will release him from his chains and wink at his departure. I fear that this is a vain fantasy, but I do not tell him so.

I will close now. The guard is ready to take our messages to the outside world. How long is it since I saw you, Charles? It seems a lifetime away, a different world. Do not imagine that, because I have found a friend here, that I have forgotten you.

Your servant
BL

Chapter Nine

My naval career prospered. So impressed was Captain Moore with my performance, both as barber and lover, that he decided to retain my services – and to 'lose' me as far as the English authorities were concerned. We continued our journey south to Liverpool, where Moore and the rest of the crew spent the night while I hid in the captain's cabin, safe from prying eyes. When Moore returned the next morning, he recounted an interview with General Wade's secretary at which he had concocted an elaborate story of how the 'Jacobite Gordon' had been caught stealing rum and been murdered by the enraged crew, his body thrown overboard somewhere off the Scottish coast. The secretary was furious, demanding that the corpse at least be brought in evidence, but Moore span a yarn about how sailors, superstitious souls that they were, refused to have a dead man on board. And so, in the eyes of the law at least, I ceased to exist.

The crew returned from shore leave very green around the gills, and were quite silent as they prepared for our onward voyage. I can only assume that the brothels of Liverpool had been well and truly visited; most of the sailors boasted that they would fuck as many women as they could the moment their feet touched dry land. All of them claimed that they reserved 'boy pussy' for sea voyages, although I was never sure how true this was. Some of them, Déssert for instance, with his golden brown skin and dirty blond hair, seemed more than casually interested in the male sex.

The *Florida* continued its journey towards Ireland, where we were scheduled to pick up a group of nuns en route for a convent in England. God only knows how the *Florida*, with its crew of debauched sex-fiends, had ever secured this commission. I can only assume that Captain Moore had sweet-talked a gullible priest somewhere along the way.

As the captain's 'body servant' I enjoyed almost total privilege for the rest of the voyage, and began to forget that I was supposedly engaged on a quest of honour. I was so pleased at having escaped the clutches of the redcoats, for which I greatly congratulated myself, that I was content to enjoy this maritime adventure for all it was worth. Remember, I had never set foot outside Scotland before, had been raised in seclusion by women and was hungry to see the world. The longest voyage I had ever taken was the crossing to and from Rum. And so I spent my days on the deck, where I was now immune from the baser attentions of the crew, and the nights in the captain's cabin.

Moore himself was besotted by me. He dressed me in his smartest clothes; they were too big for me, but I fancied that I cut a swagger among the crew. We bathed every day, and I grew accustomed to clean skin. We slept in the best sheets, and, when they were stiff with a night's spendings, sent them down on to deck to be washed by whichever poor unfortunate was on the laundry detail. How I loved my pampered status! I could order Déssert around, and he dared not disobey me. I deliberately walked over expanses of wet, freshly washed deck, just so that George or one of the other sailors would have to scrub them again. I know that they were furious with me, and would have liked nothing better than to catch me one night on deck and fuck some sense back into me; I found the sense of brooding resentment intoxicating.

The captain did everything he could for my pleasure. We spent the first week of our voyage exclusively in each other's arms, but then he suggested that I might like to play with some of the crew. To that end, Déssert was ordered up to the cabin, forced to strip and suck my cock, then the captain's. I lay down on the bed and ordered Déssert to straddle me, and watched with delight his grimaces as my cock slid up inside him. The captain approached him from behind and added his cock to Déssert's already stretched hole. The midshipman shot a considerable load across my stomach while he was being thus doubly abused.

A few days later I suggested that my friend from the hold, with whom I had spent an interesting morning among the potato peelings, be brought to the cabin. I had been thinking a good deal about him, remembering his firm, hairy body, his sleepy, slightly simple expression, and the vigour with which he had fucked me. Much as I enjoyed playing the stud with the captain and Déssert, I was eager to get a dick up my arse again. The sailor stood nervously in the doorway as Moore gave his orders; within minutes he was naked, pushing his fat prick into my arse as I bent over the captain's table. Moore sat nearby, his feet on the table, watching our every move, encouraging us to shift ourselves so that he could see more clearly the sailor's cock ploughing in and out of my arse.

On another occasion, after we had been partaking more freely than usual of the captain's stock of excellent wine, we descended on to deck and called George from the wheel.

'The boy needs fucking,' said the captain. George's eyes lit up, and he stood to attention.

'Yes sir!'

And there, in front of the eyes of all, I was stripped and plugged by his gargantuan black penis. Moore watched from the bridge; the rest of the sailors were less distant. They crowded round us, slapping me in the face with their cocks, always mindful that they were observed by the captain. I didn't care; they could be as brutal with me as they liked. I came while George was fucking me, but ordered him to continue, and within a few moments I was stiff again, with Déssert's cock in my mouth and another in each hand. How I loved playing the slut!

We docked in Dublin, picked up our religious cargo and returned with all despatch to Liverpool, hiding our sexual activities behind closed doors. The men were all under strict instructions not to molest the sisters, on pain of immediate death. I can only assume they obeyed, or if they did not, there were no complaints. Our nightly orgies raged below decks while the nuns above us sang hymns and prayed for a safe crossing.

We left Liverpool and turned north again. I am ashamed to confess that during all this time I had as good as forgotten Lebecque. It was only the knowledge that we were returning to Scotland that pricked my conscience. Oh yes! I would resume that heroic quest when opportunity allowed. But for now, I had no choice: I told myself I was a prisoner on the ship, however indulged. The truth is that I had become accustomed to reigning in my own little kingdom, and was in no hurry to abdicate. The life suited me. I had all the pleasure I could want; the appetites of a nineteen-year-old boy are more prodigious than those of a forty-year-old man, but when Moore was tired of my advances he was happy to allow me to play with the sailor – or sailors – of my choice. I fucked, or was fucked, never less than three times in every twenty-four hours.

This unwonted activity, combined with the healthy influence of sea air and the little work that I did on board, suited me well. I had dropped the last traces of puppy fat, and my muscles now stood out on my arms, chest, stomach and back. My legs were strong; I could shin up the main mast with the best of them. My arse was still as round and pert as ever, but now it was muscle rather than flesh that gave it its tempting shape. The sailors could not take their eyes off it; they longed, I know, to tear into my smooth white cheeks and fuck me ragged. I teased them; I walked around the decks naked, sometimes, daring them to touch me. Often, I would drag one of them up to the wheel and let him fuck me while he steered the ship.

It was not just my arse that was in demand; the captain, to my surprise, had an insatiable appetite for my prick. Indeed, after George, mine was the biggest on board; perhaps all the exercise had made it grow. Moore was quite shameless about his enjoyment in getting fucked; he deliberately positioned the mirror so that he could watch his arse being stretched around my bloated cock. Some of the other sailors enjoyed it just as much, but were more secretive. Déssert was known to be a good bit of 'boy pussy', but after a few weeks all of them had accommodated me both orally and anally, even George. The sight of my fat pink shaft disappearing between his smooth black buttocks made my pleasure complete.

But before long my appetites became jaded. I would like to say that my conscience won through, and that I was spurred on to my escape by a sense of honour. That was partially true, but more pressing at the time was the *ennui* and claustrophobia that began to plague me. Much as I enjoyed the constant debauchery of our seagoing life, I sickened of it too. After a month in which I had been constantly mauled, fucked and sucked, I began to long for the purer joys of solitude and contemplation. What a spoiled creature I had become! I indulged myself in gloomy contemplation of my fate, I worried about my mother, I even spared a thought for poor Lebecque; and then another cock would be in my hand, another arse offered to me, and I forgot them all again.

f

The day came when my desire to escape transformed itself from a vague longing to a definite resolution. We had done two more round trips from Oban to Liverpool, Liverpool to Dublin, back and forth across the Irish sea. With every league I grew more discontent, and the image of Lebecque burned brighter before me. He had started to visit me in my dreams; before long, I was consumed throughout the waking hours by a sense of guilt and failure. The allure of clean sheets and hard cocks was as strong as ever, but one day, as we plied further north than usual, I thought that I recognised the shape of a distant headland. With nothing more than the clothes I stood up in, I slipped over the side of the *Florida* and began to swim towards the shore.

It was harder than I anticipated. Down in the water, I could no longer see the land that had been so clearly visible from the ship's deck. The sea was freezing, and I had to fight for every breath. Strong as I was, the currents were stronger, and before long I had not the slightest idea of which direction I was swimming in, only that I must keep swimming in order not to drown. Waves lifted me to terrifying heights and then dropped me into sickening chasms below. Time after time the water closed over my head; time and again I fought to the surface. I regretted my folly, thought again of the warmth and security of the ship and the friends that I would never see again. But there was little time for reflection. If I didn't find land soon, I would freeze to death.

The waves buffeted me so strongly that I was barely swimming a stroke, just struggling to keep breathing and to survive each fresh assault. The currents were dragging me somewhere, and I was powerless to resist them. I could only pray that they were carrying me towards land rather than further out to sea. If the latter were true, I was dead for sure.

Finally one massive wave caught me just as it was breaking. All the breath was slapped out of me, I rolled over and over seeing now dark blue, now white and green as I tumbled helplessly like a piece of seaweed in the foam. The water roared in my ears, my lungs felt as if they would burst from the effort of holding my breath, I kicked my legs furiously in one last attempt to break the surface and saw, as my head emerged, the rapid onrush of land as I was thrown into the air by the fury of the waves.

I landed with a thud on the sand, winded completely. Another wave was coming up fast behind me, white hands reaching out to drag me back into the sea. I struggled with all my might, catching on to handfuls of sand which disappeared between my fingers, leaving me with nothing to grip. The second wave broke over me, crashed on the shore and then returned with a hiss into the sea, taking me with it. I flailed around, tumbling in the undertow, and my hands found a rock. I grasped and slipped and was dragged back. My hands found another rock – this one, mercifully, with a hole in it the size of an egg. I buried my fingers in it and clung on for dear life. Yes: I was still there. The waves had receded. I struggled to my feet and ran like a drunk man up the beach and beyond the waves' reach.

I lay for a while resting my head on the ground, thanking God that I had been spared. Then, content that arms and legs were unbroken, I tottered to my feet. How strange the ground felt beneath them! It was many weeks since I had last stood on dry land; I felt at each moment the phantom swell of the water which all sailors miss so much when a voyage ends. And then it dawned on me – I was free! I would find help from my fellow countrymen, beg clothes and food from some kind family, and resume my journey.

I ran up the beach into a sparse wood; beyond this, I guessed, must lie the nearest settlement. My feet crunched through bracken and moss; how good it was to smell the earth again, and all its riches! I had been too long at sea. Time to return to reality! Time to find myself once again among decent people whose interests were focused chiefly above my waist.

The wood thinned out, and a patch of sandy heath extended beyond it, with a few clumps of heather twisting their woody roots into the sparse soil. Oh Scotland, my homeland! My heart was jumping for joy as I sank to my knees and smelled the sweet herb. Then I ran on, up a bank, through some more trees and out onto a grassy plain cropped short by sheep or rabbits. Now, surely, I would see the smoke from a homely cottage, and would run towards the honest welcome of a humble Scottish family!

I looked around me, and all the breath seemed to drain from my body. I was on the highest point of land; everything around me sloped downwards into scrubby woods and patchy heath. And then, on all sides – the sea.

I turned to each point of the compass and stared down in disbelief. North: the sea. West: the sea. South: the sea. East: the sea. The island on to which I had been washed was, perhaps, no more than half a mile from tip to tip. And I could see, with a painful clarity, that there was no sign whatsoever of human habitation. Far away on the eastern horizon, perhaps four miles distant, I could see land. I could no more swim the distance than I could fly it.

Panic rose in my throat for a moment. Had I escaped the *Florida* just to expire on this desolate dot of land? I felt like throwing myself on the sod and weeping, but I am glad to say that reason did not utterly desert me. Instead I thought of my more immediate needs, and undertook a survey of my new kingdom. Breaking through the woods into a grassy clearing, I surprised three dozy-looking sheep who were cropping the grass in peace; they stared blankly at me, then lumbered away through the trees. This was my first piece of good fortune: where there were sheep, there must soon be men. Livestock was not just abandoned on an island. Farmers must pass by at some time to shear or slaughter them. It was winter now; surely, at worst, they would come for lambing time.

A few charred bits of timber on the beach supported my theory. Mankind had set foot on the island, and not so long ago; the wood was still black and soft, not crumbled away by the rain. Further exploration revealed a source of clean water, one of those miraculous burns that come from nowhere to feed beast and flower. I lay down beside it and drank deep. Somewhere behind me I heard a stamp and the crack of twigs; the sheep again, I assumed, and carried on drinking.

The wind was picking up, and soon I was cold. My clothes, of course, would not dry, and I was acutely aware that I must find shelter before night fell. I looked around for suitable caves or large rocks that would protect me from the elements, but the best I could do was a pile of leaves in one of the denser knots of trees. I covered myself and waited for dawn. Somehow, I slept.

The next day was fair, with white clouds racing across a sky of eggshell blue, and I awoke with a ravenous hunger. Of course, I had brought nothing with me from the ship; besides, even if I had filled my pockets with provisions, they would all have been lost at sea. There was nothing in the way of fruit that I could eat apart from some shiny black berries that I did not know; I was not yet so desperate that I would risk poisoning myself. But after two hours of searching the island for edible scraps, I was so desperate that I was almost ready to try. Then, sitting in despair on a stone, I saw a young rabbit come creeping out of a bramble thicket to nibble on the grass. Slowly, quietly, I picked up a stone and then, when it had wandered within my reach, I deftly brained it.

Delighted by my catch, I had spared no thought as to how I was to prepare it. There was no means of starting a fire at my disposal. I used a sharp flint to skin and gut the rabbit, and a sorry mess I made of it; but finally, there the little shiny pink body lay, looking good enough for the pot. I had always heard that rabbit was a wholesome meat that needed little cooking. I tasted a little scrap of flesh that clung to the skin. It tasted good enough; a little sour, perhaps, but not bad. And so, I picked up the poor little corpse and gnawed every scrap of meat off its bones.

I felt better instantly – partly, I suppose, from the relief of knowing that I was not going to starve to death. I ran up to the highest point of the island, knowing that my survival depended on catching sight of any boat that came within hailing distance. The sun rose in the sky, seagulls cried above my head and I felt, for the first time in weeks, an exhilarating sense of well-being. Happiness, in my case, has always found its most immediate expression through my body, and before many minutes had passed I was stretched out on the grass with my shirt pulled up under my chin, my trousers round my knees and my hard cock in my hand. The air felt so good on my skin, blowing through the light golden fuzz on my chest, stomach and legs, tickling my balls and my arse. I threw my head back and settled in for a good wank, licking my fingers and sticking them shamelessly up my arse, fucking myself as I bucked my hips and shot a big load of sperm up into the clear island air. I must have presented a strange spectacle to the sheep; just as I came, I heard one of them creeping up nearby – then stampeding away into the trees.

I opened my eyes when the come had turned cold on my stomach and was running down my sides on to the sandy ground beneath me. I sat up, wiped myself and admired the definition of my stomach muscles, thought how fine my softening pink cock looked against my white skin and golden pubic hair. I stretched my arms above my head, looked out to sea – and just caught sight of the stern of a small boat as it disappeared round the island's rocky northern point.

I leapt to my feet, shouting wildly, and crashed through the wood to the point. The boat was visible, perhaps only two hundred yards from me. I screamed, I ripped off my shirt and waved it above my head, I jumped up and down, but the boat ploughed inexorably on, and soon it was little more than a speck on the horizon.

The waves were boiling around the sharp grey rocks beneath me, and I felt like throwing myself to their mercy. There was my chance to escape, my chance to resume my journey and save Lebecque, and I had been too wrapped up in my own pleasure to take it. That was all I had ever thought of: my own pleasure! When

Alexander was sent away, all I had cared about was the fact that I had been deprived of a good fuck. I thought nothing of his safety, or the good of my country. I resented Lebecque because he stood between me and pleasure – I could not see him as I knew him now to be, a good and honest man. I had degraded myself and abandoned my quest at the hands of mercenaries and sailors, who had turned me into passion's willing slave. Oh yes, I called myself every name under the sun. I was truly ashamed.

For the rest of the morning I mooched about the island feeling very sorry for myself, plagued by the sheep who seemed to follow me always just out of sight. I heard them stamping around in the undergrowth, concealed by the trees; no sooner did I turn than they had disappeared.

By the afternoon I was feeling very sorry for myself indeed. The meal of raw rabbit that had sustained me so gloriously for breakfast had started to disagree with me, and my stomach was gripped by the most terrible pains. I wanted to be sick, but nothing would come. When I opened my bowels, however, I was practically knocked over by the force with which several pints of foulsmelling fluid shot out of me.

This was extraordinarily bad news. I had been sick like this once before, from a poisoned trout, and I knew how debilitating it could be. My head was light, and I felt unaccountably hot; I realised with terror that I was running a fever. Making my way back to the stream, my legs gave way beneath me, and I had to crawl to the water on hands and knees. When I reached it, I was shivering so violently that I could barely open my teeth far enough to get the water in. Somehow I made my way back to the wood and crawled into my pile of leaves, fully expecting never to wake.

I must have sweated the worst of the fever out while I slept; when I woke, I was soaking wet, and night had fallen. A full moon was above me in the sky; I felt disgustingly weak, with a raging thirst and a mouth like dust. I had to make my way back to the stream – a short distance, but forbidding enough in my debilitated state. I staggered from tree to tree, astonished to find that the sheep were following me still. I had never known sheep to be stealthy before. As a child it had been my favourite game to surprise them in the fields and tip them over. These island sheep were a more intelligent breed, as they hid behind the trees and waited until my back was turned before advancing.

I cleared the wood and lurched across the heath, stumbling in rabbit holes, twisting my ankle, falling face-first into clumps of heather. The sheep – or whatever it was – pursued me still. I kept turning to catch it, but all I could see in the moonlight was a shape hunched upon the ground. Perhaps it was not a sheep after all, but a beast of some other kind. A wild cat, maybe. That was not a pleasing thought.

I tried to run, but the shadow stuck to me, always a few yards behind, crouching down each time I stopped, running when I ran. I was still half crazed from the fever, and imagined myself pursued by some fearful monster. I had forgotten my need for water, and ran aimlessly across the heath, along the beach, up the banks and through the woods. The beast stuck close behind me.

Finally I ran out of strength and collapsed on the ground by a small patch of scrubby bushes, past caring whether I was savaged by a lion or not. I could hear the beast's breath close to me. It sounded, to my astonishment, human.

Nothing happened. No claws or fangs tore into me. The breathing subsided, but stayed where it was. I lifted my head from the turf and tried to make out a shape in the moonlight, but suddenly it rose between me and the sky and bore down upon me. A hand covered my mouth, and I felt a knife at my throat.

'Don't move, soldier,' a voice hissed in my ear. A huge domed head was silhouetted against the moon. I stopped struggling and lay still. A thick metal bracelet or armband was digging into my neck where he held me.

'Where are the others?'

I tried to speak, but his hand gagged me.

'Come on, soldier, don't play games with me!' He let go of my mouth and shoved the blade even closer to my windpipe; any further, and it would break the skin.

'There is nobody!'

'What?'

'I'm alone.'

'Don't lie!'

'And I'm not a soldier... oof!' He dropped me on my back and raced up to the highest point of the island. Now I could see him clearly: he was a huge creature with a shaven head, manacles around his wrists and ankles. An escaped convict.

He returned to where I lay shaking on the ground.

'What are you doing here?'

'I was washed ashore.'

'Where from?'

'The *Florida*.'

'Escaped prisoner?'

'Yes.'

'Hmm.' He put his knife away. 'How long have you been here?'

'A day. What about you?'

'A week. Broke out of Fort William.'

I jumped in astonishment. 'Fort William? But that's where my friend is!'

'Your friend? What?' He roared. 'You're a friend of the governor's? You dirty scum, I should kill you now, you traitor's brat.'

'Not the governor, not the governor!' I squealed, hardly aware of what he was talking about.

'Then who?'

'Lebecque!' I screamed as the knife glinted in the moonlight.

'Lebecque?' He seemed astonished. He dropped the knife on the ground. 'The French priest.'

'Yes! Do you know him? Is he alive?'

'Of course I know him.'

'And is he well?'

'He was alive when I last saw him.'

'But was he all right?'

'What's your name, boy?'

'Charles Gordon.'

He was silent for a while, then lifted me into a sitting position and stood aside so that the moon fell on my face.

'Charlie.' He seemed rapt in contemplation of my face, tracing its contours with his thick, dirty fingers. 'The very image.'

'What?'

'A face in a picture...' His voice tailed off. 'But you're sick, boy. What's the matter with you?'

'I was washed ashore. I ate a rabbit and it made me ill.'

He surveyed the disgusting state of my clothes; I'm ashamed to say that I had soiled them in the night, and they still clung to me. I must have stunk like a pig; fortunately for me, the fever had wiped out my sense of smell. He felt my brow, prodded my stomach and looked up my nose.

'No bleeding at least. You'll survive. What in God's name possessed you to eat a rabbit raw?'

'I was starving.'

'You're lucky to be alive.' He picked me up and cradled me like a baby in his arms. We crossed the heath, clambered over the rocks and found the mouth to a clean, dry cave which had escaped my notice before. I drank from a battered tin cup, and felt instantly better. I wanted to ask him all about Lebecque and their adventures together, but he stopped my mouth with his finger, lay me down on an animal skin and I slept immediately.

When I woke in the morning, I was naked and clean with another fur thrown on top of me. My clothes were hung over a rock; they had been washed. I was alone in the cave, and I dropped off to sleep again. When I came round this time, the man was squatting on his haunches beside me. He was gnawing on a loaf of bread and a piece of cheese.

'Where did you get that from?' I asked. He laughed and tapped the side of his nose.

'That would be telling.'

'There are no houses on the island.'

'That's what you know.'

'But I've been all over it.'

'Your eyes don't see, Charlie. But come on, get up. It's time to work.' He tossed me the heel of the loaf and I swallowed it greed-ily, then dressed and followed him out of the cave.

'What's your name?'

'Morgan.'

'Where are we going?'

'Fishing.'

'Why were you in Fort William?'

'Aren't you full of questions?'

I had no breath to ask any more; his strides were twice the length of mine, and I had to jog to keep up with him. I was still not up to my usual strength, and it took all my efforts to keep moving, let alone talking.

We reached the mouth of the burn that ran from the top of the island to the sea. A wide sandy bed was covered in perhaps four feet of fast flowing, clear fresh water. Rock and weed dotted the sand, and on each thick ribbon of weed I could see dozens and dozens of shellfish.

'What month is it, Charlie?'

'December, I think.'

'Correct. Now, follow me.'

He rolled up his trousers to reveal massive, curving calves above the cruel iron fetters that dug into his ankles. I followed him until I was stomach-deep in water; it came up just below his waist. He reached down, pulled on a piece of seaweed and came up with a handful of gleaming white shells, shook off the water and tossed them on to the sandy bank. I attempted to do likewise, and came up with a handful of slime and a few broken bits of twig, one of which had a tiny but very angry-looking crab clinging to it.

Morgan put his hands on his hips and laughed, then showed me once more how to do it: he grasped the base of the weed with one hand, ran the other swiftly up its length popping each clam from its sticky perch as he did so, catching them all and landing them with aplomb. I tried again; this time I had a handful of weed and, perhaps, half a dozen clams.

We carried on fishing in this way until we had a good pile of shellfish glistening and gaping on the sand. Morgan waded a little further out into the sea.

'Come out here, Charlie, and I'll show you how to catch a bigger fish.' I followed him; the water was up around my chest. 'You have to hold your hands open in front of you, like this' – he demonstrated above water – 'and see what swims into them. Then you grab it' – he mimed a two-handed grip – 'and pull.'

I did as I was told. We stood there like idiots, our hands freezing beneath the water.

'Anything yet, Charlie?'

'Nothing.'

He came a little closer.

'Anything yet?'

'Nothing. Can I get out?'

'No, something's coming, I can tell. Be patient.' He edged a little nearer yet so we were standing hip to hip.

'Careful now. Something's on the way. Watch it, Charlie, watch it!'

Just as he turned to face me, something very large indeed seemed to swim into my hands. I caught it and gripped and for a moment wondered why I couldn't move it. Then I realised what sort of fish I had caught. I looked up to see Morgan, his arms crossed across his barrel chest, smiling down at me.

'What have you got there, Charlie?'

'I'm not sure. Feels like a big one.'

'Let's see if we can land it, shall we?'

He stepped forwards, I stepped backwards, never loosening my grip on the great fish that wriggled and stiffened in my hands, and thus we made our way back on to the beach. As soon as we were on firm ground, I dropped to my knees and took him in my mouth. His cock was salty and, after the chill of the water, amazingly hot. It hit the back of my throat and I gagged; fortunately, I was now so adept at taking even the hugest of pricks down the back of my throat that I relaxed, breathed deeply and swallowed. Soon my nose was buried in his wet hair.

'Oh, God!' Morgan yelled above me; I suspect that nobody had ever been able to accommodate him in this manner before. Excited by the thought that I was the first to introduce him to this pleasure, I threw myself into my work and lavished upon that sturdy giant all the benefit of my education on board the *Florida*. Up and down the entire length of his cock I went; I swirled my tongue around the shaft and the head; I teased the sensitive little thread of skin that ran from his piss-hole down to the underside of his shaft. I sucked his balls, first separately, and then stuffing both of them into my greedy mouth, pulling on them as his cock soared above me. Shielding my teeth with my lips, I chewed up and down each side of his mighty length and finally, swallowing the whole thing and tugging on his balls, I took his load deep, deep inside me. His knees buckled and I thought we would both sprawl in the sand.

He righted himself, gasping, while I choked around his cock, unwilling to relinquish it from my throat. Gripping it with increased suction, I savoured every hard inch that filled me as I pulled my own cock out of my soaking trousers and, with a few quick strokes, splattered my come on to the wet sand.

Finally we parted. Morgan gathered up the clams in his shirt and we returned to the cave in an amicable silence. He lit a fire, foraged for a few roots and fruits and left me to rest. We dined in the moonlight on clam soup – to this day the most delicious thing I have ever tasted.

†

That night we shared his makeshift bed, glad of each other's warmth and the fullness in our bellies. Morgan was aroused again, and lay back with his arms behind his head while I slowly sucked and wanked him and then, when the stiff heat of his cock became too much for me, climbed over him and steered it up my arse. He lay there, smiling, half asleep, as I writhed and bounced on top of him, then, extending one massive arm, he gripped me and tossed me off until I spewed all over his belly. He came deep inside me, and we slept for a while.

When we woke, it was still dark, but Morgan set about clearing out all signs of our occupation, stamping the ashes of the fire into the sandy floor of the cave, throwing the clam shells out on to the rocks where they would soon be carried away by the gulls.

I dressed quickly and stood shivering in the cold air.

'We must move quickly, Charlie. I've been here too long.'

'Do you have a boat?'

He laughed quietly. 'No, you fool. Come on, look lively. Here, finish the water.'

'Where are we going?'

'I don't know about you, Charlie. I'm going home.'

'I must find Lebecque. Won't you help me?'

'I fear you may be too late, Charlie.'

'Why?'

'They took him away from Fort William.'

My heart sank. 'Why? Where?'

'I don't know. But you'll find him. I know you will. Just be careful. Keep eyes and ears open. Disguise yourself. Become a spy. Do all that is necessary. I know that you will find him.'

'How do you know?'

'Because you love him.'

I was glad it was still so dark; Morgan would not see my blushes.

'And he loves you, Charlie.'

'What do you mean?'

'We spoke of you in prison. He loves you, boy. He and I were… together, on occasion, in the same way that you and I have been. We were close, Charlie, close friends. And he trusted me. So that is why I know you'll find him, just as I know that I will find my Margaret. Come on, now. It's time to go.'

We emerged from the cave and walked down to the easternmost point of the island. And there, to my utter astonishment, where yesterday was just the grey, crashing expanse of the sea, now stretched a long, broad causeway of wet sand. I stood amazed.

'It's only open for a few hours. We must start now.'

Morgan grabbed me by the hand and we ran from the island.

Chapter Ten

The time had come to face up to my responsibilities in a more adult manner. I was no longer the silly child who had waltzed out of Gordon Hall with his nose in the air and a head full of glorious adventures gleaned from the pages of novels. Only a few months had passed since I left home, but I had grown up. I had learned to trust nobody, to consider the consequences of every action, to keep my own counsel. I had learned to think, as well as to fuck, like a man.

For the first week after my delivery from the island I travelled north with Morgan, glad of his protection as we proceeded with caution from Barrow-in-Furness (where we struck the mainland) through the Lake District. We slept mostly under the stars, shunning human company; Morgan, as an escaped convict, had more reason than me for keeping a low profile. Sometimes, in our makeshift beds of leaves and furs, we rekindled the flame that Morgan had lit in the cold waters of the island; more often, though, we huddled together for warmth and companionship, too tired from our day's march to do anything more than sleep.

After Carlisle, our ways diverged; Morgan judged it safe to return to Edinburgh, where his Margaret was waiting for him. I was headed north-west, to Glasgow and ultimately Fort William. Perhaps Lebecque was no longer there – but someone, somewhere along the road, would know his whereabouts. If nothing else, I would join the English regiment at Glasgow and perhaps, by keeping my eyes and ears open, find out what I needed to know. It was a vague plan, but the best available to me. Morgan's counsel – disguise yourself, become a spy, do all that is necessary – seemed to me the only course of action.

So, travelling under the name Edward Nicholls (my mother's maiden name; how pleased she would have been by my discretion!), I made slow progress through the Borders, forced to earn my crust with casual work (scarce enough at the turn of the year) and by honest begging. If I had avoided the cities altogether I would have starved, but I stayed long enough in each place only to earn sufficient coin to convert into bread to sustain me for the next leg of my journey. In Dumfries I struck gold; a wealthy merchant spied me pissing in the privy at the back of an inn, liked what he saw and offered me a good rate for the use thereof. I spent a weekend working hard satisfying the old man's depraved appetites, and by the Monday morning had spent so much energy that I felt weak and debilitated, my cock sore from its heroic efforts. The old man, who had grown accustomed to the taste of my come, offered me a ridiculous sum to stay with him as his 'secretary', but I was firm, took the money that we had originally agreed on (and he was grudging enough when it came to handing it over) and left Dumfries for good. Nothing, this time, was going to stand between me and my quest. I regretted the loss of soft beds, hot baths and clean clothes – but it felt good to be back on the road, however hard the conditions. Now I could exchange coin for food at the farmhouses and inns along the way, and I proceeded with a lighter heart.

Another week saw me crossing the Lowther Hills and well on my way towards Glasgow, thanks to a kind carter who wanted nothing more than my company on the road from Moffat to Lanark. Along the way we ran across a huge convoy of redcoats escorting supplies, as I took it, south towards Carlisle. We were stopped and searched but no harm was done, apart from the insults to our national pride that were heaped upon us. The carter was patient, however, and we went on our way.

It was in Lanark that my plans misfired. I fell in with a group of English soldiers at an inn; mindful of my experiences at the hands of the mercenaries at Auchindarroch I was a little more chary of my companionship. These, however, seemed to be regular soldiers, well disciplined even when they were off duty, offering no immediate threat to my person. And so I allowed myself to be drawn into conversation, sticking carefully to the story that I was Edward Nicholls, an itinerant tutor travelling to the house of a family in Hamilton, evincing an almost cretinous naivety about the political situation in Scotland. I was taciturn, a little shy, peppering my few sentences with classical tags – persuading the soldiers that I was a feckless scholar who could pose no possible threat to security.

Behind the mask, however, I was taking in every shred of information I could possibly glean. The company was bound for Glasgow, where they were to 'deliver' something to General Wilmott, controller of all the English forces in the area, a man of 'extraordinary intelligence' according to Sergeant Blair, a tall, slim blond soldier, who seemed to enjoy chaffing me for my ignorance about military affairs.

'The ancient generals,' I said, with a scholarly air, 'were the greatest tacticians. Look at Alcibiades, if you will, who, according to Xenophon –'

'Ah, but General Wilmott has spies in every town, in every prison, even in every regiment.' The blond soldier winked. 'And so, you see, nothing can happen in Scotland without him knowing about it.'

This was my first important discovery. The second, although less immediately useful, seemed to hold the key to my success. I had noticed as soon as I joined the company that one of their number held himself apart. While the rest of the seven-strong band enjoyed their meat and their ale around the fire, boasting and singing like any group of well-tempered soldiers, the eighth sat in the corner looking on, lit fitfully by the flames, drinking nothing and eating only the barest minimum. He did not appear to be a prisoner; on one occasion, he left the room to relieve himself, and returned to his place without exciting suspicion. And yet he was not of the band. The other soldiers looked slightly askance at him; once or twice I observed them making whispered comments to each other, nodding towards the corner of the room and laughing raucously. Nobody addressed him directly, but he watched all.

He was younger than the rest of the soldiers: about my own age, I would guess. But where I had the pale, open face and ginger hair of a typical Scot, the other was dark, spoilt-looking, his large mouth fixed in a permanent pout that sometimes seemed on the verge of a smile. His hair was cut short, and he wore civilian clothes – a clean white shirt, a brown leather tunic, trousers of a fine, expensive wool. He kept about him at all times a large purse of thick brown leather, which he wore slung about his neck on a sturdy strap and fingered idly. When Blair had made reference to spies in the camp, I thought I detected a faint nod towards the silent boy in the corner. This, then, was one of General Wilmott's all-seeing, all-knowing band of informers. If anyone would know where Lebecque was, this, I guessed, was he.

The evening wore on, and I enjoyed a modest meal and some agreeable conversation with the soldiers. Sergeant Blair had generously offered me a bed for the night 'if you don't mind bunking down with a rough and ready soldier'. The accompanying wink led me to suspect that there was more behind the offer than just a bed, and I was sorely tempted: not only by the prospect of missing out on another night under a cold hedgerow, but also by the juicy-looking bulge at the front of Blair's tight buff trousers. It was now some time since I had enjoyed another man and, despite my resolve to conduct myself more seriously, I was hungry for some loving. The merchant in Dumfries had exercised my cock but not my imagination, beyond the self-regarding thrill of being treated as a sex-object. Blair, however, was a much tastier proposition.

But first there was business to attend to. I felt certain that the boy in the corner held the key to my quest, and if I could only pump him for information I could continue my journey with fresh purpose, perhaps even rewarding myself with a night spent swinging on the sergeant's cock into the bargain. By eleven o'clock, after the ale had been flowing liberally for some hours, the party was almost ready to break up. Blair had become quite demonstrative, and had manoeuvred me to a dark corner behind the bar where he was whispering the most obscene suggestions in my ear, kissing me on the neck and scratching me with his stubble, a sensation which always has an instant effect on my groin. I was trying to keep my eyes on the boy in the corner during all of this, but it was becoming difficult to concentrate; Blair, when he felt that I had become erect, was grinding our groins together and mauling my backside, telling me in explicit detail just exactly what delights awaited me if I'd only come upstairs with him.

The dark boy in the corner took all this in; not for nothing was he a professional informer. While Blair buried his face in my neck, I looked over his shoulder to see those deep, sparkling eyes glancing over at me with a mixture of contempt and amusement, the full, sulky lips parting for a moment to reveal a pink tip of tongue. I was surprised to see that none of the soldiers tried to engage the boy in the way that Blair was engaging me; in their shoes, I would have thought him a very agreeable bedmate. But they restricted themselves to a few ribald remarks, and left the boy alone.

When I saw him rise to his feet and slip out of the bar, I knew I had to make my move. Screwing up my resolve, I attempted to break away from Blair's embrace, but it was not so easily done. By now he had one hand down the back of my trousers, and was kneading my buttocks with a will. When I tried to move, he impaled me on his middle finger and started stirring my guts around. My cock was all in favour of retiring to his room and letting him have his wicked way; my head, however, was telling me otherwise. Remembering Morgan's advice, I realised I would have to dissemble.

'Oh God, what are you doing?' I whispered in his ear, resuming my role of the naive scholar.

'Doesn't that feel good?' he murmured, his voice thick with lust.

'I don't know... I've never had anyone touch me there before...' My cynical plan worked; Blair was so excited by the idea of taking my virginity that he became even more frantic.

'Just you wait, boy, until I get this up there...' Never taking his mouth from my neck, he fumbled around in his groin and pulled his cock out, placing my hand around it. It was certainly a handsome piece, and ready to go off.

'It's so big and hard,' I whispered, staring into his eyes and licking my lips. 'How are you going to get that into my little arse? It's far too tight. You'd have to push really hard.' My charade was having the desired effect; Blair's eyes seemed to be filming over, and he was breathing through his mouth. I started moving my hand up and down his shaft, playing him like an instrument.

'Oh, I want you to fuck me so badly, Sergeant. I don't care what you do to me. I just want that big hard cock inside me...' I started moaning and writhing around his fat finger, which was now as far inside me as he could get it. I clamped the muscles of my ring around it, giving him a taste of things to come, and continued wanking him. He may have thought he was in control, that I was an innocent just waiting to be debauched, but he little suspected that I was an expert in such matters, as practised as the most professional whore. Within another minute he was spewing his load all over my hand; it splattered on the floor around us. Poor Blair opened his eyes in surprise as his cock started to go limp. He pulled his finger out of my arse.

'Sorry... I got a bit over-excited...'

I kissed him on the mouth in promise of future bliss, then told him that I had an urgent need to go to the privy which, considering the intrusion into my 'virgin' arse, was a plausible excuse. I slipped out from his grasp and left him wiping the end of his cock, still with a look of confusion on his handsome mug.

But instead of slipping out to the privy, I bounded up the stairs in pursuit of my quarry. He had only been gone a few minutes; his would be the only occupied room, and easy enough to find. Sure enough, a thread of light shone from underneath one of the doors where all else was darkness. He must have lit a candle.

I listened for a few moments; nothing. I applied my eye to the keyhole and saw, to my momentary bewilderment, the two perfect globes of a naked male backside, slightly downy around the crevice. Then the buttocks parted and I caught sight of one of the pinkest, prettiest arseholes I have ever seen. The boy was bending over – perhaps removing a last item of clothing? – and in my still-aroused state I had an overwhelming desire to shove my tongue, and then my hard cock, into that inviting little twat.

After the best part of a minute the boy stood up and his hole was lost to my view. He walked away from the keyhole and, I assumed, towards the bed. I saw a flurry of white linen and all was still.

I should have known immediately that I was up against a more practised dissembler than myself; the show, of course, had been entirely for my benefit. As usual, though, I was so excited by the erotic possibilities of the situation that I failed to listen to the voice of reason. The results were almost disastrous.

Standing up and attempting to conceal my erection, I slowly turned the door handle, expecting to take my young quarry by surprise. But there was no sound, only the creaking of the hinges. Surely he had not fallen asleep already? I opened the door further; still no response. He must have been aware of my presence. A few more inches, and I stepped into the room, bracing myself for a surprise attack. But no: he was not hiding behind the door with a cosh; instead, as the candlelight all too clearly displayed, he was lying face down on the bed, his head resting on his forearms, his legs spread wide apart. Somewhere in the soft, downy shadows between his buttocks, I knew that delightful pink hole was waiting for me. My cock was jutting straight out in front of me once again, despite my efforts to control it.

I must have stood like an idiot, staring at this appetising prospect. Suddenly I realised that the boy had turned his head and was watching me watching him, with a smile on his face. Instead of reprimanding me, or calling for help, he ground his hips on the mattress and raised his arse a little. Oh, I was so pleased at my devious handling of Sergeant Blair just a few moments before, and here I was falling into the hands of yet more cunning player. I had come up here determined to extract information from him, by violence if necessary; now all I could think of was how hot his arse would feel around my prick. I stood like a fool unable to speak. I suppose the bulge in my trousers was eloquence enough.

Catching sight of the leather purse slung over the back of the chair, I came to my senses for a moment. Information was what I had come for, and information I must have. If he sought to trap me with sexual pleasure – well, two could play at that game. I advanced towards the bed and stood at the foot. He reached one hand round and pulled his left buttock aside, probing himself with a finger.

'Go ahead, schoolteacher,' he said in a sneering, arrogant voice. 'Help yourself.' Well, he had fallen for my disguise so far. I had the upper hand.

'What do you mean?' My voice was shaking; it was not entirely assumed.

'You've been looking at me all evening, even when that sergeant had his tongue down your throat. Come on, fuck me. I know that's what you want.'

'I don't understand.'

'Get that big hard cock out of your trousers and stick it up my arse.' Well, he was being direct enough now, and to avoid any possibility of confusion he knelt up, held his cheeks apart and gave me an uninterrupted view of his moist, velvety hole. 'It's the best pussy in Scotland. Very popular with the English generals. You really can't say no, can you?' He extended a foot and rubbed my cock. My mouth was watering.

But for once I looked before I leapt. If he was so popular with the generals, and such a successful whore, why was he offering himself to me? Had he discerned my intents, and was simply trying to put me off? Or was he trying to double-cross the soldiers downstairs, using me as some kind of escape route? I thought quickly. What could his plan be? Lure me into his bed, knock me out, take my clothes and leave in disguise – well, that's what I would have done under the circumstances.

I needed to know more. Perhaps he would talk if I played along. I sank to my knees and buried my face in his arse, licking and slurping and finally sticking my tongue into his hole. I heard him gasp in surprise; he hadn't expected the naive schoolteacher to be such an adept. Well, it was no great hardship; eating his arse was like enjoying the finest of sweetmeats. When I broke away, I was gratified to see that his cock, limp at first, was now fully erect. He was only play-acting before; now, however, he was genuinely excited. This, I felt, shortened the odds between us.

The temptation to plough straight into his arse was overwhelming, and my cock was begging for relief. He wanted it as much as I did, I could tell: he was arching his back and sticking his tail in the air like a cat on heat. I had to take advantage of the situation. If I gave him what he wanted, satisfied him and allowed him to recover his *sang-froid*, then the opportunity would be missed. I knew that I'd be able to think clearer if only I could empty my balls inside him, but that would have to wait. I had to keep him on the boil.

'Come on then,' he said – and now he was not sneering. 'Can't you see I'm ready for you?'

'God, you're a dirty wee bastard, aren't you?'

'Oh yes, I am.' My aim had hit home; I guessed that he was the sort who liked to be treated a bit rough, while keeping the upper hand. I knew the game well; I had played it myself often enough on board the *Florida*. Let them think they're in control, pander to their masculine pride, but all the time get them to do exactly what you want them to do...

'I should tan that arse of yours before I fuck it.'

He buried his face in the bedclothes and gave an 'Mmm' in reply, wiggling his bum provocatively in my face. He thought he was being so clever. But we were both playing a role.

I smacked his right buttock gently, then his left. He squirmed. 'Harder!'

This time I gave each cheek a good whack; the sound was loud in the small chamber. He groaned in delight. 'More.'

Moving round beside him I gave his pert arse a good thrashing, and watched it grow pink and then red under my hands. The pain was goading him on; he was now pushing his cock back between his legs to show me how hard it was, to inflame me even further. Oh no, my boy, I thought, you won't trick me that easily.

Still belabouring his bum with one hand, I reached over the chair with the other and picked up the leather purse; the boy was so far gone that he didn't even notice. The shoulder strap was made of good strong leather, about two inches wide: just right for a good whipping. I doubled it over and brought it down with a crack across his cheeks. He moaned, pushed his cock further back and wriggled his arse. I whacked him again, then let the leather strap dangle between his spread buttocks, playing over the hole.

Suddenly he realised what I was doing. His head whipped round and he made a grab for the purse, which I held just out of his reach. As quick as lightning he was up on his knees facing me, grabbing for the purse. I held it above my head. He was red in the face from his recent beating, and his stiff cock bounced around with every movement.

'Give me that!'

'Come and get it!'

He stood up on the bed and reached; I took a step back, and he nearly crashed to the floor. As he regained his balance I caught him round the waist, threw him down on his back and held on to his knees; he twisted and turned his torso, but there was little he could do. I was a good deal stronger than him. The purse I slung round my neck.

'What's so special about this old leather bag, then?'

'Nothing... Just give it to me.'

'Oh yes, I'll give it to you.' I pressed my groin against his arse, which was spread open at just the right level. He shut his eyes and groaned, but he wouldn't give in that easily.

'Let me go, schoolteacher.' The sneer was back in his voice, but his cock was still as stiff as a post, drooling at the tip. He was a lithe, slim-hipped young man, smooth-bodied – and his cock looked huge on that slight frame. I longed to see it shooting over his slender belly. But that would have to wait.

'Tell me what's in the package and I'll let you go.'

'Letters. That's all. Now shut up and fuck me.'

'Letters to whom?'

'General Wilmott of course. Didn't your friend downstairs tell you? I'm one of his spies. That's why they won't lay a finger on me. Dirty rabble. I know what they want to do. What you all want to do. So come on. I'm ready for it.'

'What are they about? The letters?'

'You're suddenly full of questions, schoolteacher. I thought you were only interested in the ancients...'

He was catching on too quickly. I had to distract his attention, and so with one hand I undid my trousers and let my cock spring out into the open. He should have used the opportunity to struggle free and raise the alarm, but the moment he caught sight of my weapon all the fight went out of him.

'My God.'

'You want this, don't you?'

'I... yes.'

'You want it inside you.'

'Yes. Please.'

'What's in the letters?' I could see the struggle going on inside him. I made my cock twitch, and pressed it against his bum.

'Information.'

'About what?'

'Prisoners. They're moving prisoners all over Scotland. It's all in code, you won't be able to read it. That's all I know. Now will you just stick that fucking thing up my arse and get on with it.'

'Oh yes, I'll get on with it.'

I launched myself on top of him and stuck my tongue down his throat, letting my cock batter against his hole, which was practically sucking me in. Then, with a dexterity that still surprises me, I whipped the purse over my head, looped the strap around his wrists and tied them quickly together. There was little he could do; the bucking and writhing beneath me was half complaint, half encouragement. When his hands were firmly tied, I sat up and admired my handiwork. His arms stretched above his head; he was sweating. Our cocks were playing together down below.

'What... what are you doing?' For the first time, he sounded uncertain.

'I'm double-crossing you, you dirty little spy.'

He was about to cry out, but I shunted quickly up his torso and stopped his mouth with my cock. With a pitiful look in his eyes, he swallowed the whole thing. He was not content just to gag on it; within a minute he was sucking on it with enthusiasm. He was very good at it, too, and I could feel a good head of steam building up inside me. But if I came, he would lose interest in me.

While he was guzzling on my prick, I opened the purse and had a cursory look at its content. A large outer envelope was clearly addressed to General Wilmott, Glasgow; it bore the royal seal, and a Latin inscription on the reverse which I immediately translated as 'The Bearer is to be Trusted'. Oh yes, he was to be trusted all right; but he was not to be the bearer they were expecting. I would take his place. I slipped the package back into the purse and concentrated on fucking his face. Looking over my shoulder, I saw his cock pulsing on his stomach, where a pool of sticky juice had collected. This was turning out better than I had expected. I reached round and gave it a squeeze; I heard him moan in gratitude.

I pulled out of his mouth when I felt I could bear it no longer, and waited for the boiling in my balls to subside. The messenger boy had lost all interest in shouting out for help; he could think about one thing only now. He licked his lips, unwilling to relinquish the taste of my prick, and I must admit that I would have been more than happy to give him a mouthful that he could savour at his leisure.

First, however, I had to secure my plans. I hooked his bound wrists over the headboard, looped the purse through it and thus secured him at one end. Then I picked up his shirt from the floor, ripped it into two pieces and deftly bound his ankles to the knobs at the foot of the bed. He put up a token resistance, but a few slaps around the face with my hard, wet cock were enough to shut him up.

There: I had him where I wanted him. If he cried out I could kill him, and he knew it. Instead he just lay there, looking to me for the next move.

I was in two minds. Uppermost was the fact that here lay this beautiful young man, slim-hipped and well-hung with the juiciest arsehole it had ever been my pleasure to lick. He sucked like an angel; I could only imagine what it would feel like to bury my prick in his guts. On the other hand, a plan had formed in my mind. I wanted satisfaction on both counts.

For a while, I stood at the side of the bed and looked at him. He was certainly appetising. Dark nipples stood out of his smooth brown chest like organ stops; I licked my fingers and teased them, pulling on them until he sighed with pleasure, then I rubbed the head of my dick over them, leaving a trail of slime over each one. He lifted his hips off the bed, begging me to pay some attention to his arse, and so I gave him a finger, then another, and fucked him that way for a while. God, his arse tugged and pulled at those fingers! I added another, and went as far as I could go; it was far enough for neither of us. How much more satisfaction I would get with my prick, longer than my longest finger by a good four inches.

And then there was his hard, silky cock lying against the taut skin of his stomach, framed by a little tuft of hair. I lifted it and played for a while with the loose foreskin, pulling it back to expose one of the best-shaped heads I have ever seen. I couldn't resist it: I bent down and ran my tongue over it, then placed my lips around it and kissed it. The boy was muttering a string of obscenities in a half-whisper. He hated me, of course, but he loved what I was doing to him.

I stood up and stripped, watching with delight the look of hunger in his eyes as he took in every inch of my body. He was accustomed to the English generals; I would show him the body of a true Highlander, and he'd see what his treachery had cost him. He was transfixed – as, in truth, was I by the sight of him bound and writhing on the bed. I could hear the heavy footsteps of the soldiers as they pounded up the stairs and along the corridors to their own chambers. Between us, there was a pregnant silence. I wanted nothing more than to fuck him.

I clambered over the foot of the bed, in between his legs, and lay at full length atop him. Our cocks pressed together; our mouths locked, and with one hand I caressed his head while with the other I brutally fingered his arse. Then inspiration struck. I leaned over and blew out the fat tallow candle that was burning on the night stand. We were in total darkness. Now, he must have thought, he was going to get what he wanted.

I pulled the candle out of its holder, pinched off the wick between finger and thumb and spread some of the molten tallow over the other end, where it had been cut down slightly to fit into the candlestick. It was just the right size: as fat as my cock, and a little longer. I hoisted the boy's legs in the air and shoved the candlestick up his arse. He groaned and writhed in ecstasy at first, then spat in disappointment.

'What the fuck are you doing?'

He was too late. I had used those few seconds to bundle up his clothes. I put on my own shirt (his I had used to tie him to the bed) and stuffed his mouth with a scarf. He would look a pretty sight when the soldiers found him.

I slipped the package of letters out of the purse, dressed quickly and quietly and crept into the passage, just in time to see Blair, my lover of the evening, disappearing into his room.

I went to his door.

'Blair! Blair!' I whispered, doing my best to impersonate the messenger boy's sneering tones.

'What is it?' He was clearly drunk.

'He's waiting for you.'

'Wha –?'

'The schoolteacher. He's waiting for you in my room. He wants a good fucking, although I suggest you light a candle first.'

I heard Blair stumbling around, and made my escape down the stairs before I saw him leave his room.

Well, if both were willing, the messenger boy would get fucked, and Blair would get a piece of arse. Only I would leave the inn unsatisfied. But I had something far more precious: the letters and a new identity.

I left the inn as quietly as possible and stole a horse. By the time Blair discovered my deception, and the messenger had dared to confess that I had tricked him so easily, I would be well on the way to Glasgow.

Chapter Eleven
Carlisle, 2 March 1751

Dear Charlie

You must by now have assumed that I am dead or disappeared for good. Perhaps you spare the odd thought for me and wonder what became of your old tutor. Perhaps these letters never reach you at all.

To my astonishment, and maybe yours, I am still alive, no longer in prison, living in relative comfort and safety although not, I am afraid, enjoying my liberty. My situation now may be more dangerous than before, but at least I have a bed to sleep in and a bowl to wash in.

You will see from the address that I find myself in Carlisle, way down over the border in England. Charlie, I hope you never have cause to venture this far south; it is a dismal place, squalid and dark in comparison to the glorious open spaces of the western Highlands. My lot, however, could be worse: I am billetted in a handsome property just outside the town, and have almost forgotten what hunger feels like. The flesh is returning to my bones, and I am even able to exercise outdoors.

You will be wondering how I find myself in such comparable comfort. When last I wrote I was chained to the wall like an animal in a stinking dungeon, my only comfort another prisoner who contrived to escape from the castle (at the cost, I fear, of a corrupt soldier's life) and gained freedom. I pray that he has found his way home to his wife and child and that no accident has befallen him along the way. He was a good man, if violent.

My status in Fort William was, as you know, extremely parlous. There were those who wanted me killed without delay; word had obviously reached them that I was not an innocent priest, but some kind of French agent at large in Scotland. But my clerical garb served me well, and I was spared that time. My heart sank, however, when I was once again summoned to the Governor's office. This time, I felt certain, the die was cast. I was interrogated again; I was silent in response. Certain accusations were made; I did not reply, although I was impressed at their accuracy. I was a spy sent from France to help high-ranking Jacobites, they told me. I said nothing. A rescue party had been sent from France, they said, and was thought to be on these shores. I hung my head; indeed, I still know nothing of the truth or otherwise of this allegation.

They dared not kill me, that much was clear; I suppose the fear of reprisals was a major consideration. Instead, however, I was to be transferred from Fort William to an undisclosed destination. I was placed, bound and blindfolded, in a closed carriage among sacks of meal and bundles of firewood that had been 'requisitioned' from the Highland farms, and taken under guard on the road out of Scotland. The arrogance of the redcoats never ceased to astonish me as they stopped and searched every traveller they met. It was only the patience and dignity of these persecuted Scots that avoided outright violence.

Finally we passed through Lanark and over the Lowther Hills, across the border and into Carlisle – or so I gathered from the shouted conversation of my escorts. At least I was fed and watered regularly, and on the third day one of the soldiers suffered me to have my eyes uncovered.

I was unloaded alongside the rest of the cargo outside the garrison at

Carlisle where, had it not been for the thick cords that bound my hands (I was tethered to a railing like a horse) I might have slipped away. Instead I was transferred to an impressive coach and driven alongside a surly, taciturn redcoat to my current address – Leigh House, a well-proportioned red-brick edifice, perhaps fifty years old, obviously the work of a successful, status-hungry merchant with money to burn. The only thing that marked it out from a normal burgher's house was the high wall around the park, the deadly-looking railings atop them, and the armed guard patrolling the perimeter.

I was escorted into the main hall, where my host, Mr William Leigh, awaited me. I disliked him at once: his long, grey hair, his shiny, smooth forehead, the plump, perfumed jowls and white hands that had never done a day's work in their lives. I guessed that his father had made the family fortune, and that the incumbent enjoyed a life of idleness. He greeted me in a brocade dressing gown and a smoking cap with a tassel dangling foppishly from the top; his feet were shod in tiny, delicate chamois slippers.

'Oh, for heaven's sake, take his boots off!' he squeaked when I was pushed forward on to the Turkish carpet. The guard obliged, and I stood barefoot in my prison rags, a sorry sight to see.

Leigh looked me up and down, circling around me for all the world like a Roman patrician about to purchase a slave. I expected him to prise my mouth open and look at my teeth.

'Well,' he smirked, 'you're my little boy's new tutor. I suppose you'll have to do. I don't know what they think they're sending me these days.' He rolled his eyes to heaven. 'But I suppose we shall have to make the best of a bad job.'

Leigh, I guess, is one of those infamous types who benefit from civil strife, who offers his services and influence to the governing powers in return for financial and business favours. Leigh House had been converted into a kind of private prison, where awkward cases like myself could 'disappear' for any length of time under a guise of respectability. So, I was to be a tutor once again. The contrast between my two pedagogical appointments struck me at once.

I sensed that Leigh himself would have been quite happy to 'learn' from me, such was the appraising manner in which he ran his piggy little eyes over my frame. He insisted on attending while I was taken to the bathroom and sluiced down by his 'valet', a taciturn brute who I imagined was called upon for any number of intimate services. I tried to maintain my modesty while this creature rubbed me down, and while Leigh peeked around the door like a naughty schoolgirl, giggling and blushing when he saw my nakedness. There was little I could do, however.

Washed and issued with clean clothes, I was summoned to join the family in the parlour. Leigh was there, strutting around like a peacock in his dressing gown. His wife, a semi-cretin, sat in an armchair by the window petting a constipated-looking toy dog. The son, dressed head to foot in embroidered blue velvet, stood by the fireplace with his back very pointedly to the room.

'Ah, Monsieur!' chirruped Leigh, as I noticed an armed soldier patrolling past the window, 'how kind of you to join us.'

'Monsieur Leigh. Madame.'

'This is your charge, sir. Jonathan. Introduce yourself.' Leigh snapped like an old woman.

Jonathan, the young prince in blue velvet, turned lazily around and leaned against the mantelpiece and stared; he made no move to greet me. He was a tall youth, with a great flop of blond hair over one eye, skin as soft as a girl's and huge blue eyes fringed by absurdly long eyelashes. His mouth was startlingly red in his pale face, his bone structure as exquisite as any of the porcelain figures that adorned the fireplace. I was fascinated and repulsed.

'*Bonjwaaaah,*' he drawled, in an exaggerated French accent. '*Commong sah vaaaah.*' He extended one long, pale hand and held it out with the fingers pointing down, as if I should kiss it. I wanted to punch him.

'Jonathan, behave yourself, you little... This is your new tutor.'

'So I see, father.'

'Shake hands properly.'

'Very well.' Jonathan slouched towards me and took the hand I held out. His finger tickled my palm, and he moistened his lips.

'Welcome to Leigh House, sir.' He stared into my eyes, trying to discomfit me. 'I hope you will be very... comfortable.'

Leigh Senior clapped his hands. 'Very well! Enough! Show our new guest to his quarters. Double quick!' The soldier who had been my constant attendant snapped to attention and marched me out of the room. I was led upstairs to a chamber – a bed behind a screen, a small barred window looking over the lawns, a washstand, a press and a desk with writing materials. It was not dissimilar to my quarters at Gordon Hall, but there was one crucial difference; when the soldier left me, he turned a key in the lock behind him. I was still a prisoner.

Food and drink had been left on a tray covered with a linen napkin. I ate, washed myself and lay down to rest, but not for long. After half an hour the key turned in the lock, the door was opened and my young student was admitted to the room. The door closed and locked behind him.

'I'm ready for my lesson, Monsieur.'

'What am I to teach you, sir?'

'Oh, I think anything would be an improvement. I'm terribly, terribly stupid. Which, when you look at my parents, is not surprising.' He was right; it was astonishing that his parents had managed to have a child at all, let alone one as fine-looking as him.

'Do you have any Latin, sir?'

'Latin? *Amo, amas, amat...* Beyond that I'm a complete dunce, and I have no desire to learn any more. Why should I? All this is mine one day, when those two die. I don't need education. I shall do as I like. Just as I have always done.' I detected a meaning behind the surface of his words, but chose not to acknowledge it.

'And Greek, sir?'

'I have little interest in the Greeks apart from what I have seen in my father's library.'

'Ah, and what is that?'

'Pictures of boys getting buggered.'

I had fallen into that one, and changed the subject.

'Perhaps you would rather not keep up the pretence of lessons, then, sir.'

'Oh, I'm afraid I must, Monsieur. Papa absolutely insists. You see, he's determined to get as much out of you as possible. Not that he doesn't get a decent amount of money for keeping you here, I know he does. But he thinks he can get a little extra for nothing. The last one painted Mama's portrait up here, and probably fucked her into the bargain, which would delight Papa as it would save him the trouble of such a distasteful task. She gets fractious if she doesn't get a regular fucking. I suppose that must be where I get it from. Thank God I didn't inherit anything else from her.'

He was scrutinising my face for any sign of reaction; I gave him nothing.

'Anyway, there is a guard outside the door who will report everything to Papa, so we'd better at least look as if we're learning something. Just keep your voice low and we'll be all right. I'll tell him what a marvellous teacher you are and we'll all be happy.'

He pulled the other chair up to the desk and we sat down together. I pulled a book off the pile in front of me – it was an edition of Aristophanes – and we set about a charade of education. The guard would go away happy, and I would earn my keep. In fact, our conversation had little to do with learning.

'Is it true that you're a priest?'

'Yes, sir.'

'I don't believe you. I think you're a spy. It's all right, I don't care. I hope you are. I hope you betray the lot of them.'

'Indeed.'

'I wish Father and Mother would just hurry up and die and let me get on with my life. I'm not interested in politics or money or anything really. I just want to enjoy my life. I like pleasure, Monsieur, that is all.' He stretched out his long arms and legs, then, as the guard peered through the peephole cut into the door's central panel, pretended to pore over our text. The peephole shut, and again he was sprawling in his chair.

'If you were a priest, which I don't believe for one moment that you are, you could take confession, I suppose.'

'Yes, sir.' I was on very shaky ground; posing as a priest was a very different matter from faking the sacraments.

'Oh, I do so long to confess all my sins,' he said, putting his feet up on the desk (they were shod in very pretty dark-blue leather).

'Perhaps we should concentrate on Aristophanes.'

'To hell with Aristophanes! If I don't like you, Monsieur, I can tell my father that you refuse to teach me and you will be transferred to the dungeon. It's happened before. Is that what you want?'

He read my eyes; I had no desire to return to the misery of confinement.

'I thought as much. Now we understand each other. So, where was I? Oh yes, I was going to tell you what a naughty, naughty boy I've been.'

'How old are you, sir?'

'Why do you ask?'

'Simply out of curiosity.'

'I am eighteen.'

'I see.'

'And you? How old are you, *mon professeur*?'

'Thirty-two.'

'Mmm... Well now, let us get something straight. I have no desire to learn Latin, Greek or anything else from you. You have no desire to be stuck down in the prison. We can help each other out. You can spare me the boredom of an education, I can spare you further suffering. I would say that's a fair deal.'

'And what shall we do in the meantime?'

'I shall talk about the most interesting subject in the world: myself.'

'Very well.'

'And you will fall madly in love with me and want to be my slave forever.'

He looked teasingly at me from beneath his long eyelashes. I thought it best to say nothing.

'My last tutor fell in love with me. That's why he was dismissed. That was a long time ago, over a year, and I haven't had a day's education since then, thank God. He bored me to death and so I had to think of a way of getting rid of him, so can you guess what I did?'

'No, sir.' I could guess perfectly well.

'I came up to his room one day – this very room – and while he was construing a Latin verb I took off all my clothes. And do you know what he did?'

'No, sir.'

'He got down on his knees and he put his mouth on my thing. Now, why do you imagine a man would do a thing like that to another man?'

'I have no idea, sir.'

'He didn't just kiss it, either. He put it in his mouth and moved it in and out until it went very big and hard.' Rather like my own cock was becoming – and Jonathan's own, as I could see quite clearly through the blue velvet knee-breeches.

'Then he made me lie down on top of that desk,' he said, pointing with his foot and leaving his legs spread wide apart, 'and he started to lick me down there.' He indicated his bum. 'It felt so strange... Monsieur.'

'Doubtless.'

'Do you know what he did then?'

'I can't begin to imagine, sir.'

'He took off his clothes, and he stuck his great big prick right up my arse, just like those awful Greeks used to do, and he fucked me and fucked me until he came inside me.'

'I see.'

'And after that he fell madly in love with me and wanted me all the time. But do you know what?'

'I imagine, sir, that you withheld your favours in order to drive the poor soul to despair.'

'Exactly!' He laughed with delight. 'And it worked magnificently. So no more boring Greek and Latin for me, and soon after he was sent away and I never had to see him again.'

'A most effective campaign.'

'But do you know what the strangest thing of all is?'

'What, pray?'

'I really quite enjoyed it. And so I got one of the soldiers to do it to me, and that was even better, because he was a good-looking chap, though not as good looking as you, Monsieur...'

I said nothing.

'But really rather handsome in a brutish English sort of way. And when I got bored with him I tried another, and another, and another. I've had all the soldiers in the garrison now, you know. They love my arse. They say it's better than fucking a woman. I wonder if that can be true. What do you think, Monsieur Lebecque?'

He was sitting there with his legs wide apart, his cock straining quite obscenely against his velvet-clad thigh.

I was spared the necessity of answering by another rattle at the peephole. Jonathan quickly moved his legs and pretended to be studying. His hand, however, was busy under the desk. When the peephole dropped back into position, he pushed the chair back and there, sticking out of his fly, was his erect prick, standing straight up in the air.

'Look at that, Monsieur. See what you've done to me.'

'I see, sir.' I had to clear my throat. I was blushing like a child.

'Is yours like that as well?'

He could see perfectly well that I was as stiff as he was, but I was not about to show it to him.

'I think, perhaps, the lesson is over.'

'Don't say that, Monsieur. I'm not sure I've learned enough.'

'That will do quite well for one day.' I got up and banged on the door. The guard was there in an instant; Jonathan hurriedly stuffed his cock back into his trousers.

'Master Jonathan is not feeling well, guard,' I said. 'He is asking to be taken down to his Mama.'

Master Jonathan shot daggers at me as he left the room. 'Very foolish, Monsieur,' he whispered. I assumed that the guard would be pressed into service before they had descended the stairs.

Our 'lessons' continued in this way for some time. On each occasion Jonathan tried to press himself on me; every time I managed to resist the temptation. Much as I despised this arrogant, selfish Englishman, I grew a little fond of him: he was stupid and depraved, but at least he was honest in his desires. I think he also respected me a little – at least, he didn't have me put into the dungeon, which he could easily have effected with a word to his father. And so we continued at our studies, he 'confessing' his latest sins, me listening in silence and trying not to succumb to temptation.

But of course I couldn't resist forever. I am only human. I held out for as long as I could, painfully aware that this student-teacher relationship was a gross parody of our friendship, Charlie. I felt that if I succumbed to the young man's blandishments I would somehow be betraying you. Ah well: my intentions were good.

One pleasant day at the end of February, when the sun was shining through the latticed window, Jonathan was recounting his latest adventure while I stared vacantly at a page of Ovid. He had lured three soldiers up into the attic the night before, he said, and had forced them all to fuck him twice. Whether these epic debauches actually took place, or whether they were concocted to arouse me, I never knew. Suddenly, in midstream, he stopped.

'I need to use your thing.'

'What?'

'Your chamber pot.'

'Oh. I see.' I extracted the pot from under the bed and handed it to him; he retired behind the screen. I went to the window and opened it, breathing in the fresh spring-like air. Two minutes passed, and he was still behind the screen. Another minute, and I called out to him.

'Are you all right, sir?'

'Yes, thank you, Monsieur.'

I returned to the window, but still he did not come.

'Is everything in order, sir?'

'Oh yes, Monsieur. I was just looking at one of your books.'

'Which one?' I knew I was being tricked; I allowed it to happen.

'I can't read it. It's in Greek. Perhaps you could help me.'

I couldn't help myself; I walked heavily from the window, like a man in a trance, and stood by the screen.

'Hand it to me, sir.'

'Oh no. I think you'd better come and get it.'

'Very well.' I stepped to one side and looked behind the screen. There, stark naked, was my student with a book in one hand and a very stiff prick in the other. His body, freed from the ridiculous foppery of his clothes, was surprisingly well made: broad shoulders, a strong torso and long, lean legs. I stood beside him; the heat from his skin was tangible.

'Look. I can't make it out.' He handed me the book. I took it, tossed it aside and threw my arms around him. I didn't care what happened. I kissed him on the mouth, his lips parted and we sank to the floor.

'Strip.'

I did as I was told, hurrying out of my clothes.

'No. Slower.'

He lay on the floor playing with himself while I peeled off my shirt, my stockings, my trousers. Finally I was as naked as he was. He seemed delighted with the darkness and hairiness of my body, and was soon sucking on my cock with more energy than I had imagined him capable of.

'You must fuck me. I insist.'

I took little prompting. Spitting into my hand, I slicked up my prick, pushed him face forward over my bed and steered myself in. He let me in immediately, then his arse clamped around my cock like a vice and he started shifting back and forth on the balls of his feet. I didn't have to do a thing; he was clearly used to getting what he wanted.

He flipped over on to his back, held his legs in the air and guided me back in, pulling me down on top of him so he could run his fingers around my chest.

'Harder, Monsieur. Harder.'

I fucked him like a machine, driving all my force into his arse, which absorbed every stroke and still wanted more. Soon it was too much; I came inside him.

Jonathan's arse wouldn't let me go. He wrapped his long, slim legs round my waist and used me like a dildo, wanking himself until he squirted all over his stomach. The screen had long since been kicked over; I turned and saw an eye glued to the peephole. My fate, then, was sealed.

Finally my cock was relinquished, Jonathan stood up and dressed himself once more in his hideous garments. I expected words of contempt, but instead he kissed me lingeringly on the lips and looked into my eyes, stroking my face.

'Till tomorrow, Monsieur.'

'Yes, sir.'

The door was opened, and Jonathan issued forth. I lay down on my bed and slept for an hour.

To my astonishment, the door was opened a little before the usual feeding hour, and an armed soldier beckoned me outside. I was escorted through the main hall and out into the garden, where I was allowed to roam at will – always under the watchful eye of my guard. I wondered if he was the same who had spied on my sport with the young master?

The fresh air revived me enormously. I returned to my room after half an hour to find a better dinner than normal awaiting me.

And so it has continued ever since. My 'student' is a quick study and has rapidly overtaken me in his chosen subject. I am permitted to correspond with my friends – Jonathan is eager to do anything that he thinks will undermine his father's position. I have only taken advantage of my freedom on this one occasion, and have couched my letter in the accustomed Greek to avoid falling into traps. Nobody in this household understands a word of the ancient languages. I had always imagined that an English gentleman possessed all the academic accomplishments, but I am sadly disabused of that illusion.

Thus another chapter in my strange saga comes to an end. Perhaps I will write to you again from Leigh House. Perhaps there really is a rescue party on the way to Scotland. I can do little but wait for fate's next turn of the screw. Escape is impossible.

Believe me, Charlie, to be your devoted friend still, despite the strangeness of my circumstances.

Ever your
BL

Chapter Twelve

For once, luck was on my side. I was neither pursued on the road to Glasgow, nor did news of my treachery precede me; the gamble I had taken must have worked. Blair, terrified of the consequences of his failure, had disappeared into thin air, taking the messenger boy with him. Let us hope that they live happily ever after; two more sexually greedy men I have never met.

I rode into Glasgow early on a Sunday morning in March; the streets were quiet, apart from a few well-dressed citizens making their way to church. Upon asking the way to the garrison, I was coldly but politely directed across town to Cowcaddens. The good people of Glasgow obviously took me for a collaborator, and resented my presence in their city. I wanted to lean down from my horse and assure them that I was as good a Scotsman as they – but for now my disguise would have to remain intact. Dissembling had become second nature to me.

The garrison at Cowcaddens was an impressive set of buildings, clearly intended to last. As I rode up to the iron gates, set in thick, freshly plastered walls, the message was loud and clear: the English are here to stay, and any attempt at insubordination will be quickly crushed. I must admit that my heart failed as I dismounted; I was about to enter the very heart of the enemy's camp. Now was no time to turn back, though; I had wasted enough time already.

Lebecque, for all I knew, could be dead – thanks to my selfish dalliance along the way.

I hailed the guard and presented myself as a messenger for General Wilmott. Where from? Carlisle. Who's company? Blair's. At any moment I expected to be challenged and unmasked, but to my astonishment my extempore answers seemed to be the right ones. The guard looked me up and down, and I pulled the packet of letters out of my tunic. When he saw the royal seal, he unbarred the gate and admitted me – with a salute.

I was taken with all despatch across the cobbled courtyard, up an exterior staircase and straight into the general's presence in a well-furnished room that looked over an extensive parade ground and barracks beyond. The guard announced me, saluted to the general and left us alone.

General Wilmott was every inch the professional soldier: tall, weather-beaten, impeccably turned out from his freshly-barbered silver whiskers to the polished toe of his black boots. He was, perhaps, fifty or more, balding, with short grey hair, thick black eyebrows and an impressive set of sideburns that tapered down on either side of his lined, brown face. He had the air of a man who had seen and done everything, and yet his sharp grey eyes had a lively twinkle. His uniform fitted him like a glove; for all his years, he was as solidly-built as a man twenty years his junior.

Wilmott stood to greet me, grasped me firmly by the hand and indicated that I should sit.

'You arrived alone, I understand?'

'Yes sir.' I was desperately trying to think of a plausible reason.

'Good. I dislike escorts. They draw attention. Well done.'

I tried not to show the relief on my face.

'You have the documents?'

'Yes, sir.' I pulled the package out of my tunic again and handed it over. Wilmott checked the seal, scanned the Latin tag on the back and smiled.

'I see you're to be trusted, young man.'

'I hope so, sir.'

'Coming from General Wade, that is high commendation.' There seemed to be a hidden meaning behind his words; I could only guess at it.

'Thank you, sir.' Wilmott cocked an eyebrow and looked at me for a moment, then returned to his reading. I cast the odd glance over the papers; all I could see were rows of meaningless letters. Clearly the contents were in cipher.

Wilmott scanned the pages, then locked them in a drawer.

'There is no name.'

'Sir?'

'Wade hasn't told me your name.'

Was this a trap? 'Nicholls, sir. Edward Nicholls.'

'Edward. Good. And did you enjoy your stay in Carlisle, Nicholls?'

'Yes, sir, very much.'

Again his eyebrow went up, the eyes twinkled. 'Wade says that you're very skilled.'

'Sir?'

'Good with your hands, eh?' This time he winked, quite unmistakably.

'Oh. Yes, sir.' I began to understand that I, or rather the boy that I had replaced, was part of the 'delivery' alongside the documents that I had carried.

'Perhaps you need to rest after your journey.'

'Thank you, sir, I'm quite refreshed.' In truth I was fascinated by the turn that the conversation was taking, and was unwilling to delay its outcome. Wilmott seemed pleased by my answer.

'Good. Then perhaps you would oblige me by stepping next door for a while.' He held open an interior door that led into a smaller, darker room.

'Yes sir.' Inside was a day bed, a washstand, a chair and a small table piled high with books and documents.

'I shan't keep you long. Make yourself... comfortable.' He winked again, and closed the door on me. I heard him ring a bell on his desk, and the guard returned.

'Take these to Lexington and have them deciphered immediately,' said Wilmott in an undertone which I was not meant to hear; I, however, had my ear pressed to the door.

'Yes, sir.'

'Inform Edinburgh of the contents as soon as possible. I shall be *incommunicado* for the rest of the morning.'

'Yes, sir.'

I heard the guard leave, and then Wilmott moving around in his office, locking drawers, tidying papers. I took a quick look at the pile of documents on his desk, enough to see that there was nothing there of interest to me, and awaited his arrival. 'Make yourself comfortable,' he had said. I removed my tunic and my boots and socks. Perhaps he expected me to be naked when he came into the room. I had little doubt that I had been passed on as a 'gift' between generals, and that favourable reports on my skills (or, rather, the skills of the one I had replaced) had accompanied me. Fortunately, I had been granted a preview of the kind of skills that my predecessor practised, and prepared myself to evince all of the sluttish eagerness that characterised his performance.

Wilmott was in no hurry to join me, it seemed. I pressed my ear to the door again and heard the clank of metal on metal; by peering through the keyhole I could see him standing at the window, meditatively removing his sword and belt. Then he unbuttoned his scarlet tunic and cast it aside, pulling the shirt over his head to join it on the floor. My first impressions had been correct: the general was in excellent physical shape for a man of his years, a little thicker round the waist than he once might have been, but impressively powerful in the chest and shoulders. His torso was covered in thick, silver hair, from which two large, dark nipples stood out in dramatic contrast.

I was no longer in any doubt of the kind of reception that he expected when he joined me in the little room, and so I quickly pulled off the rest of my clothes in readiness. Needless to say, I was already half hard; my prick had that agreeably heavy feeling that precedes full arousal. It swung around in front of me at forty-five degrees from my thighs. One of the general's tunics was hanging on a peg behind the door; I hastily donned it, and caught sight of myself in the mirror. The scarlet accentuated the redness of my hair and the paleness of my skin; the cut of the garment, stopping just around the waist, emphasised the roundness of my bum and the length of my cock. I was pleased with the effect; my impersonation of the enemy was complete.

The doorhandle rattled, and I quickly took up my position by the window, leaning against the embrasure with one foot resting on the wall behind me, my hands on my hips. The door opened, and there stood General Wilmott stark naked apart from a pair of long, white woollen socks which came up to his knees, his great shaggy thighs towering above them. He caught his breath when he saw me; obviously, the reports of my eagerness to please had not been exaggerated.

Wilmott locked the door behind him and regarded me for a while in silence. I thrust my hips forward, making my cock sway lewdly from side to side, then, thinking that perhaps his interests were more focused at the rear, turned round and offered him my arse.

'Very good, Edward,' said Wilmott. 'I shall have to thank General Wade for his generosity.'

'Yes, sir.'

'Now, let me see. What shall we do first?'

I was so far gone in my role of whore-to-the-enemy that I quite forgot the real reason I was there – to discover Lebecque's whereabouts – and instead gave serious consideration to the general's question. I decided that what I wanted most urgently was to get fucked, quick and hard: a look at Wilmott's thick, hammerheaded cock stiffening as he gazed at my arse was enough to persuade me of that. So I bent over, braced myself against the wall and brazenly wriggled my arse in reply.

The general needed no further answer. He picked up a jar of pomade from his washstand, scooped out a big glob on two of his fingers and proceeded to grease up my hole with an expertise clearly born of practice. I was already writhing around in pleasure; I could feel the blood rushing to my head, the veins standing out on my neck and forehead.

'Wade not taking care of your arsehole, boy?'

'No, sir.'

'He always was a little squeamish about that area, even at Sandhurst. I, however, can think of nothing I like more than a nice tight bum. How does that feel, Edward?' With two of his fingers working the grease into my hole, all I could do was grunt in reply. Wilmott gripped my cock with his other hand, realised that I was ripe for fucking and prepared to mount me.

With one strong, hairy arm round my waist, he lifted me until I was on my tiptoes then, bending his knees to bring his prick in line with my hole, he aimed and fired. There was nothing subtle about his technique: the moment he had breached me he stuffed the full length right up to the hilt and began a steady, rhythmic in-out movement. I shifted myself a little higher so that he went as far into me as possible, and settled down for the ride.

What Wilmott may have lacked in subtlety, he more than made up for in stamina. While most men shoot their load after only a few minutes up me, Wilmott seemed in no hurry to finish the job. After he'd fucked me in a standing position for five minutes, he pulled out and sat me down on the edge of his desk, scooped up my knees and ploughed into me again. I hung on round his neck while he pistoned in and out of me, enjoying the brush of his whiskers against my cheek as we pressed our faces together. His breath smelled of cigars.

I knew that if I so much as touched myself I would come instantly, and I was unwilling to do so: such was the hammering that Wilmott was giving my arse it would be a lot more painful without the anodyne of sexual arousal. The temptation, however, was enormous; I had learned by that point that I love nothing better than the sensation of an orgasm while a well-hung man is fucking me good and hard. I busied my hands with his ears and his tits, which pleased him – and inspired him to fuck me even harder.

The desk was becoming extremely uncomfortable, so Wilmott carried me (with his rock-hard prick still buried inside me) over to the day bed, where I could lie in comfort and get my legs higher and wider for him. Thus relaxed, I concentrated entirely on the sensations that were emanating through my body from my guts. Wilmott, sweating gently, pushed my balls back so that he could see his cock disappearing into my arse. The sight must have triggered something in him: soon he was fucking me like a lunatic, and came inside me with a great, grunting shudder.

He lay down panting on top of me for a while, kissed me deep on the mouth and then righted himself, took my cock in his broad, hairy hand and started stroking. To my delight, he had remained as stiff as an iron bar inside me, and so it did not take long for me to start spewing my come all over his fingers. He finished me off, brought his fingers to his mouth and licked off every drop.

I had assumed that this would be the end of the game, but the general had other ideas. Instead of pulling out, he set up a small rocking motion which soon took on the character of a renewed fucking: my new lover, it seemed, was one of those lucky men who can remain hard after an orgasm and be ready to go again in a few minutes. It takes me longer to recover, so for a while I lay inert and limp while he gently fucked me, bending down occasionally to kiss me on the lips. The taste of cigars on his tongue was now joined with the savour of my come, and the combined effect had a powerful aphrodisiac effect on me. Soon my prick was filling up again.

The general was pleased. 'Good, Edward. I like a boy who can keep up with me.' Now that I was primed and ready, he pulled out of my arse and let my feet down on to the floor. I stretched luxuriously, enjoying my role tremendously. The general stood back for a moment and looked at me, then knelt between my legs and started licking my cock and balls. I grasped his head, let my fingers cling on to his sideburns and pulled him down on to me.

He sucked me for a while, putting his fingers back into my arsehole which, to be honest, was hungry for something to fill it. Soon I was bucking and thrashing away as if I had not come once already. I did not want to shoot a second load too soon, and so gently eased the general's head off me and joined him on the floor. He held me in his arms with such tenderness that I completely forgot for the moment that he was my enemy, the man who held Lebecque's life in his hands; all I was conscious of was the warmth and strength of his body, and the rigid heat from his cock which was pressing insistently into my thigh.

Wilmott lay back on the floor and put his arms behind his head – a clear indication that his wonderful, strong, mature body was mine to do with as I pleased. And so I approached it with relish, exploring every inch of him with my hands and tongue, licking the sweat from his chest, chewing on his hard tits, running my hands up his massive thighs until I could bury my fingers under the huge pouch of his scrotum. I straddled him, rubbing my arse and balls against the thick, matted hair on his stomach. I kissed him with a passion and ferocity that took both of us by surprise. I found the danger and dishonesty of the situation profoundly exciting and yet, above that, I found Wilmott himself overwhelmingly attractive. I badly wanted him to fuck me again, and I told him so.

He pulled me forward so that my cock and balls bounced over his chest, neck and chin, resting finally over his face. His tongue found the sensitive band that runs from balls to arse, then hit my hole and started working. God knows what muscles he had in his mouth, but his tongue fucked me almost as effectively as his fingers and his cock. His hands kneaded my buttocks like two pieces of dough, and the sensation of his whiskers on my inner thigh was almost too much.

When I was good and wet again, Wilmott lifted me slightly, shifted himself backwards on the floor and pressed his cock against my bum. I put my weight on to the soles of my feet, raised myself and sat on it. In this position, I was in control of the fuck, and could let my hands roam all over his chest while I bounced around on his prick like a child on a rocking-horse. I tore off the scarlet tunic which I had worn all through our masquerade; Wilmott reached up and took one of my nipples and then the other between thumb and forefinger, pinching and rolling them until they stood out like little cocks.

After a few minutes of this, I was ready to come again, and the general's stomach was slick with the droolings from my over-stimulated dick. But before the crisis was reached, he stopped my bucking and lifted me off.

'My turn now, Eddie.'

'Sir?'

'You don't think I'm going to let you go before I've had that thing inside me, do you?' He gave my cock a playful squeeze. 'Wade said nothing about that. What's wrong with him? I've never seen a better.'

Thank God his brain was clouded by lust; sooner or later he'd start guessing that I was not the same boy who had been taking care of General Wade for the last few weeks.

Wilmott rolled over on to his front and raised his arse in the air like a dog. 'Take it easy, son. It's a long, long time since anything went up there.'

I couldn't believe my luck. The general's arse was as solid as the rest of him, densely furred, warm and sweaty. I dived in with my mouth, burrowing through the thick black hair until I hit my target. I swirled my tongue around it, getting as much spit into the area as possible; the hair now lay flat, exposing his pink ring more fully to the eye. It was a memorable sight: the veteran campaigner offering his arse to a twenty-year-old, his hand working on his cock in anticipation of the onslaught to come.

I lost no time in plugging him before he changed my mind. I guessed from the way that he'd fucked me that the general was not one for gentle treatment; instead I just spat on my cock, slicked myself up and tore in. He bellowed with pain, and his hand just worked faster on his prick. I fucked him as hard as I could, the thought going round and round in my brain that I had one of the most powerful men in the country squirming on the end of my fat cock. I suspect that the poignancy of the situation was not lost of General Wilmott either, as he slammed his arse against me to increase the battery. I felt him tighten around me as another huge load spilled out of his horse-cock on to the rug; five strokes later, and I let loose inside him. I collapsed on top of him and we lay together in each other's arms until we dozed.

The general was greatly pleased with my performance and, when we had woken and had dressed, he announced that I would be the guest of honour at a 'small private party' in the officers' mess that evening. He informed his chief of staff that he would be taking the rest of the afternoon off, and invited me to join him on a tour of the camp which, he said, 'I would like you to regard as your home'.

This was by far the most tempting of the many propositions I had received on my journey. As the general's companion I would be well fed, watered and housed, I'd have all the sex I could want with a man whom I genuinely desired and admired, and I could see scope for all sorts of amorous adventures with the soldiers who populated the camp. Judging from the number of appraising glances that were directed towards my posterior as we crossed the parade ground, the general was not alone in his taste for boys. Had I been of a less tenacious disposition, I might be living there still; might, perhaps, be keeping a boy of my own.

The garrison housed one hundred and twenty men in clean, comfortable dormitories around two sides of the courtyard. In the main block at the front were the officers' quarters, the kitchens and the messes; at the rear, stretching along most of the fourth side, was a slightly shoddy building that resembled a small hotel, in and out of which members of all ranks were issuing regularly.

'That,' said Wilmott, indicating the house with a sweep of his arm, 'is my favourite brainchild, the whorehouse.'

He led me in through the main door, where a group of soldiers were sprawling in chairs, reading newspapers, smoking pipes. They sprang to attention.

'As you were, men. An unofficial visit. Just showing a visitor round the village shop.' The men relaxed and laughed. 'Looks like a busy day, soldier,' he said to one handsome young brute, no older than me.

'Yes, sir. We all have to wait our turn.'

'Time to recruit some more girls, I suppose.'

'Yes, sir!' The men greeted the suggestion with wolflike eagerness. The general and I left them in peace.

'Nothing is so dangerous as an army that isn't getting its oats, Ned,' he said, putting an arm round my shoulder as we strolled across the parade ground, 'and, unfortunately, not all the soldiers share our excellent good taste in these matters. Life would be so much easier if they'd all just fuck each other, and I could save a fortune in board and lodgings. As it is, I've made provision for a dozen or so local women. They're paid and well housed, and they have the best-looking clients of any whore in the kingdom, as you can see.' Indeed, I had been thinking just how lucky the women were in their choice of clientele.

'Aren't you tempted to take care of a few of the men yourself, sir?' I asked, intrigued by the potential for relations between the ranks.

'Of course!' Wilmott laughed. 'But only those who are interested. Plenty of them have... what shall I say? Paddled in those waters. They know where to come if they have the urge. Most of them, however, lack the imagination.' He sighed. 'And it's not in my interests, as the commander of an army of occupation, to upset them.'

It was difficult to fault his pragmatism. My heart sank, though, when I thought of all those hard cocks going to waste (as I'm afraid I thought) in the hands of a bunch of women. How glad I was to be of the services of that whorehouse I would soon discover.

We spent the afternoon over tea in the general's private quarters, and I was disappointed that he didn't fling me to the floor and ravish me among the silver muffin dishes. 'No, Ned,' he said with a smile, as I kept reaching for his cock, 'we must save ourselves for this evening.' No questions of mine would elicit further details about the forthcoming entertainment. 'You will simply have to wait and see. I want it to be a surprise.'

At around six o'clock the general went to inspect the men, and I was escorted to a small room where luxurious washing facilities had been provided for me. I bathed, availed myself of the various perfumed oils on offer, and dressed in the freshly-pressed shirt and suit that had been left out for me. Inspecting myself in the mirror, I felt every inch the dandy. My shoes had been taken away and cleaned while I soaked in the tub; the leather shone as never before. I watched the general in action on the parade ground beneath me, strolling up and down the uniformed ranks with a friendly word here, a touch on the shoulder or the chin there. The men seemed well disposed towards him. Perhaps, I thought, the English army wasn't all bad. I began to consider my future in a different light. Of course, for the moment I had completely forgotten the existence of Benoit Lebecque, so susceptible was I to bodily pleasure.

I had drifted off into a pleasant daydream about my life as an army whore, and looking forward to my next bout with General Wilmott, when my lustful reveries were disturbed by a sharp rap at the door, followed almost immediately by the entrance of a young soldier.

'Message from the general, sir!'

His words were respectful, but the grin that accompanied them was anything but. His eyes had lighted immediately on the erection that my new suit trousers did little to conceal.

'Yes?'

'Your presence requested in the officers' mess.'

'Lead on.' I stood up, making sure that he got a good eyeful. I would take care of this one at a later date, I decided.

'Yes sir!' The soldier conducted me downstairs and opened a large pair of polished oak doors. All was dark within, with just the glint of candlelight on silverware.

'The young man, sir!'

Wilmott's voice sounded from the gloom. 'Very good, show him in.'

The soldier stood aside and motioned me inwards, imparting a pinch to my bum as he did so. The door closed behind me.

At first all I could make out was a multiplicity of candles in glass jars standing in a row about three feet from where I was standing. Each was backed by a tin reflector, directing the golden light straight into my eyes; beyond that, I could make out little except vague shapes.

'Good evening, Ned!' Wilmott's voice again, rising above the muted conversation of half a dozen others.

'Good evening, sir.' I shaded my eyes and peered into the room. There was Wilmott in full dress uniform, his sword strapped on; around him sat five of his fellow officers, most of them younger than him, none of them less than thirty. They whispered in each other's ears and looked up at me. I seemed to be standing on a raised platform, about two feet above the floor. Combined with the lights, it created a pretty good makeshift theatre. Beyond the party of smoking, laughing, drinking officers, a banquet was laid out on a long mahogany table.

'Ned, I would like to introduce you to the *crème de la crème* of the Glasgow garrison, who have gathered here tonight to welcome you as a valued new member of our community.' As he called out their names (I forget them now) each stood and saluted. They were of various heights, builds and colourings, some fair, some dark, some of them bald like Wilmott, others with fine heads of hair falling across their foreheads. One in particular struck me – his name, I think, was Miles – an aristocratic-looking English soldier with floppy, pale-brown hair and a kind expression.

'Now, Ned, I'm afraid I have given you something of a build-up in your absence, and my fellow officers here have accused me of exaggeration in my description of your charms. I wonder if you would care to settle the argument?'

How could I refuse? 'Certainly, sir. How would you –?'

'Perhaps if you could entertain us with a little display.'

I was not quite sure what he meant. 'Sir?'

'Take your clothes off, boy. Slowly. We would like a show. A performance.'

The idea of an audience was certainly appealing; the element of humiliation inherent in the situation added spice. One of the officers, a dandified forty-year-old of Mediterranean appearance, struck up a tune at the spinet – a slow, blowsy sounding number.

At first I stood still, uncertain what to do. But Wilmott was looking up with an encouraging smile, squeezing his crotch in promise of future bliss. I took centre stage and began to dance.

The audience was appreciative, and regaled me with a running commentary on my performance, mostly relating to the curve of my arse when I turned round, or the volume of my bulge when I faced front. First of all I removed my jacket and unlaced the front of my shirt, making sure that they got a good view of my hard, defined torso, even pulling the fabric aside to show my nipples, which were once again as hard as bullets. The show was going well; a couple of the officers were openly rubbing their crotches.

I pulled the shirt over my head and danced around for a while, allowing them to appreciate the details of my upper body which showed up well in the golden glow of the candlelight. Next I kicked off my shoes and peeled off the thin cotton socks that had been provided for me; Wilmott snatched one of them up and pressed it to his face. My accompanist, impatient perhaps for what was to come, sped up the pace of his playing.

There was nothing for it: the trousers had to go next. I inched them down, then up, down, then up, earning myself a barrage of good-natured abuse from the audience who had decided that I was a prick-tease of the most delightful nature. Miles, the handsome creature with the floppy hair, was rubbing the outline of a hard cock that seemed to stretch halfway to his knee.

Finally I threw the trousers in a corner, and was left in a pair of loose white shorts which did little to restrain my manhood, which was bouncing around inside them and leaving little damp evidences of my excitement all over the front of the garment. I turned round and pulled the back down, revealing my bum – to a gasp from the assembled company. Then I turned and pushed my cock down so that the head, still half sheathed in skin, appeared at the opening of my left leg. One or two of the officers had their hands inside their clothes, blatantly masturbating.

I was consumed by a desire to be fully naked and at their mercy, and so I whipped off the pants and continued my performance in the nude, bending and thrusting in order to let them see every detail. The music had stopped; the only sound was my feet thumping on the boards, and the heavy breathing of the officers. They had left their chairs and were clustering around the front of the stage, reaching out towards me; at first I evaded their grasp, but soon allowed one or two of them to take liberties with me.

Wilmott and a couple of his colleague moved a few of the candles from the front of the stage to allow me to sit on the edge; they stood around me, illuminating my body to the maximum, while I stretched out and started to pleasure myself. Hands were all over me, stroking, tweaking and pulling, delving underneath me to find my arse, running over my face and hair. I closed my eyes and settled back for a good wank, which was not of long duration. I came, copiously, to a round of applause from the officers.

The come was licked from my body by a couple of eager tongues, and I sat up and jumped down on to the floor. I had assumed that we could now proceed to dinner, that I could dress and take a more conventional role in the company. On the contrary: Wilmott took me by the hand and led me over to the table, where a large space had been cleared amidst the dishes and covers.

'Now then, Ned, if you would oblige us.'

'Aren't we going to have dinner?'

'Oh yes, most certainly.'

'And... what is for dinner?'

'You are, Ned.'

For one hideous moment I wondered if I had fallen among cannibals, but the general's kind expression assured me otherwise. The other officers were taking their places round the table, two on each side, Miles at the foot and Wilmott at the head; I was soon lying at full length among them.

If I was not actually to be the food at this banquet, I was certainly the platter. One of the officers, a rugged-faced veteran who had stripped to the waist, scooped up a handful of butter from a silver dish and started to spread it over my chest. The sensation was delightful, and became even more so when he started using his tongue to lick it off. All around my chest he worked, around my neck, the butter melting and running down my sides as fast as he could eat it.

Another – the floppy-haired Miles, who I so liked the look of – picked up a jug of whipped cream and, spreading my legs, started to apply it to my arse. It was cold and slippery and absolutely delicious. Of course, I was hard again. His fingers worked the cream all around my crack and into my hole, then his head disappeared and started to sup the melting white liquid. When he surfaced, he had shiny cream all over his face, and his hair was plastered down and dark with the stuff.

General Wilmott, at my head, took the cover off a dish of asparagus and dangled one above my lips; I extended my tongue to catch a drop of butter hanging from the end, then opened wide and took the whole spear as he dropped it slowly into my mouth. It was delicious; I ate another, and another. Meanwhile Miles was going to town with the cream at my rear end, plastering the entire contents of the jug over my arse and his face. His tongue was finding its way further and further up my chute with each assault.

As Wilmott fed me asparagus, the rest of the officers were shucking their uniforms and preparing to join the feast. God, they were a handsome crew! Not one of them was saggy; all of them had soldiers' bodies. That is all I can say. The details are lost to me. Suffice to say that soon I had a prick in each hand and hands all over me.

Wilmott broke off from feeding duties to pull out his cock, which he dangled above my mouth in place of the vegetable. Once again I licked a drip from the tip and then swallowed the entire spear; with my head bent back over the edge of the table, I had no difficulty taking his whole length down my throat. Soon I was plugged at the other end as well: Miles had replaced tongue with cock, and was fucking me gently as the squishy, slippery cream squirted out of my arse and around his prick with each thrust. It didn't take him long to come, adding another dollop of cream to the pint or so that had already been piped into me.

My arse was not left empty for long; fingers were sliding in and out, and then something thick and hard. It was not a cock; I was so surprised by the sensation that I released Wilmott's dick from my mouth to look south. Two of the other officers – the Italian musician and another, older one – were making selections from a basket of raw vegetables which they were inserting up my anus. A carrot had been the first; now I was enjoying a cucumber. I was slightly alarmed to see a vegetable marrow in the basket.

The feeling, however, was not unpleasant, and I grasped my knees and spread my legs to give them better access. When I looked back up, Wilmott was spreading chocolate sauce all over his genitals and waving them lasciviously in my face.

'Time for dessert, Ned,' he said, as I started licking his balls and shaft, savouring the combined sweetness and saltiness of this latest course. My arse was being severely stretched, I knew not by what; I was quite prepared to wrestle free if it became too much. I was relieved when the *crudités* were replaced by the more familiar feeling of a warm cock inside me, and I glanced down just long enough to register that the Italian had taken his turn.

By now, of course, we were all absolutely filthy, covered from head to foot in a *mêlée* of foodstuffs and come. Miles took up a bottle of red wine and poured it all over me, licking as he went; he was hard again, and I was eager to taste his cock. I didn't have long to wait; the chocolate-coated general was soon wanking himself off in my face, while the Italian was coming up my arse. I took my chance, sat up and launched myself on Miles, who slipped over in a pat of butter and landed on the floor with me on top of him. I lost no time in sliding down to his groin, and swallowed his cock in one go. As I sucked and sucked on this delicious piece of meat,

I naturally assumed a kneeling position – and my arse was open once again to assault. Fingers, tongues, vegetables, a silver salt-cellar and a variety of serving implements were tried for size; eventually, of course, every cock in the room was up there pumping out another load of cream.

When the company was replete, having come at least twice each, I emptied another bottle of wine over my head, shoved a handful of butter up my arse and rounded off the evening by a particularly lascivious wank show. The final load of the evening received a rapturous round of applause, and dinner was over.

Chapter Thirteen

How long I might have stayed as chief whore to the boy-lovers of the Glasgow garrison I do not know; as it was, my holiday had an abrupt termination. Wilmott and his fellow revellers, exhausted by the epic of sodomy they had just enjoyed, dozed and drank in the banqueting hall; I felt in need of a bath, and so found my way back to my room. Fortunately, there was no one to observe me; covered in the debris of my recent excesses, I would have presented a pretty spectacle to any onlooker.

Passing through the general's quarters I noticed a file of papers that, I was sure, had not been on the desk before. Sleepy and satiated as I was, my curiosity was pricked. The word CONFI-DENTIAL only made me more inquisitive. I left the door ajar – any approach would be easy to detect – and opened the file. Of course: it was the translations of the ciphers that I had delivered that morning.

A letter from General Wade formed the bulk of it; I was amused to discover that the writer had 'enjoyed many nights with my cock down the young man's throat', and suggested that Wilmott do likewise. I scanned further down; rapturous descriptions of 'his doe-like brown eyes' and 'chestnut hair', 'his olive skin' and 'smooth chest'. Aha, the game was up. Worse was to come; the boy's name, Peter Rendall. My imposture could not have been more completely uncovered. I had to move fast. I was about to run next door to change into my old clothes, when my eye was caught by a piece of paper pinned to the back of the letter. 'Movement Order' it read, 'for Prisoners in Scotland, April 1751'. There followed a long list of names and destinations. My eye ran down the column and found what it was seeking.

'Lebecque, Benoit, French spy, Leigh House, Carlisle to St Leonard's Castle, Edinburgh. Priority: immediate.'

I was about to pocket the paper, but thought better of it; I wanted to leave no clues as to my real business in Glasgow. I dashed next door, wiped myself quickly on one of the general's shirts (that would have to suffice as a souvenir), pocketed some money that was left on the washstand and ran downstairs as quietly as I could.

The front gate was barred and guarded; obviously I would not be leaving the way I came. Someone in the building – the cryptographer Lexington, perhaps – knew of my deception already. The alarm could be raised at any second, and my life over the next. There was no way out that I could see – unless – of course! Skirting the parade ground, I headed with all despatch for the women's quarters.

There it was quiet enough; most of the soldiers were in bed. I saw one staggering out, stuffing his cock back into his trousers; he saluted me with an exhausted bonhomie and wove his way across the courtyard. I was about to try my escape through one of the inner doors (it must surely lead to the rear of the building and thence to the outside) when a young woman popped up from behind the front desk where, it seemed, she had been concealed all along. I jumped.

'Sorry to startle you, I was just putting the towels away.'

'That's quite all right.'

'We're closed for the night, really.'

'Oh, I see.'

'You're new here, aren't you?'

'Yes. I'm a guest of the general's.'

'Oh!' She smiled. 'Well I don't imagine you'll find much to entertain you here, then.'

'No...' Looking back through the still-open door, I saw a couple of soldiers walking purposefully towards the banqueting hall. 'Could I come in, just for a few moments? It's important.'

'Of course. What's the matter?'

God bless her, she didn't wait for an answer, but instead led me into the inner room and locked the door behind her. I held my finger to my lips and listened. There was nothing. I breathed again.

'Are you in trouble?'

I looked at her; she had a beautiful, kind face. My experience of women was pitifully limited: the few bloodless spinsters that my mother had employed, Ethel my old nurse, the occasional landlady. My new companion seemed more congenial than any of them: a girl of about my age, height and colouring. She could have passed for my sister.

I had no choice but to trust her. 'Yes, I'm in a great deal of trouble and I have to get away immediately.'

'What have you done?'

'You don't want to know.'

'Highlander?' She must have recognised my accent.

'Yes, Loch Linnhe. You?'

'Arisaig. I'm an orphan,' she added, by way of excusing her unpatriotic employment.

'Will you help me?'

'What can I do?'

'Get me out of here.'

She pondered for a while. 'The back of the building is heavily guarded. We can't come and go as we like, you know.'

'Then what am I to do?'

'There might be a way...'

'How?'

'It's difficult, and dangerous, but it will get you out. And it will serve me a turn as well.'

The plan was simple enough. Later that night, around two hours past midnight, a coach was to arrive from Kilmarnock bearing one Captain Robert, en route for Stirling, Perth and Dundee, 'a most fearsome soldier' according to Anne, my new friend. His visit to Glasgow had a twofold purpose: to change his horses, and to change his woman. Anne had been designated as his 'companion of the road' for the next stage of the journey; the captain, it seemed, was a man of prodigious appetites and a short attention span. If I would take Anne's place in the captain's coach, I would be ensured a safe passage out of the garrison – and would enable Anne to stay near the soldier that she loved and was planning to marry. What happened to me beyond the garrison gates was, of course, my own affair; it would not be the first time I had jumped out of a moving vehicle, albeit my first attempt in women's clothing.

At first I demurred; the plan was simply too bizarre. But gradually it dawned that it was my only chance, and that Anne was putting herself at considerable risk by agreeing to help a countryman. Perhaps it was her way of atoning for her own betrayals; whatever the reason, I could not resist her for long.

She led me upstairs, through a locked door ('We need a safe haven here, believe me') and into the dormitory, where a dozen narrow beds were laid out in rows down either side of a cheerless attic. And all around – in bed, at tables, gossiping together on chairs – were the women of the house, combing their hair, washing their faces, dressing for the night. At my entrance, there was a collective gasp and giggle, but Anne signalled silence and went about closing all the shutters and extinguishing any unnecessary candles.

'Ooh, Annie,' said one of the girls, a big-boned brunette who was a good six inches taller than me, 'you really shouldn't bring your work home with you!'

'Let's have a look at him,' said her friend, a petite blonde who approached me with a candle. 'Why, Annie, he's as cute as a button! Where did you find him?'

Soon they had all gathered round me and were examining me like a new pet, stroking my hair, pinching my cheeks and my backside.

'That's enough!' whispered Anne. 'There's work to be done! Quick, Charlie, strip!'

I have never been bashful about nakedness; why, only a couple of hours earlier I had performed for the lusty officers of the garrison. Now, however, in the company of women, I was shy and awkward, blushing like a little boy.

'For heaven's sake, Charlie, hurry up!' said Anne. 'The garrison's waking. Something's afoot.'

Indeed, I could hear voices below. I undressed hastily and stood amidst the circle of women, who discussed me as if I wasn't there.

'It's bigger than your David's.'

'Aye, but it's not so bonnie.'

'Will you look at the skin on him? White as milk!'

'But he's got a hairy arse, and look, a hairy little tummy.'

'We'll have to shave him.' This was Anne who, to my horror, was whetting a razor. 'It's all right, Charlie, we occasionally have to shave our legs and armpits for men with specifically smooth tastes. I know what I'm doing.' Swiftly she lathered me up from the washstand, and in a few painless strokes had removed the offending tufts. She dabbed me dry and applied some scented powder to the freshly denuded areas. My backside felt, in truth, as soft as a woman's.

'There, now you'll pass muster in the dark. I just pray to God that the captain doesn't have bright lights in his coach.'

I joined that prayer most fervently. Smooth I may be, but it would be a foolish man indeed who believed me to be a woman. Clothes improved the illusion: I was swiftly dressed in a long petticoat, a pair of silk stockings that fastened to a belt around my hips, and a blue dress of sprigged muslin that was thrown over my head and tightened at the back. Shoes, some false curls and a bonnet completed the illusion. Anne even added a touch of paint to my cheeks and lips.

'Well, you're a pretty lass and no mistake,' she said, surveying her handiwork. 'It's just a shame we couldn't find a pair of knickers to fit you. Just remember not to cross your legs.' She dabbed my nose with powder and kissed me on the cheek. 'What a shame we're losing you. I'm sure you could have given the boys a little extra something, Miss Charlotte.'

The rest of the girls giggled, and I blushed prettily. Our fun was interrupted by three loud bangs from the front door. Anne squeezed my hand and ran downstairs to open up. Soon she was back in the dormitory, followed by two soldiers armed with rifles. I recognised one of them as my escort from earlier in the evening, the one who had pinched my bottom before delivering me to the officers. Anne was remonstrating.

'This is disgraceful! How dare you come bursting in here? As if you don't give us enough trouble throughout the day without depriving us of our beauty sleep!' The soldiers started poking around under the beds, searching through cupboards, opening chests. My disguise seemed to be complete. One of the other girls, the pert blonde, busied herself with my bonnet as if helping me to undress for the night. The soldiers approached us, looked us both in the face – and moved on. Anne slammed the door behind them.

They had no sooner left than we heard the scrunch of wheels on the gravel at the back of the house; peering through the shutters, we saw a coach pulling up.

'Captain Robert! Ready now, Charlie. Remember: speak as little as possible. Stay in the dark. As soon as you can: run! And God bless you, little brother!'

The horses were changed, the coach awaiting, and I was

escorted downstairs on the arms of my companions. A dark figure within the coach held the door open, and I climbed in. Another moment, and the horses were cantering down the road and we were away.

Out of one dangerous situation, I now had to face another. My eyes grew accustomed to the gloom of the coach; the blinds were down, and besides, it was still pitch-dark outside once we had cleared the lights of the town. A little illumination came from the driver's lantern, which shone through a gap at the top of the window; enough to see that there was only one other passenger. Captain Robert, no doubt. For the first five minutes of our journey, he was silent.

We rattled out of Glasgow, and I assumed from the change in the road surface that we were now in open country. The coach slowed as we climbed a hill; I tried, discreetly, to find the door handle. There – easily within reach. I gripped it and pulled. No movement. I tried to lift it; nothing. It was locked. The other door, through which I had entered the coach, was barred by Captain Robert's legs. There was nothing for it; I would have to wait until our next stop.

From the reports that had preceded Captain Robert, I assumed that he would be attempting to force himself upon me the moment we were under way; I was relieved and astonished, then, to find myself unmolested. No word had yet been addressed to me, and we remained in silence for perhaps half an hour. I was about to nod off, exhausted from the day's excesses, when the captain drew a bottle from inside his jacket, uncorked it and took a swig of what my nose told me immediately was brandy.

'Would you care to join me, my dear young lady?'

'Oh,' I piped, in what I hoped was a passably feminine voice, 'no thank you.'

Silence from the captain, who took another draught.

'I beg your pardon?'

'I said, no thank you. It... er... disagrees with me.'

'Say that again?'

I feigned a cough to explain the hoarseness of my voice. 'Pardon me, Captain. I have a cold.'

'Indeed.' He seemed to be laughing; I could not be sure. After another silence, he said 'But my dear, there is nothing like a little drop of brandy to help a cold. Come along, it would really be the best thing in the world for you.'

'No, really...'

'I insist.'

'Very well.' I expected him to pass me the bottle; indeed, a tot of brandy would be a welcome tonic for my nerves under the circumstances. But he sat back in his chair and made no move towards me.

'Won't you come and get it, my dear?'

Ah: I saw his game.

'On second thoughts, I don't think –'

'But you must.' He grasped my hand and pulled it towards him. I was not altogether surprised when, instead of closing round a cold brandy bottle, my fingers came into contact with a hot, hard cock.

'Oh, good gracious!'

'Come, my dear, it's surely not the first time you've had a soldier's prick in your hand, is it? Not in your line of work.'

'Of course, but –'

'If you'd prefer the brandy...'

'No...' Judging by the extraordinary dimensions of the piece I was holding, there was nothing I would rather have had in my hand. But I was mindful of the dangers of my predicament.

'Come on then, my girl,' said the captain, thrusting his hips forward, 'take care of me. That's what you're here for.'

Gingerly at first I rubbed the captain's shaft, but he was not for half measures. 'Don't just play with it! I was told you were a professional.'

Unwilling to arouse his suspicions, I grasped his cock more firmly and started wanking him in earnest. The captain sighed and stretched out his legs. By the dim rays of the driver's light, I could just make out a dark face and a full moustache.

Obviously a hand alone was not going to be enough for the captain, so I sank to my knees on the floor of the coach and applied my ruby-red lips to his helmet. The sooner I could make the captain come, the better: maybe then he would sleep, and I could spring from the coach. My chin brushed the silky skin of his shaft, and I felt certain I was lost; instead, he just grunted with pleasure and started toying with my curls. I prayed that they would not come off in his hand.

The captain spread his legs and I knelt between them, quite ruining my skirts on the coach's dirty floor. His prick stretched my mouth to its utmost but, as an 'experienced whore' I had to manage. I squeezed his gigantic balls and was delighted to find that they were tightening already. The job would soon be over.

Of course, my companion had other ideas. Until now he had been happy to lie back and take it; now, however, it seemed he wanted something more from me. His hand had strayed from my head to my shoulders – I cursed the muscles I had developed there! – and down to my chest, which Anne had padded with cotton. He passed over my bust quickly enough (perhaps he was not one of those men who favoured breasts above all other bodily parts) and travelled down. Now I was really in trouble. He found an opening at the side of my gown and slipped a hand inside, ripping the muslin quite carelessly as he went. His fingers made contact with my stomach; thank God for Anne's skill with the razor! He seemed delighted by the smoothness and firmness that he found there, and let me know by enthusiastic moaning that he approved. I guzzled more vigorously on his swelling cock.

But of course, like many men, he wanted pussy. His hand was rummaging around inside my garments trying to find its goal;

indeed, he made contact with my pubic hair, and stroked it appreciatively. Any minute now he was going to get the shock of his life. I was holding my cock out of the way by clamping it backwards between my thighs, a feat that caused me no little discomfort for, despite the perils of my predicament, I was now as stiff as a post. His fingers were straying lower; something had to be done.

I raised my mouth off his cock and whispered. 'Not there, Captain. It's my time, you understand...'

'Ah! Of course. The curse of Eve. Well, what a shame.'

I had to keep him busy. 'But of course, if you'd like to go round the back...'

'What a splendid idea! And in many ways my preferred route.'

The moment he had disengaged his hand from my front, I quickly opened my thighs, let my cock bounce up against my stomach then trapped the whole package in the forward position. It was not a moment too soon; the captain was already lifting my skirts and petticoats. Soon my bum was exposed to the air.

'Ah, what a smooth, fragrant arse!' he said, running his hand over my shaven cheeks. 'Please, my dear, carry on sucking my cock.' I did as I was told. One finger, then two, then three, slid into my hole at the rear. Thank God he was satisfied with that – for the time being.

'I must fuck you now, my dear, in that tight little box. Bend over the seat.' I gathered up my skirts and did as I was told; the captain lost no time in pressing the huge, swollen head of his cock against my ring. 'Here I come!' he exclaimed, and breached me. With the jogging of the coach and the thrusting of his hips, it was not long before my arse had opened sufficiently to allow all of him in.

'My God, I've never experienced a fuck like it!' he said, gripping on to my hips and ploughing into me. He spoke truer, perhaps, than he thought.

I called on every trick in the book to make his ride the more enjoyable, hoping to hasten the moment of my escape. I clamped my sphincter around him; I pushed my arse back to meet him; I wriggled in a corkscrew motion that had had other men spewing their loads in a trice. Not the captain: he held on for grim life and rode me as if he were breaking a frisky young mare. 'You're a hot little trollop, Miss!' he said as I let out a great grunt of excitement.

We hit a particularly bad piece of road, and I was being thrown around the coach like a rag doll, conscious only of the effort of concealing my manhood and keeping the captain firmly occupied up my arse. Finally his thrusting took on a greater urgency, and he soon approached his crisis. In truth, I was so stimulated by the battering of my tender parts that I, too, reached orgasm at the same time, and drenched my petticoats with hot sperm.

The captain withdrew with a satisfied plop, wiped his cock on my skirt, kissed me passionately on the mouth and settled down to sleep. I had manoeuvred myself round to the other door, and made ready to escape the moment we slowed down.

Running water: we were about to cross a ford. I reached for the handle and prepared for a soaking and a bruising.

The door was locked.

Stunned by disappointment, I joined the captain in sleep.

†

Dawn was well advanced by the time the coach juddered to a halt; a sickly grey light crept in round the blinds, and made the rays of the driver's lamp look sulphurous and unearthly. I awoke with a sore arse and a familiar taste in my mouth, and the horror of my situation returned to me with full force. The captain was already wide awake, and when he saw that I had regained consciousness he drew the blind.

'Good morning, my dear.'

'Good... morning...' I whispered, trying to shield my face from the light. I felt sure that, by now, my beard had grown enough to give me away. My companion seemed to be in excellent good spirits, and noticed nothing.

Now, for the first time, I had a chance to get a good look at the man who had fucked me so hard in the night. He was of medium stature, perhaps only a little taller than me, around five foot seven or eight, and a good ten years my senior. He was clearly one of those men who loses their hair early, and it suited him; his hairline swept dramatically back above each temple, then forward again in the centre, and back. What hair remained was brown tinged with grey, and cut short. Any lack of hair on the head was more than made up for by a magnificent thick moustache, and what looked like the beginnings of a serious forestation at the neck of his shirt. He was dressed, of course, in military uniform, with a Scottish sporran hanging at the front of his trousers – a dangerous concession to the banned Highland garb, I thought. I was surprised to see that one of this arms was in a sling, the hand and wrist in plaster. That explained something that had puzzled me the night before; I had only ever felt one hand on me. I had been too preoccupied to think about it then; now I was glad that his injury had prevented my unmasking.

That, however, could only be a matter of time. I felt my knees turning to jelly. I would have given anything to flee, but the captain offered no opportunity. He handed me down from the coach with his sound limb, and we proceeded arm in arm to the door of an inn. I fumbled to secure my bonnet, attempting to shade as much as possible of my face. My make-up was just a memory, all of the rouge smeared over the captain's cock and transferred thence, I assumed, to my arse. Please God, I prayed, don't let him look too closely at me! I scratched my chin and was horrified to feel the stubble growing there. I must shave – or die!

Just before we entered the inn, the captain leaned towards me and whispered in my ear. 'God, I cannot wait to get you upstairs, my girl,' he said. 'After last night, I want nothing more than to see you naked and skewered on the end of my prick.

I thought I would throw up.

We made it into the hall, where a bleary-eyed young porter gave us a key and indicated that our room was on the second floor at the rear. He unloaded the captain's trunk from the back of the coach and hovered at the foot of the stairs, awaiting his reward.

'Ah, my dear,' said the captain, never taking his good arm from mine, 'there's a coin in my sporran if you would do me the favour.'

'Of course.' Perhaps I could escape while we were on the stairs. I did not want to alarm him by any show of disobedience now.

I reached across and unbuckled the front of the pouch, lifting the leather flap and sticking my hand in. And what did I find? Not coin, not leather, but warm skin and hair and a half-hard cock. The captain whispered in my ear, 'Can you not find the money, my dear? It must be in there somewhere. Have a good look.' I let my hand wander further; it was, indeed, an ingenious arrangement. The sporran seemed to be sewn to the front of the captain's trousers, which had been cut away to allow his cock and balls to rest inside the leather pouch.

I let my hand run up and down his stiffening member, executing a pantomime of confusion for the benefit of the porter who, thankfully, was too sleepy to notice much. 'No, Captain,' I trilled, 'there's nothing in there but my breakfast.'

He chuckled. 'Ah, of course, that's where I put the victuals. Here, in my jacket.' He rummaged around inside the garment, and found a small piece of silver which he handed to the porter, who stood aside. My arm remained clamped to his ribs.

'Well now, if you would like to precede me, my dear.'

I trotted up the stairs; there was no getting past the captain, who was bringing up the rear. On the landing he grabbed my arm and fumbled with the key in the lock, pushed me into the room and locked the door behind us. The key, to my despair, he planted in the inner recesses of his tunic.

'Alone at last!' he said, licking his lips and looking, with that great moustache of his, disturbingly like a wolf. I tried to keep my back to the light. Perhaps I could jump out of the window? I edged across the room and looked out; it was a sheer drop on to some lethal-looking railings.

'What is your name, my dear?'

'Er... Charlotte.'

'Charlotte. Charlotte.' He rolled the name round on his tongue. 'What a beautiful name. It suits you. It's a long time since I have met a girl as lovely, as wonderful, as you.'

'Thank you, Captain.' I feigned modesty and hid beneath the brim of my bonnet.

'But please, let me see that beautiful face. Ah, the true Scottish complexion. Peaches and cream, my dear, peaches and cream.' I stepped quickly backwards to avoid the hand held up to chuck my chin.

'Ah, you are shy now, in the morning light. And yet last night ... that was the real you, my dear girl. True passion. True open-mindedness. A willingness to explore. Why, you're my ideal! There is something truly extraordinary about you. You're quite unlike other girls!'

I smiled weakly. How long could I delay the fatal moment?

'Now, help me to undress.' He struggled out of his jacket (and took good care to kick it, and the key, out of my reach) and waited for my assistance with the rest. He sat, I kneeled and pulled off his boots and socks. He had, I couldn't help noticing, particularly beautiful feet, high-arched and well-moulded.

The shirt was a little harder; I took care not to wrench his injured arm. His torso, as I suspected, was furry and powerful. On his right shoulder, just at the top of the arm, he had a tattoo, which intrigued me. It showed, quite clearly, the Stuart coat of arms.

'Surprised?'

'Oh... no, sir.'

'Continue.'

I undid his belt, unbuttoned his fly and pulled down his trousers. As I knew from my previous fumblings in his sporran, he wore nothing underneath. I grabbed them by the bottom of the legs and pulled; he raised himself slightly from the chair, and the garment was off.

Naked, he was everything I could desire. I cursed the bad luck that had made our liaison so fraught with difficulties. Oh well – I would just have to make the best of a bad job. I grabbed his cock and started sucking.

'No, my dear, that won't do just now. I must have you as I want you: naked.'

'Oh sir, I can't...'

'Why not?'

'I... I'm not... I'm ashamed...'

'You're a whore, aren't you?'

'Yes, sir, but my time of the month...'

'It doesn't concern me. Do as I ask.'

'Please sir, I beg you, don't make me.'

'I insist. Lay aside this modesty. There is nothing that can shock me, I assure you. Now please. Stand up.'

There was nothing for it. I stood up and unbuttoned the front of my dress. I kicked off my shoes.

'Leave the stockings on, please.'

I pulled the dress over my head; fortunately the fashion for petticoats was such that my body was still concealed. Just as well: despite fear, I had a roaring erection. I hesitated. The captain was masturbating with his good hand. Lust made me careless. So: he would discover my secret! Too bad. The last laugh was on him. He had fucked a boy – and not even known!

I turned my back on him, and undid the fastenings at the back of the petticoat, and let it drop to the floor. It caught for a moment on the fuzzy stubble that was growing back on my arse, then glided down my legs. Now I was naked, apart from the stockings and garter belt, and the absurd hat and false hair on my head. I stood up and gave him a good view of my back, and the arse he had fucked last night.

'Very good. Very good indeed. Now turn round.'

Well, I could die as well as any man. I grabbed my headgear, whipped it off and discarded it as I turned to face him. There was no longer any mistaking my gender.

The captain said nothing. His hand stopped playing with his cock, but held it, still erect.

He spoke calmly. 'You are a traitor.'

'Yes.'

'And a spy, no doubt.'

'What you will.'

'I should kill you.' He reached for his sword. My cock fell, but I was not afraid.

'If I die, I die in the service of my country,' I said, before my voice gave way in the onset of tears. I had no choice but to be silent; I would not betray my fear with a womanly display of crying. For all my recent masquerade, I was still a man of Scotland, and not ashamed to die as such.

The captain stood up, his sword in his hand. His cock, I noticed, was as stiff as his sword, and he waved both at me.

We stood facing each other for a long moment, eye to eye. Then I dropped my head, exposing the back of my neck to him.

'Go on. Kill me. Make it quick.'

I shut my eyes in anticipation of the blade. Instead, I felt a hand on my hand and, in the next second, a tongue seeking my mouth. The captain's sword crashed on the floor beside him, and we staggered over to the bed in an embrace. His prick was pressing into my belly; my own manhood, which had drooped with fear in the preceding minutes, sprang instantly to attention.

I could say nothing at first: Captain Robert's mouth was locked over mine, our tongues doing battle within. At last he broke away and sat up, his thick hairy thighs straddling my waist, pinning me to the bed.

'A fine spy you make, my boy!'

'What?'

'You thought you had me fooled, did you not?'

'I –'

'Little Miss Charlotte, indeed. Even in the dark I could tell you were no woman.'

'But...'

'I fucked you. Of course. The masquerade amused me. Do you think I would have done so if you had been a woman in fact, as well as in dress?'

'I thought, as you had ordered a whore for the road –'

'And look what I got!' He reached round and squeezed my cock, which had lodged between his buttocks. 'Appearances, my dear Miss Charlotte, are important in our line of work. The masquerade must be complete. Captain Robert, the fearless soldier, the scourge of the Jacobites, is a loyal supporter of the English king, a good fellow and a devil with the ladies. The truth, as you see, is somewhat different.'

'The Stuart tattoo...'

'Indeed. And this' – he indicated the arm in plaster – 'a little reminder of the dangers of my profession. I was nearly discovered in the Borders, led astray by a young English soldier who let me take his arse, then tried to betray me.'

'What happened?'

The captain said nothing, but the terrible look in his eyes told me enough. This was not a man to be trifled with.

'And you, young man, are you a traitor?'

'No, sir.'

'Prove it.'

A dozen plausible lies skimmed through my mind, but the captain's face told me that truth was the only option.

'My name is Charles Gordon. My father was a Jacobite general. I am bound for Edinburgh in search of a French agent named Benoit Lebecque.'

'And what were you doing at the garrison in Glasgow?'

'Looking for information.'

'Dressed as a woman?'

I blushed. 'That was the only way I could escape.'

'You weren't very convincing, Charles.'

'Oh.' I was disappointed that my brilliant plan had been so easily rumbled.

'The moment you opened your mouth you betrayed yourself. Perhaps a less perceptive man would have been fooled. But then there were other things... The feeling of your mouth upon my prick. The scent of your arse. The slimness of your hips. I know what a boy feels like, Charlie. I know what it's like to fuck a boy.'

He climbed off me and, with his good hand, grasped my ankles and raised them in the air. I held myself behind the knees and spread my arse for him. With the stockings and garter belt, my nether parts were prettily framed. Captain Robert stood for a while in admiration, then dropped to his knees and got to work with his mouth. He licked my arse, sucked my balls, tickling me all the while with that great hog's moustache. He licked up and down the column of my prick and then swallowed it in one go, his whiskers mingling with my wiry red bush. He roughly kneaded my buttocks, which were itching like mad now that the hair was growing back, adding to the inferno that was igniting in my hole. I remembered what he'd said to 'Miss Charlotte' outside: 'I want nothing more than to see you naked and skewered on the end of my prick'. Well, he would get his wish.

The captain stood up and lifted my arse into position, tearing off my stockings as he did so; they hung in shreds from my ankles.

He hawked into his hand and slicked up his cock; my arse was already so juicy that I could have taken him dry. Then he was inside me. Holding on to the garter belt he pulled me towards him, and I slid all the way down his rock-hard cock. God, he was a good fuck! Rough and energetic, just as I like it, but concerned that I should enjoy the ride. He grasped my prick and pinched my tits; something about the sight of his injured arm in its white sling bandage against his dark, hairy chest excited me enormously. My dick was drizzling quantities of fluid over his fingers, which he plastered down the length of my shaft.

We were both close to coming when he pulled out and bent over a chair, offering me his arse. I had assumed that my great captain was strictly a one-way man, but no: it seemed that he wanted me to take as well as give.

'Come on, Charlie. Give me what that piss-eyed little English bastard couldn't do. I need a fuck, boy. That's an order!'

I knelt behind him and dived into his furry crevice with my tongue, licking the hair into whorls against each cheek. His hole was warm and salty; within moments I was tasting his insides. But the captain was impatient.

'Please, Charlie, give me your cock. I need it.'

I was happy to be playing the man again; my recent excursion into womanhood fuelled the fires of my lust, and I fucked Captain Robert as hard as he could wish. I took him over the chair, I had him face down on the floor, and I finished with him on his back, his legs wrapped round me and our mouths locked together as I filled his arse. The captain had come sometime during the fuck, without touching himself; I suppose that the friction between our stomachs had been enough to do the trick. When we parted, we were both coated with his sperm.

I helped the captain to wash, then we retired to bed; after the events of the night, we were both tired. We must have slept for a few hours; when I awoke, disturbed by a sound in the room, the sun was well over the zenith and was streaming straight through the west-facing window, casting a latticework of shadows on the wall opposite. I was certain that I had heard a click and a knock. Mindful of the captain's parlous position in Scotland (and indeed my own) I was wary of sabotage. But I heard nothing more, and turned to more interesting matters.

The captain was still asleep beside me. Throughout my sexual career, I have always been fascinated by the sleeping male. It is, I suppose, something to do with the combination of strength and vulnerability that excites me. Captain Robert, with his powerful body and his broken arm, looked particularly striking as he lay against the white sheets, his mouth slightly open, his good arm crooked behind his head so that the biceps swelled outwards in a casual display of force. I could not resist it; I carefully peeled the sheet back to reveal his great hairy torso, the dense bush at his groin, then pushed the sheet down over his legs until his full nakedness was revealed to me.

For a while I was content simply to gaze, but soon I wanted more. His cock was half erect; I hoped he was dreaming of me. Carefully, I moved down the bed and kissed it; it stirred and swelled a little. I kissed again, marvelling at the smoothness of the skin in contrast to the roughness of the hair all around. Then I opened my mouth and drew him inside; I love to feel a man grow to full hardness between my lips. Soon he had done just that, and I had woken him in the process; one lazy hand was running through my hair as I began to suck him in good earnest.

I was just picking up the pace to pleasure Captain Robert to the best of my mouth's ability, when again I heard a knocking from somewhere close at hand. The captain had heard it as well; he was up and alert in a trice, his wet hard cock swinging between his legs like a weapon. He motioned me to be silent, picked up his sword from the floor and leapt across the room. It all happened fast; he grabbed the door of the wardrobe, reached inside and within a split second had pulled forth the cowering figure of the porter, who sprawled on the floor at his sword's point.

'A spy! Die!'

'No sir, I beg you!' gibbered the porter. I realised then that his trousers were open at the fly and his cock, a monstrous fat thing, was hanging out.

'Say your prayers, scum,' hissed the captain, pressing the point of his sword into the porter's neck. The poor man closed his eyes in terror; I looked up and saw Captain Robert smile and wink at me.

'Tell me who sent you, spy!' he demanded, standing over the terrified man (who, I couldn't help noticing, sneaked a few glances at his captor's great prick despite the fact that a deadlier weapon was at his throat).

'Nobody... I... I came in to change your linen, sir... I didn't mean –'

'What?' roared the captain in mock fury. 'You lie!'

'No, sir! I swear on my mother's life!' The poor man was trembling; his prick had shrunk to the size of an acorn.

'Then what were you doing in the cupboard?'

'I came in and I saw the young... er... the young gentleman in bed with you and I was... surprised, sir.' Well he might be; when we had checked in, I was a young lady. 'And then when he awoke I was afraid, and I hid in the cupboard, and, and –'

'And spied on us!'

'Yes, sir. Sorry, sir.'

'And what did you see, dog?' Captain Robert was enjoying himself, I could tell.

'I don't know, sir... I saw the young... er... gentleman... touching you down there, sir...'

'You watched him sucking my prick, did you?'

'Yes sir.'

'And what did you think about that? Hmm? Tell me?'

'I thought it was strange, sir.'

'Never seen anything like it before, I suppose?'

'No sir.'

'But not so very disgusting, was it.'

'Sir?'

'Not so strange that it didn't make you want to wank, is that it?' The captain lifted the porter's shrivelled cock on the point of his sword.

'No, sir. Sorry, sir.' The poor man was terrified that he was about to lose his manhood; his persecutor was deftly playing with it with the blade's end, pushing it from side to side, lifting up the scrotum, running the tip of the sword down towards the porter's arse.

'We don't like spies, do we, Miss Charlotte?'

'No, Captain.'

'What do we do with them?'

'We punish them, Captain.'

'And how shall we punish this one, my dear? You must decide.' God, he was a cruel bastard; the poor man looked ready to shit his breeches. But I was enjoying the perversity of the game.

The porter was not a bad-looking creature – a little on the stocky side, as if he had spent too long sampling the delights of the kitchen, but handsome enough, with a slightly dim-witted expression. I remembered that his prick, although it was tiny now, had swollen to prodigious proportions when he had tumbled out of his hiding place.

'Well, Captain,' I said, as if making a serious judicial decision, 'I think the normal punishment under these conditions would be appropriate. Prisoner!'

The porter faced me, wide-eyed with fear.

'Sir!'

'On your knees!'

He lifted himself to a kneeling position. I clambered over the bed and stood before him.

'Drop your breeches!'

He did as I commanded, revealing a big, meaty arse. Captain Robert leaned against the mantelpiece, watching the performance with amused satisfaction, and gave our prisoner a stinging swipe across the cheeks with the flat of his sword. The porter stifled a cry.

'Open your mouth.'

He obeyed. I stepped towards him, my prick now completely hard. He looked at it with a mixture of terror and curiosity. His tongue trembled out of his mouth. I rested the head of my cock against it; it felt like a cushion.

'Now suck it.'

He gazed up at me in consternation.

'Come now, you saw what I was doing to the captain, didn't you, my peeping spy? That's all the instruction you need. Suck it.'

He tried his best, choking and gagging at first until tears ran out of the corners of his eyes. It was not particularly pleasant, but the novelty of the situation (and the sight of the captain playing with himself) kept me hard.

'Mind your teeth, prisoner!'

'Sorry, sir.' The porter made a concerted effort to improve the quality of his performance; perhaps he was genuinely afraid that his life would be forfeit if he didn't. Soon his lips were sliding up and down my prick to much greater effect.

'Well, Captain,' I said, 'he's taking to cocksucking quite satisfactorily. I think it's time for the next stage, don't you?'

'Whatever you say, Miss Charlotte.'

I pulled the porter off my cock (I was glad to see a look of disappointment on his face) and stepped back. 'On the bed!' I barked. He waddled towards the bed, hampered by the trousers round his ankles, and sat down. 'Now, prisoner, make yourself hard.'

'Sir?'

'Your cock. Make it hard.'

He frowned in concentration and set to work on himself,

pulling on his cock, coaxing it back into life. At first nothing happened, then he sighed, grunted and it began to swell. A little at first – then suddenly it ballooned. The captain and I stood slack-jawed in astonishment; neither of us, I think, had ever seen such a metamorphosis. Soon the porter was shyly holding a great bloated thing, looking sheepishly up at me for further instructions. I wanted nothing more than to shove the monster in my mouth, but I had to maintain the pretence of authority.

'Good. Now keep it that way.'

'Yes, sir.'

'Prisoner, have you ever been fucked?'

'Sir?' He clearly didn't understand what I was saying.

'Fucked, man. Do you know the meaning of the word?'

He made a crude gesture with his finger and closed fist, but looked confused. 'A man and a woman, sir?'

The captain laughed. 'Show him, Miss Charlotte!'

'Lie back and spread your legs in the air, prisoner.' He did as he was told. He had a nice, clean, pink arsehole. I spat on my fingers and rubbed them around his crack; his great prick twitched to an even greater size, and he looked surprised. I worked a finger in; he was shocked, but dared not complain. Another finger, and he grimaced with pain.

'Relax, prisoner. Here, let me help you.' I grasped the great organ that I had been longing to touch, and slowly wanked him. He sighed and closed his eyes, the muscles inside his hole loosening.

'That colt is broke for riding now, Miss Charlotte. I suggest you mount him.'

'Yes, Captain.' I had no particular desire to hurt the porter, but when I removed my fingers and replaced them with my cock he looked surprised by the pain. Again, I teased his prick until he was ready to take me, and pushed all the way in. The captain, eager to join the game, jumped on the bed and sat on the porter's face, commanding him to 'Lick my arse!'. The porter obliged, only to find his mouth plugged with the captain's cock. And so we rode him, watching each other breaching him at each end; I was glad to see that he remained erect throughout. Captain Robert pulled out and came all over the porter's face, while I shot a load up his arse.

We climbed off him.

'Shall we let the prisoner go now, Miss Charlotte?'

'Not quite yet, Captain. There's just one more thing.' I felt sorry for the poor man, who was writhing around on the bed like a cat on heat. I dived down and practically dislocated my jaw trying to get his prick into my mouth; finally I had to be content with just the first couple of inches, making a tunnel with my two hands down the shaft while the captain shoved three fingers up the man's arse. Thus employed, it took us no time to bring him relief.

Finally we allowed him to get up and dress; he kept glancing down at the captain's cock, half fearful, half eager that he would get hard again and commence another fucking.

'Tell nobody of this, or your life is worthless!' hissed the captain with full melodrama.

'No sir. I promise. Thank you, sir.'

'Now bring me a chamber pot. I need to piss.'

'Yes sir!' The porter dashed out into the corridor and returned a second later with the requisite article, which he placed on the table.

'Not there. Hold it.'

As the porter held the chamber pot at waist level, Captain Robert strode over and, never taking his eyes from the porter's, hoisted his prick into the pot and half filled it with piss, then stood nonchalantly shaking the drips off.

'Now for Miss Charlotte.'

The porter obediently shuffled over to me and held out the pot. I filled it to the brim and let my prick dip into the warm yellow fluid.

'Now go.'

'Yes, sir. Thank you, sir.' The porter, cradling the pot of piss, backed out of the room. We heard him slowly descending the stairs.

The captain threw back his head and laughed heartily.

'Well, Charlie, you're as debauched as I am, and that's a fact. Now we must make haste. Dress yourself from my trunk and we'll take fresh horses from the stables. And on the road, I'll tell you who I am and where I'm bound.'

Chapter Fourteen
St Leonard's Castle, Edinburgh
June 1751

My dearest Charles

This is the last letter you will receive from me – if, indeed, you have received any of the letters that narrated my sorry decline since that disastrous day when I was taken from your side.

I have found great strength and solace in my trouble from the certainty that you are safe and well, and from an inner peace that has come from certain fundamental truths that I have finally acknowledged about myself. My only regret is that I should have come to this too late. I pray that you will find happiness in your life, Charlie, and that you will remember one who loved you. Perhaps, if God wills it, I will have knowledge of you when I am on the other side.

I write this in what I believe to be the last hour of my life. I have no reason to think that it will ever find its way to you, although the guard has promised to smuggle it out of the castle. Ah well, I must believe that he is telling the truth, as it comforts me to make these communications. Surely, Charles, there is nothing in this world as important as love. It is easy to see that now that I face death; less easy in the pride and turmoil of a man's life.

Politics, allegiance, war, intelligence, rank – all of these are nothing compared to love.

My holiday at Leigh House continued for a month or so, and I sank into a satisfied stupor, thanks to Master Jonathan's expert attentions. Every once in a while he invited a soldier to join us in the study, commanding us both to fuck him, making the soldier suck me off while he watched, and so on. Occasionally he insisted on leaving the door to the chamber open so that we might be 'discovered'; he loved the sense of danger and transgression that accompanied our liaisons. I went along with him, fooling myself that there was nothing I could do about my position, but in truth intoxicated by the affair, lured into the boy's dangerous web of deceit.

Well, I have nobody to blame but myself. One day, Jonathan arrived in my room, accompanied on this occasion by not one but three soldiers. This was extravagant even for him, but they were handsome fellows and I was curious to see what he would force us to do. I was feeling the first tingling in my groin, when Jonathan stepped aside to make way for his father.

'There's the fellow, sir,' he said, pointing at me.

'So I see,' lisped the father, dressed on this occasion in a peculiar Turkish outfit. 'Get up, Lebecque.' His face was cold.

'Sir?'

'Do you confess to debauching my son?'

'Sir?'

'Don't play games with me, Lebecque. Is it true? That you have sodomised my child under my own roof, as a guest in my house?' Oh, I saw it all now. The injustice of his accusations made my blood boil: I was no more a 'guest' in that prison than I had 'debauched' his son. The soldiers, seeing my anger, put their hands on their swords.

I was silent.

'You, a priest, a man of God! Are you not ashamed to be caught in so disgusting a vice?' He was working himself into a mock fury – I suppose he needed to muster a show of anger in order to render his next move more convincing.

'I have no option but to hand you over to the Sheriff, Monsieur. I suppose you know what the punishment for such a disgusting crime is? Well, I need not spell it out...' Just as well, I thought: if all in Leigh House were punished according to the law, there would be a quick end to the family line. Still I held my tongue. This infuriated Leigh even more.

'Have you nothing to say? No excuse? No lies? Ah, I see, guilty as charged!'

'You have made your mind up, sir. There is no need for me to speak.' I looked at Jonathan as I spoke. His smooth, bland, smiling face betrayed no emotion. After all the times we had spent together, he was happy to hand me over to certain death.

'Take him away,' said the treacherous young man. 'He disgusts me.'

The soldiers dragged me to my feet; as we descended the stairs I could hear father and son shrieking at each other like fish wives. God knows what hateful coils had led to my betrayal; I understood now that Jonathan's sexual appetites had been nothing more than a trap to catch me. Just like the cowards at Fort William, they could not kill a priest – but a convicted sodomite was a different matter. Defrocked, discredited, nobody would oppose my death. That there were political motives behind my arrest and removal from Leigh House I have no doubt.

Strangely I have no bitterness towards Jonathan Leigh. His judgement will come in the next world, I suppose.

I was taken in a closed carriage across country, without food, for three days. Arriving at our destination, I saw from a few familiar landmarks that we were in Edinburgh. Then I was bundled inside the castle and have not seen the light of day since.

I was placed in a cell with two other souls, both of them imprisoned for the same 'crime' as myself. There was no talk of a trial. We were there to await death. We were not chained, at least; there was no escape from the cell, and we were under constant observation through the bars like animals at a zoo. There were always one or two guards outside, just to make sure that we didn't cheat the hangman by harming ourselves. There was little opportunity to talk; occasionally, when the guard slept, we enjoyed a few whispered conversations, from which I learned where I was and what my fate would be.

My two companions had been clerks in the King's service, working together on the land records that legitimised the shameful seizure of ancient lands from their rightful owners by the English crown. They were both lowland Scots, good, peaceable men who had taken the King's money to feed their families. They were friends since childhood, and had been lovers since their teens. They had been caught – betrayed, like me – by enemies within the corrupt administration. Accused, they had done nothing to defend themselves, eager to spare their families the shame of a scandal.

Steven, the more talkative of the two, was a slim youth of about 25 with abundant curly brown hair, an open, friendly face and, even in these horrific circumstances, a ready smile. Sam, his companion, was the same age, shorter and more muscular, with a cropped head and sideburns down to his chin. His eyes were the palest grey, with pupils like pinpricks; his jaw worked constantly, as if, beneath the silent exterior, there was fury within. They seldom spoke to each other; they sat, touching perhaps at the knee or the shoulder, in silent communion. I felt as if I was intruding.

I had been in the cell for twelve hours when we had our first opportunity to speak.

'My name's Steven,' whispered the curly-haired one. Sam was asleep with his head on his shoulder. I introduced myself and cautiously held out a hand, which was gripped warmly.

'You're like us.' It wasn't a question. They had been told of my arrival – and my crime.

'Yes.'

'We only have a few days now.'

'All of us?'

'Yes.' He actually smiled. And so, in fragmentary conversations over the next few days, I pieced together their story and learned something of my own fate. The gallows were to be built at the end of the week. It was a Sunday when I arrived. It is now Thursday night. We hang at dawn. False information has been released to the authorities, claiming that we are held awaiting trial next month; the trial, however, will never happen for the prisoners will be dead. Given the nature of our crimes, it is unlikely that any complaint will be made. And for the political puppeteers behind my incarceration, this is most eminently desirable. Word will never reach France, and I will rest in an anonymous grave far from home. My defeat is absolute.

Yesterday I asked Steven if he was content to die. He smiled sadly and grasped Sam's hand.

'I am content, sir, that we die together. If there was anything I could do to save Sam, I would do it, but there is nothing. I am only glad that he is not dying and leaving me alone. That I could not bear. At least we leave this world together, and go, I believe, to a better place.'

His simple faith touched me, and I thought of you. How lucky they were, these two who faced death with such composure; they knew that they were loved, and they were together as equals in the face of death. I, who have never told my love, who have never known what it is to have a love returned, die alone. I have tasted pleasure along the way, thank God; my body, at least, has known ecstasy. But my heart dies unfulfilled.

The priest visited us late yesterday evening, and mumbled a few platitudes. I begged him for pen and paper that I might write a confession; I flattered him enough that he conceded to my wishes. The guard took pity on me and agreed to deliver this letter on my behalf. Perhaps he was saying it only to make me feel better; ah well, it has worked. And so I write these last lines to you.

†

The evening wore on, and we were left alone for a while. Sam cradled Steven in his arms; occasionally they kissed. I saw a look of imprecation in Sam's eyes, and I understood; they wanted for one final time to be fully together, without the intrusion of a third party. I walked to the bars, and turned my back on them as they began to make love. The muted noises of their activity had the predictable effect on me, so when the guard returned to the cell I was able quickly to distract his attention by offering him my erect penis through the bars. My gamble paid off; instead of raising the alarm, he sank to his knees and started sucking. I kept him busy for long enough for Sam and Steven to finish; they lay in each other's arms as I shot my come into the guard's upturned face. He, perhaps, was conscious that this was my last chance for sexual pleasure, and he gave me the best that circumstances allowed, for which I thanked him.

I must now finish my letter and give it to the guard before it is too late. I can hear hammering from beyond the wall; I guess that the scaffold is being erected. Thank God, Sam and Steven are still asleep. Soon they will be at rest forever – together.

Charles, I have no time. I wish my life could have been otherwise. I love you more than man has ever loved.

Pray for me
BL

Chapter Fifteen

Captain Robert's command of the situation astonished me. We had been on the road barely a day before he had apprised himself of all the facts relating to Lebecque's whereabouts that I had been unable to discover in weeks of searching, although he had the good grace to tell me that my paltry little bit of information, gleaned from General Wilmott's confidential files, was the key to the whole mystery. He laughed long and loud when I told him (in detail) what I'd had to go through in order to get it, and promised me that we would stop for 'asparagus' at the very first opportunity.

And so I came under the tutelage of perhaps the most accomplished double agent in the history of these islands. Captain Robert – that is the name I knew him by, although not his real one, which he never revealed to me – was in the pay of both the English and the French governments, playing the one off against the other when it suited him, loyal at heart to the Stuart cause (as his tattoo suggested) and willing to risk everything in order to help one that he considered worthy of his support. One such was Lebecque. Robert had, indeed, been sent from France to discover Lebecque's whereabouts, although his brief had been information rather than rescue. As far as his French masters were concerned, Lebecque could live or die; they cared only that someone should continue to smuggle wealthy Jacobites out of Scotland that they might bring their money across the Channel. 'Ah, Charlie,' laughed Robert, 'there are no good men and bad men in this muddle. The French are as dishonest as the English, and, I'm glad to say, just as partial to a bit of cock up the arse.' I had no doubt that the good captain spoke from extensive experience on both sides of the water.

'But I'll say one thing, I've never met one yet who could match my appetites, with the honourable exception of your good self. Here's to you, Charlie Gordon, the best fuck in Christendom.'

We were riding in broad daylight along the great eastern road to Edinburgh. The captain was known to all the patrols along the way, and we passed by with nothing more than a wave and a friendly greeting. Outside Armadale we enjoyed a four-man military escort, having been warned by the young sergeant at the English garrison there (who 'fucked like a rabbit', according to Robert) that there were 'dangerous Jacobite bandits' abroad who would kill us if they could. 'Arse bandits, to boot,' muttered Robert in my ear; little did these good soldiers know that they were delivering the most dangerous of them all to safety.

Robert was in high good humour. He could not believe his luck in finding me along the way, and chuckled constantly over the coincidence of our shared interest in Lebecque. Riding by my side, he unveiled his plans: we would make our way to the outskirts of Edinburgh, raise a small force and storm the castle, rescuing Lebecque – who was to be held there indefinitely awaiting trial, according to 'impeccable sources'. Aloud, he boasted to the sergeant about his latest sexual conquests, how he had fucked a certain 'Miss Charlotte' who had 'squirmed around on the end of my cock like a stuck pig'. Poor sergeant; he would have loved to trade places with that fortunate young lady. He licked his lips and rode along in sullen silence.

Rid of our escort, we struck off south into the Pentland Hills where, said Robert, we would lie low and rally our forces. There was no hurry; Lebecque was in prison, uncomfortable perhaps, but in no immediate danger. We stopped at the Water of Leith to bathe in the cold, clear streams, where the captain painfully eased the dressings and splints from his wounded arm and decided that it was sufficiently healed to be put back into use. He chased me, naked, through the heather, brought me down in a flying tackle and fucked me under the open sky, both of us bellowing at the top of our lungs as we reached the climax, our only witnesses a startled capercaillie.

Late one Wednesday afternoon in early June we rode down into Penicuik, a few miles outside Edinburgh, where the captain commandeered quarters and announced that we were setting up in business as recruiting officers. As I undressed for bed, he conversed in whispers with a man on the stairs. 'No fucking tonight,' he ordered, as we climbed between the sheets. 'You'll need your energy for the morning.' He kissed me, and I fell asleep with the impression of his moustache still on my face.

†

Thursday morning dawned fair, and we made a hasty breakfast of coffee and rolls before descending to the main room of the house, a substantial parlour about twenty feet square. I was curious to know who the house belonged to, and how we could take it at such short notice; the captain answered all my questions with a smile.

'You really don't need to know, Charlie. I have a lot of friends.'

'So I see.'

'Now, to business. We have to rescue Lebecque, yes? But we cannot do it alone. St Leonard's is well guarded. A detachment of twenty men is stationed there. It is to our advantage that the castle is isolated beyond the town; the larger garrison could not be reached in less than fifteen minutes. That gives us, I suppose, ten minutes to storm the place, grab our man and quit the environs.'

'Then let's go!'

'No, Charlie. We need an army.'

'Oh, I see. And where are we going to get an army from? I suppose they're just going to walk in off the street, are they?'

The captain laughed, ruffled my hair and went to the door, beckoning me to follow him. There was a queue of men, perhaps some thirty or forty strong, waiting patiently outside.

'There, Charlie. There's your army. Come in, one and all.'

I watched in astonishment as the men filed into the room and seated themselves at Robert's bidding on the wood floor.

'Thank you for coming, gentlemen.' He used the term of address with a smile; they were anything but gentlemen. Labourers for the most part, I guessed; a rough, layabout lot, but young and strong. I guessed that, since the defeat of the Jacobite cause, there was no shortage of under-employed young Scots just itching for an opportunity to try their muscle against the English oppressor.

'As you may have heard, I am in the market for a few good men to help me with a little project that I have in hand in Edinburgh.' That explained the whispered conversation on the stairs; word had been sent around the area that Robert was raising an expeditionary force.

'This is not an ordinary assignment, gentlemen, and it will not be suitable for all of you. I am looking for what I might politely call special forces. My lieutenant here' (he indicated me) 'and I shall interview you during the course of the day and assess your suitability for the job. We shall be taking a force of twenty men tonight. I ask you all to hold yourselves in readiness, and I say to those of you who don't succeed – there will be other opportunities. You know me well, don't you lads?' There was a hearty cheer.

'Right, now, if you will give us five minutes and then come upstairs two at a time, please. We'll be as quick as we can.'

Robert took me by the arm and we raced upstairs. He was like an excited schoolboy.

'What exactly is going on?'

'I've got a plan, Charlie, oh, the most wonderful plan. And it's all thanks to you and your little masquerade.'

It sounded insane. We would lead the attack on St Leonard's Castle, a band of twenty men – all of us, bar the captain and I, dressed as women.

'Don't you see, Charlie? They'll not turn us away. You know what soldiers are like, my boy. You've fucked enough of them. Most will do anything for pussy. Well, pussy we shall give them, but not quite the sort they are expecting. They'll let us in, the "girls" will disarm them and then, at my signal – action! We take the castle, leave them to fight it out with the guards, take Lebecque and ride like the wind. Isn't it perfect?'

I thought it was stupid, and told him so.

'And you, great strategist, have a better plan, I trust?'

I held my tongue; of course he was right.

'Very well. Now, Charlie, we have a lot of work to do. I know these men. They're rough bastards, but they're keen to have a go at the English. Most of them would do anything – and I mean any-thing – to get the chance. So we've just got to weed out the ones who are too squeamish to go through with my brilliant plan –' he shot me a humorous look from beneath his black brows '– and the rest we'll send home to raid their wives' and mothers' wardrobes. Ah yes, Charlie!' He rubbed his hands. 'I shall march at the head of an army of queens!'

It was impossible to resist his enthusiasm, and so I stationed myself at a chair behind a table and waited for my first 'recruit'.

'Up you come, boys, first two please!' yelled the captain down the stairs. They appeared – brothers, I assumed, both dark-haired, both farmers from their clothes. Robert took one into the bed-room; the other stayed with me.

'Name?'

'Harvey.'

'Age?'

'Twenty-six, sir.'

I couldn't think what to ask him next. I hesitated a moment.

'Er... and are you sound in wind and limb, Harvey?'

'Yes, sir.'

'No broken bones?'

'No, sir.'

'No infectious diseases?' I was warming to my theme.

'No, sir.'

'If you wouldn't mind quickly slipping out of your clothes for me, Harvey.'

He didn't even raise an eyebrow; I suppose my impersonation of a military doctor was successful. He doffed his jacket, pulled his shirt over his head and started unbuckling his belt. My eyes took in a strong, sunburnt torso, a densely muscled stomach with a line of hair running down below his belt, which broadened out as he dropped his trousers into a neat bush of black hair. His cock, as he struggled out of his boots and socks, bounced heavily on a plump set of balls. He stood up, completely naked.

'Attention!'

He straightened his spine and brought his feet together, staring straight ahead of him. God knows what he thought I was doing. I improvised, walking around him, tapping his chest, feeling the muscles in his arms, looking in his ears.

'Open your mouth, Harvey.'

'Sir.'

His jaw dropped open and I looked inside, pretending to inspect his teeth. I ran a finger round the inside of his lip, feeling the heat and wetness within.

'Good. Now cough for me.' I pretended to listen to his chest as he coughed, pressing my ear to his smooth tight skin as I did so.

'And again.' This time I cupped his balls in one hand. He coughed, and they jumped in their sac. 'Spread your legs this time, Harvey.'

He placed his feet a yard apart and coughed again. I thought I detected a slight stirring in his cock.

'Now bend over. Got to make sure that you're all right up there.'

He braced himself against the desk and bowed, exposing one of the prettiest arses I have ever seen. I pushed and pressed against his hole.

'No piles, Harvey?'

'No, sir.'

'Are you sure about that, soldier? We can't be too careful, can we?'

'No, sir.'

'I'm going to have to give you a full inspection, I'm afraid.' He looked over his shoulder; I noticed to my delight that his face was crimson and his lips slightly swollen. His cock was no longer dangling inert between his thighs, but had started to stiffen.

I wet my index finger and worked it inside him, keeping up a pretence of checking him for haemorrhoids.

'Good. Ah, yes, hmm, good, that all seems fine. Just a moment, what this?' I had reached his prostate gland. 'There seems to be some kind of small bump here, Harvey. Can you feel that?' I pressed a little harder, and he grunted.

'Yes, sir, I can feel it.'

'How would you describe the feeling, Harvey?'

'Mmmf.'

'What? You'll have to be more precise than that, I'm afraid. Is it painful, or pleasurable?'

'Pleasurable, sir.'

'And what about that, Harvey?' I added another finger, and continued to bang his prostate.

'Yes, sir.' I kept my fingers inside him.

'Now stand up straight, Harvey.' His prick, fully erect, was a tasty piece. 'Any problems in front at all?'

'No, sir.'

'Skin moves back and forward all right?'

'Yes, sir.'

'It only seems to be pulled back halfway over your helmet, soldier. Show me that it goes back all the way.'

He grasped his cock in his hand and exposed his knob; it was a dark pink colour, flaring out obscenely at the ridge.

'Now move it back and forth for me, Harvey.'

'Sir.' He did as he was told.

'I didn't tell you to stop.'

'No, sir.'

And so he stood there and wanked himself off while I fucked him with my fingers from behind and kissed him on the neck. When he came it went all over the top sheet of paper on my desk.

'Thank you, soldier.' I threw the soiled paper in the bin, and made a fresh note of his name. 'Get dressed and report here at six o'clock.' He was beaming with delight, and even saluted me.

'Yes, sir! Thank you, sir!'

Just then the other soldier emerged from Robert's room looking similarly flushed and happy. The captain gave me a thumb's up from within.

'And Harvey!' I shouted.

'Sir?'

'Send the next two up!'

'Yes, sir!'

†

And so Robert and I worked our way through around three dozen men, most of whom were more than happy to go along with our depraved little plans. Those that weren't were easy to detect; they found reasons not to undress, they confessed to ailments that they clearly didn't have, then turned tail and fled. Only one of them turned violent on me, accusing me (quite rightly, I suppose) of being 'a dirty wee fucker'. The captain leapt from his room and sent him arse over tit down the stairs.

At six o'clock the chosen twenty reported once more to the hall, where Robert briefed them on the details of the mission. At first, of course, the idea of dressing as women was greeted with howls of derision, but one look from the captain was enough to quell them.

'You will do more than dress like tarts,' he went on, in a quiet tone more commanding than any bluster. 'You will behave accordingly. You will suck cock. You will get fucked up the arse, if needs be. Do you understand? You will do everything necessary to get those poor bastards at St Leonard's so worked up that they won't know which way they're standing. Are there any questions?'

There was a certain amount of muttering, a little lewd laughter, but no complaints.

'Very good. Now, you must all go home and get yourselves kitted out. I don't want you turning up here looking like Old Mrs Miggins who opens the pews in St Bride's. I want you to look nice. Understand?'

'Yes sir!'

'We march at midnight. We should arrive at dawn. That means we have time for one final... briefing. Charlie!'

I didn't know what he was talking about.

'Yes, Captain?'

'I want to be sure that these men are all as good as they say they are. We don't want any lousy fucks in our troop, do we?'

'No, Captain.'

'Right, men. Stand in line. Charlie: take your clothes off.'

I obliged.

'Now come and sit on my lap.'

I did so. I was completely naked; the captain played with my tits and made me spread my legs.

'This, men, is the greatest fuck in the whole of Scotland, possibly in the whole of the British Isles. This is the standard to which you aspire. I want there to be no doubt in your minds about the kind of enthusiasm you bring to this mission. And so, gentlemen, if you would like to prepare yourselves, you will all get a chance to fuck Charlie up the arse.'

It was my own fault; I had complained to the captain earlier that during all the fun and games of the recruitment interview, I had not had a chance to come. Now, I saw, he was paying me back in spades.

The captain leaned back in the chair and slipped a hand round the back of each of my thighs, hoisting my legs in the air so that my bum was exposed. My cock, of course, was pulsing with excitement as I watched the new recruits pulling down their pants.

'Come on, then,' said the captain, 'who's first?'

'Me, sir!' A great brawny blond, with curly hair and a pug nose, lined himself up and gently pushed into my arse. I grunted and shuffled around on the captain's lap until I was comfortable, and the blond giant started to fuck me in earnest. My hand had crept to my cock, but it occurred to me that it would be a good idea to postpone my orgasm for as long as possible; I had an awful lot of fucking to endure.

After five minutes, the blond groaned and shot up my arse; his cock was quickly replaced by another, and another. Those that had finished wiped themselves and left; the others stood around watching and wanking. Finally there was only Harvey left. He was a handsome bastard; I'd been watching him throughout the last hour, looking forward to his turn.

'If you don't mind, Harvey, I'd like to join you,' said the captain, setting me on my feet for a moment while he pulled his own cock out and slid it up my arse, which was now so slippery with come that it gave easy access. I sat down on Robert's prick and leaned back as far as I could. Harvey could not believe what he was seeing.

'Go on, man,' I panted, 'stick it in me.'

'Anything you say.'

He pressed the head of his cock along the underside of the captain's, and soon they were both inside me. I thought I would split open. They synchronised their thrusts and started to work on me. It didn't take long; I can only assume that the heat of each other's pricks sliding together added to the intensity for them. The captain came first, and jammed himself tight inside me; soon Harvey was adding his own load. I finally allowed myself to grasp my cock and, as both men watched, milked out a huge load that splattered all three of us as the chair collapsed beneath our combined weight.

ƒ

At midnight we assembled in the town square, as strange an army as Scotland has ever seen. The boys had gone about the project with a good deal of enthusiasm ('We've your arse to thank for that, Charlie!' said the captain) and had decked themselves out in the most sluttish costumes they could find. Some of the younger ones could pass muster as women, just about; the older ones would only fool the most demented. Fortunately, they had made inventive use of shawls and gloves to conceal the more obvious signs of their true gender. In each pair of hands there dangled a pair of dainty women's shoes; for now, they were shod in their working boots for the march on Edinburgh.

We set off in high good humour, the captain leading a hearty chorus of Loch Lomond as we rode at the head of our troops. I began to believe that the scheme might work.

By two o'clock, we were silent, trudging through the freezing air as Edinburgh loomed in the distance. Another hour brought us within striking distance. We skirted the town to the south and made our way to the lonely crags of Holyrood Park, from which vantage point we could see the walls of St Leonard's Castle in the first glimmerings of the early summer dawn. Now there was no more laughter or play; with all seriousness, the men sat down on the grass and struggled into their women's shoes, trying them out with short runs up and down the rocks, modifying them by breaking off a heel here, ripping open a toe there. The captain called them to attention and began his final inspection.

There was a weird solemnity about the affair. Last night I thought Robert was insane. I had gone along with his scheme, happy to have each and every one of the soldiers empty his balls up my arse, but scarcely believing that this ridiculous escapade could truly lead me to Lebecque. Now, however, there seemed a real possibility of success. The captain was a fine orator.

'It's a simple job, men, but it must be done properly. Surprise is everything. They will not be expecting us. You must convince them that you are tired, fragile little things who have been cruelly persecuted by Jacobite bandits on the road.' I looked down the line; a less fragile group it would be hard to imagine. I prayed that it was dark in the castle gate.

'You know my signal?' The captain pulled from his pocket a small silver whistle. 'Two long blasts means attack. Short-long-short means retreat. There is no other option.'

The men nodded and stamped in the cold.

'Very well, then. Follow me! For Scotland!' He winked at me, and we rode on. We tethered the horses at Canongate and proceeded to St Leonard's Castle on foot. Dawn was breaking; the sky in the east was already tinged with pink.

St Leonard's Castle was an ugly hulk of a building, fenced around with tall spiked iron railings, its massive studded doors guarded by two soldiers with bayonets. We ran down the last hundred yards of the street; the guards were instantly on the alert.

'Oh for God's sake, boys, help us!' stammered Captain Robert in a voice quite unlike his own, an effete English accent. 'We've been attacked! Those cursed brigands have taken some of my poor, poor girls!'

The surviving 'girls' came limping up to the gate in a convincing display of wretchedness; the prettier ones had been pushed to the front, and looked imploringly at the soldiers.

'Your papers, ladies,' asked one of the guards querulously. He could not have been much older than me.

'For pity's sake, man, we're desperate! They killed poor Susie...' He feigned a sob, which was echoed by a shrill moaning from somewhere within our ranks.

'We'd better let them in,' said the other soldier, looking around in terror for the brigands he believed were on our tail.

'Please, for the love of mercy,' begged Robert, and the gate was unbarred. The temptation to charge was overwhelming, but instead we limped into the courtyard.

'Can you give these poor young virgins warmth and shelter? Do you have men who can help to tend them? They're very frightened, gentlemen, and they need comfort. The poor young maidens. Look at them. So soft, so helpless.'

The soldiers were whispering to each other, and at length beckoned the 'girls' through to the kitchens. Our plan, to my astonishment, was working.

The 'girls' displayed themselves in various attitudes of grief and terror as, one by one, more soldiers filtered into the room, roused from their slumbers by the rumour that there were women in the castle. Robert and I, feigning exhaustion in the corner, counted heads. When there were twenty in the gloomy room, and they were occupied in tending to the poor, fragile young ladies, we slipped back into the courtyard.

None of the other doors was unlocked, so, like a couple of monkeys, we scaled a drainpipe and clambered across the slate roof of what I assumed were the sleeping quarters. Robert, weaker than I with his injured arm, slipped and dislodged a tile, which broke with a crash on the cobbles below. Nobody came out to investigate; I could only assume that the soldiers were busy getting their cocks sucked.

We reached the highest roof within the castle walls just as the sun came over the battlements and gleamed back off the chapel spire. There were windows in the side of the chapel, unprotected by bars. That would be our point of entry.

We were just scrambling over the last furlong when, from a small courtyard far below us, came a sound that froze my blood. A long, low roll on the drum. Silence, then again, the long roll. Robert was poised like a cat. We hauled ourselves up to the top of the roof and looked down.

There, in the gloom below us, was a group of perhaps six soldiers. Six soldiers! Our information was wrong! We had not tricked them all into abandoning their posts. Where had these new forces come from? I glared at Robert, who signalled silence, and pointed.

A crude timber construction stood in the yard: a platform, perhaps three feet high and three feet wide, from which sprouted a long upright beam and a crossbar. A gallows. The hangman was adjusting the rope round the neck of a pale, gaunt figure.

Lebecque.

The drums rolled again. A priest stepped on to the platform, thumbed through a greasy black book, muttered something and clambered down. Standing at the foot of the gallows, the soldiers held two more captives bound and ready for the noose.

The light was increasing rapidly now; a sunbeam caught the chapel window and reflected on to Lebecque's face. I saw his lips moving in prayer, his eyes wincing in the light as he looked up to heaven and straight into my face, thirty feet above him.

He blinked, bowed his head, then looked up again. I suppose he must have thought he was seeing things.

The drum beat again, no longer the slow roll but now a steady, remorseless march as the hangman tightened the noose around Lebecque's throat. I looked up at Robert, who had the whistle poised at his mouth. But if he blew – and the soldiers attacked – we would still surely be too late. The hand that would push

Lebecque to his death was already on his shoulder.

And so this was their justice: murdered in secret, under a cloak of sham religion, without the benefit of a trial and with no friends to speak for him.

I don't remember hatching any particular plan, but before Robert could hold me back I hoisted my legs over the apex of the roof and slid down the slates into thin air, just as Lebecque was pushed off the platform. God's hand must have been upon me, for I landed with a crash against the beam of the gallows and knocked the whole shoddy assembly flying. Somehow I avoided dashing my brains on the cobbles, and landed instead on top of a *mêlée* of soldiers. The wind was knocked out of my body, and I had just the time to see Lebecque struggling with the cord around his neck, and to hear two loud blasts of the whistle above me, before I lost consciousness.

When I came to, what I thought was only a couple of seconds later, pandemonium had broken loose around me. There was blood on the cobbles in front of me; blood from my own nose, I soon discovered. I raised my head and looked straight into the open staring eyes of a dead soldier. A flurry of petticoats passed across my head as a woman – ah! one of our girls! – jumped over me in pursuit of a man in uniform. Captain Robert stood on the scaffold belabouring all and sundry with his sword; two or three lay dead at his feet. Everywhere I looked, there were mad Bacchantes brandishing daggers, swords and planks of wood, wreaking deadly havoc among the terrified men of the castle. The fat priest sat under the gallows clutching his prayer book. I could not see Lebecque.

Yes: there he was, kneeling over the bleeding form of a young man with long, curly dark hair. I dragged myself to his side and grasped his arm. He turned and saw me at last.

'God in heaven. Charlie. It is you.'

I descended into darkness again as the chaos surged around me.

†

I came to my senses in the back of a covered cart, lying on my back and conscious of a terrible pain in my leg. A cool hand was on my forehead; my head was resting on something firm and warm which, I discovered, was somebody's lap. I opened my eyes, but found it hard to focus.

'Lebecque?'

The hand smoothed my brow again, and a voice I knew well came from somewhere above me.

'Yes, Charlie, I'm here.'

Again I fell into sleep, or unconsciousness, and awoke once more with the gentle hand stroking my hair, the warmth of another body next to mine. I felt better; my leg still hurt like hell, but I knew I would survive. I tried to raise myself.

'No, Charlie, you mustn't move.'

'I must see you, Lebecque.'

Strong arms raised me a little, and I looked up into those dark, hooded eyes, saw again the dark hair falling over the pale forehead. I buried my face in his chest.

'Thank God. Thank God.'

He bent down and kissed me gently on the mouth.

'Where are we?'

'Bound for the north, Charlie.'

'Captain Robert?'

'He's gone.'

'With his army?'

I heard the smile in Lebecque's voice. 'Yes. God help Scotland.'

'Who's driving?'

'Sam. A friend.' He pointed to another body lying on a few sacks beside us. 'Steven is badly hurt. We're going to find help.'

'And then?'

'And then home, Charlie. Home.'

Chapter Sixteen

The rest of my story is swiftly told.

Lebecque and I left our friends at Stirling and took horse for the Highlands. We were shy together for the first few days; I was ashamed of myself, to tell the truth, ashamed of the heinous amounts of time I had wasted on my journey, a delay which very nearly cost Lebecque his life. I agonised over each foolish adventure, each needless dalliance. I rebuked myself for a shameful lack of purpose and manly resolve. God, if we had lingered just one more day, one more hour, one more minute, Lebecque would be dead.

Lebecque, for his part, was full of praise for my bravery in leading the attack on the castle and rhapsodised over his feelings when he first looked up and saw my face peering over the rooftops. Then he checked himself and became strangely silent, more like the Lebecque I had known at Gordon Hall long, long ago. I began to wonder, as we rode together over the rough country around Strathyre, whether all my efforts had been worthwhile. What was the relationship between us now? Would we return to Gordon Hall only to say farewell? Or would Lebecque return to his sullen, secretive ways, resuming his profession of spy and false priest? I could hardly bare to think about it.

One night, however, as we were camping under the trees and

stars after a two days' ride, we started to talk. Lebecque asked me
if I had received any of his letters. Only one, I replied, which had
sent me out on my quest. None since? None. He was silent for a
while.

'I wrote to you many times, Charlie.'

'How?'

'I found... means.'

'What happened to the letters?'

'I don't know. Perhaps they were never delivered.'

'Perhaps they're waiting for me at Gordon Hall.'

'Yes. Maybe.' He drifted off, scowling at the tiny fire we'd built.

'Charlie.'

'Yes?'

'I said many things in those letters. Things which, perhaps, I
should not have said.'

'Such as?'

'I committed many shameful acts.'

'Oh, well...' I was hardly in a position to take the moral high
ground. 'I forgive you.'

'But it was not so much my actions that those letters described,
as my thoughts. And my feelings.'

There was something about the tone of this voice that persuaded me to keep quiet. I nodded and shifted a little closer to the
fire; closer to him.

Lebecque seemed to be struggling to find words.

'Charlie, would you describe me as an honest man?'

'A good man, certainly.'

'But honest? Open and forthright?'

'No, I suppose not. I knew you under strange circumstances,
remember.'

'Yes. I could use that as an excuse. I had to dissemble my true
feelings, my true self, for the good of the cause that I served. That
is behind me now.'

'Indeed.'

'Yes. I am no longer in the service of any government, or any cause. I am a free agent. And as such, I have no loyalty except to myself... and to those I love.'

I was no longer an innocent. I knew that his words preceded some kind of declaration.

'I realised this during my last days...'

'What, Lebecque?'

'That love is all that matters.'

'Yes.'

'Charlie, do you remember when we were at Gordon Hall, when I first arrived? When you were so angry with me?'

'Yes.'

'I had sent away your friend Alexander, hadn't I?'

'That's right.'

'Did you... love him, Charlie?'

'Love him? A little. I was fond of him. I enjoyed his... company.'

'I see. But love?'

'I suppose not.'

'Why was that?'

'Because I was too young to know what it meant.'

'I see.' Lebecque pondered a while. 'Not because... he was a man?'

At last I saw what the conversation was driving at. Poor Lebecque; for all he knew I could be betrothed to some local girl by now, having put behind me the follies of my youth.

'Not because he was a man, no. *Au contraire.*' I smiled, desperate to introduce a note of levity into this serious conversation.

'Could you, do you think, Charlie, ever...'

I was beginning to lose patience. 'Love a man, Lebecque? Is that what you're driving at?'

He scrutinised my face for any sign of disgust. 'Yes.'

Words! I had had enough of them. Instead I leaned over, slipped a hand round the back of his neck and kissed him on the mouth.

'Does that answer your question, Monsieur Lebecque?'

He stared at me in disbelief.

'Don't look so solemn, Lebecque!'

'I cannot believe it.'

'Why do you think I chased across Scotland to find you? Why do you think I'm sitting here with my arm around you? I love you, Lebecque. I think I always have.' Perhaps that was not quite true, but in the heat of the moment it made sense. I had always desired him, certainly, and I had come to admire him. Now, after all my experiences, it seemed to me that there was no man that I wanted other than Benoit Lebecque.

This time he initiated the kiss, and I have never known one like it. Not just the kiss of two men who are about to fuck (although it was that as well). This one came from the soul.

Gradually we entwined ourselves until we were lying on the ground. It was hard and lumpy, and not a little damp, but to me it felt like the most luxurious feather bed. The conviction was growing that this was the moment towards which all my adventures had tended – that it was in the arms of this man that I belonged.

I could tell that Lebecque was aroused; his cock was pressing into my thigh. But he seemed diffident about making the next move. I could see his point; I suppose he was still worried, somehow, that he was abusing his position as tutor. Poor man! He had been shut up in a prison cell while I had been fucking my way round the British Isles. Oh well: as usual, I would have to play the slut.

I broke from the kiss and started unfastening his shirt. Lebecque lay back and closed his eyes, perhaps from shame. His chest was hard and dark, with a light covering of hair that was thicker in the centre, where the mounds of muscles curved in towards his breastbone. His stomach was ridged and rock hard, and heaving more than usual. I kissed Lebecque on the throat, then on the chest, I ran my tongue round each of his nipples and buried my face in his armpits. When I looked up he had his eyes open and was looking straight at me with a smile on my face; at last he had realised that I was not some virginal little soul who would be scared off by the merest whiff of sex. God, if only he knew... I was more concerned about alarming him with my evident experience. I don't imagine many young men of twenty, at least from my sheltered background, had racked up as many sexual conquests as I had.

Now Lebecque took an active part in our lovemaking. He practically tore the shirt off my back, and his eyes shone with delight when he saw my body.

'God, Charlie,' he said, 'you've grown into a fine, strong young man.' He placed a hand on my stomach, feeling every contour. It felt good, but I was becoming impatient, and so undid my trousers to expose my red pubic hair. Lebecque needed no prompting; his hand dived in and started rummaging around in my groin. Soon his fingers made contact with my cock which, as the reader must have assumed by now, was as solid as a rock. The look of surprise and delight on his face as he wrapped his hand round it will stay with me for a long time.

For a minute he was content to play with it inside my clothes, but gradually lust was getting the better of him, and he hauled it out into the open air. Of course, Lebecque had only ever seen this part of my anatomy when it was shrivelled by the cold waters of Loch Linnhe during our summer dips; he was clearly astonished by how much it had grown. He gripped it and wanked me gently, accustoming himself to the feel of a hard cock in his hand. I could see him licking his lips, and it didn't take a mindreader to know what he was thinking. I gave him permission.

'Suck me.'

As far as I knew he had never actually done the deed before, but he must have had a natural talent. He swallowed me whole, and I felt my head breaching his throat. He neither gagged nor choked, but carried on caressing me in great long strokes, while his hands explored my balls and my bum. Then he let me go and continued licking every inch of my shaft.

Now, however, I wanted to get my hands on what I had only ever seen through a window before. While Lebecque busied himself with my cock, I shifted round and undid his trousers, pulling them down to his knees so that he was naked from the neck down. His cock was stiff and dark, throbbing in its nest of black hair. I repositioned myself and took the head between my lips. I could not see his face, of course, but I assumed from the grunts and the increased vigour with which he played with my cock that he was happy with the arrangement. We carried on with this game until, to the astonishment of both, we came simultaneously in each other's mouths. I scarcely knew where Lebecque ended and I began. I had never known such a sensation of bonding with another.

Neither of us had had enough. Lebecque seemed possessed by a devil of desire, and pinned me to the ground, calling out my name again and again, kissing me wildly on the mouth as if he was afraid that I would disappear.

'It's all right, Lebecque. I'm here. I will never leave you again.'

He was hard once more, and I knew exactly where I wanted him to put it. I whispered in his ear.

'Would you... fuck me?'

He looked down at me with such tenderness and concern; perhaps he believed that he was really going to take my virginity. I didn't care to disabuse him; it pleased me to play the role, and besides, I really felt that this was the first time again. To my astonishment, I felt slightly shy – me, who had spread my legs for anyone with a handsome mug and a ready prick, who had enjoyed entire garrisons up my arse, sometimes two at a time.

'Yes, Charlie.'

Gently, he picked my knees up from the hard ground and surveyed my arse by the firelight. The stubble was still growing back, and it looked unusually gold, I suppose. He was lost in admiration – which soon had me stiff again.

We did not speak again that night; finally, we had gone beyond the fumbling of words, and let our bodies express our feelings. Lebecque spat into his hand and wet his prick, then guided himself slowly into me. It took the best part of five minutes before he was fully inside, and then he stayed still, allowing me to get used to the feeling. For once, I reined in my appetites and enjoyed the moment, rather than hastening on to the next.

Then he began a slow rocking movement within me, which soon developed into a cruder in-out, in-out. Before long he was pistoning into me, supporting himself on his toes and elbows and using his cock as a fulcrum. When he came, he stared straight into my eyes.

†

For the rest of the journey we enjoyed ourselves. Occasionally we spoke of our feelings, but mostly we revelled in the novel sensation of not having a care in the world. Nobody knew where we were, we had no responsibilities, and we were in no hurry to assume any. We sat outdoors during the long June evenings and watched the sun set over the first of the lochs. We dined at taverns and inns, and occasionally raided the last of my gold to pay for a room. By the time we had neared Fort William, my name alone was enough to ensure credit and welcome in any of the houses along the road.

And of course we fucked. We fucked in every conceivable

position, in every place, outdoors, indoors, in public, in desolate stretches of countryside. Lebecque fucked me; I fucked Lebecque. We did everything that I had ever done before, and more. None of my suggestions disgusted him; rather, they delighted him. As our animal passions became wilder, Lebecque himself revealed a side of his character that I could scarcely believe existed: playful, humorous, considerate, relaxed. Perhaps this was the young man who had been hidden so long beneath the black robes of office.

The holiday had to end. I felt exhilarated and sick when we crossed the bridge at Ballachulish and re-entered the familiar homelands. Nothing had changed. There were the same old trees of the forest, the burns and rocks that I had known all my life but which I saw, now, through the eyes of a man. How beautiful they were! Once I had thought of my home as a prison. Now, returning at last, I felt that it was where I belonged. I turned to Lebecque, who was smiling like a man who has entered the promised land.

Less happy was our arrival at Gordon Hall. The park gates, which had always been carefully leaded and oiled, were dingy and interwoven with climbing weeds. Dead leaves had blown into the porter's lodge. The gates were chained.

Of course, I knew every entrance to the estate, and so we rode on a little further until we found a gap in the fence, where we tethered the horses and continued on foot. It was about six o'clock in the evening; the sun was low in the sky.

Everywhere I looked were signs of decay and neglect. The house itself seemed dead; the shutters were up at the windows, there was no sign of light or life anywhere. But it was still standing, and it looked, somehow, safe. Somebody, I realised, must have shut it up properly after my sudden departure.

We walked round the outside of the building, unwilling to enter. I felt strange, like a burglar in my own home. I had no idea what had happened here – or if, indeed, I still belonged.

Someone in the village would be able to tell us what was going on, and so we strolled over the lawns, past the beach, past the coppice and towards the stables. We would have carried on to the village, but Lebecque suddenly stopped and pointed.

There was a horse in the yard.

It was Starlight.

I wanted to scream with joy, but Lebecque put a finger to his lips and we walked stealthily on towards the buildings. Starlight snuffled and stamped a hoof – recognising his old jockey, I suppose. Lebecque beckoned me on to the side of the stable, to the shed where, in more prosperous times, we had kept all the tackle and parked the little pony carts that I had ridden as a child. We peered in through the window; a candle was burning.

At first I could see very little, half blind as I was from the brilliant setting sun. Then, as I grew accustomed to the gloom within the shed, I noticed movement. I screwed up my eyes and tried to focus. Something looked familiar.

Yes: undoubtedly. It was Alexander's naked arse pumping up and down, as I had seen it so many times in the past. He had his back to the window, and was concentrating on giving some lucky soul a good fucking. From the hair on the legs that were wrapped round his waist, I could tell that it was a young, blond man.

Lebecque joined me at the window to spy on the show. I could make out more and more: Alexander's heavy balls banging against a smooth firm arse, and occasional glimpses of his thick cock disappearing into a stretched hole. We could hear occasional grunts and endearments; this was not, it seemed, a casual fuck. Lebecque stuck a hand down the back of my trousers and started fingering me in time to Alexander's fucking.

At length, the two lovers finished, Alexander clambered off his mount and allowed me to get a good look. He was a handsome young man, about my age; I dimly recognised him as one of the village boys, a beautiful youth who had played the organ at the church on Sundays and occasionally sang the psalm. I had often wondered if he was inclined towards men; here was my answer.

Both of them were lying on a thin mattress on the ground, their eyes closed, perhaps dozing. I allowed myself to look around the shed, and saw that a makeshift home had been made: a few sticks of furniture from the servants' quarters at the big house, a fire laid in a newly opened grate, a couple of rabbits skinned and hanging up ready for the pot. Typical Alexander: he could make the best out of the slenderest means. I looked back at him, lying there with one arm around his friend, the other crooked behind his head. How beautiful he was, my first lover!

I suppose Lebecque must have read my thoughts, for he backed away from the window a little. I grabbed him by the shoulder, unwilling that he should entertain even for a moment the idea that I wanted anyone but him. I kissed him, grabbed his crotch and wrestled him to the ground.

I suppose we must have made a noise, for suddenly the door of the shed crashed open and there stood Alexander with a bloody knife in his hand – the knife he had used to skin the rabbits, I suppose.

'Who's there... My Lord! Charlie!'

I broke away from Lebecque's embrace and stood up. Alexander was grinning from ear to ear.

'Alexander.'

'Charlie! At last!' Naked as he was, and still sticky with his lover's sperm, he threw his arms around me, held me by the shoulders and looked at me.

'I thought you must surely be dead. I've waited month after month for news. Where the hell have you been?'

'It's a long story. I'm glad to see you well, Alexander.'

He saw me staring at his body, and suddenly remembered that he was naked.

'Excuse me, gentlemen!' He grabbed a cloth and attempted to

wrap it round his waist; it only emphasised his nakedness. Lebecque stood up and held out his hand.

'Alexander. I am Benoit Lebecque.' Alexander scowled. 'You have good reason to hate me, I suppose. I apologise for any harm I did you, or your family, in the past.'

Alexander, too manly to hold grudges, took the offered hand and shook it. The blond boy had got up from the bed and was standing beside him with an arm on his shoulder. His cock dangled against Alexander's arse. They made a very pretty pair.

'Who's your friend, Alex?'

'Excuse me! Gentlemen, this is William Bruce. Billy: may I introduce Mr Charles Gordon, and Monsieur Lebecque.'

We all shook hands.

'I see you've made yourself at home, Alex. Don't apologise. I'm glad. I assume it's you we have to thank for looking after the house in my absence.'

'Yes, Charlie. I came back when the soldiers had gone, and found the place in a terrible state. The doors had been left open, the house was filthy, there were a couple of tramps living in the hall, not to mention colonies of mice and rats. I cleaned it up to the best of my ability, but I needed some help. And that's how I got to know Billy.'

'I see. You could have slept in the house, you know. There's everything you need there.'

'Oh no, Charlie. I tried that once before, if you remember. It didn't do me much good. Now you're back, we'll be on our way.'

'What are you talking about, Alex?'

'I need to make a living.'

'Alex, your place is here.'

'Sir?'

'Don't call me sir! You're part of the family, as far as I'm concerned. You and Billy can stay here, if you wish, or move into the house, or whatever you want. Will you stay?'

'Yes, Charlie! I have dreamed for a long time of building a little house with my own hands.'

'So be it. And now, Monsieur Lebecque and I will open up the big house.'

'Will you join us for supper, gentlemen?' asked Billy.

'With pleasure.'

'Come back in two hours.'

'Thank you.'

'Just one thing, Charlie,' said Alexander, reaching underneath the mattress (his cloth, when he kneeled, exposed his arse most delightfully). 'These came for you. I've not opened them. They may be important.'

He handed me a batch of letters, most of them scrawled on filthy paper, carefully tied up with a piece of twine.

'What are they?'

'I don't know.'

I turned them over; the hand was familiar. Of course: Lebecque's letters. I looked to him, but he was already striding back to the house.

Epilogue:
Christmas Eve 1752

And so I discovered that Lebecque, far from being the chaste soul that I had imagined him, had experienced things during the time of his captivity that matched my own picaresque debauches.

At first he was ashamed and angry, and tried to snatch the letters from me and throw them into the fire. But I resisted, ran up to my old room and barred the door. After a while he gave up his knocking and retired to sulk in the old office.

I left him in no doubt as to my reaction upon completing my reading of his dispatches. His sexual confessions had ignited the fires of my lust to an unbearable pitch; his professions of love had moved me to tears. We spent the next hour fucking each other with a fierceness that was almost frightening in its intensity.

Our lives at Gordon Hall were pleasant after that. My mother, I found, had retired permanently to Rum, wishing never to set foot on the mainland again. She was surprised to discover that Monsieur Lebecque had returned to the house, but asked no questions about the nature of our lives there.

Alexander and Billy built their house on the edge of the coppice, and live there as our chief steward and housekeeper, respectively. We dine together most nights, we swim naked in the Loch in the summer and occasionally we raise a little hell together.

Mostly, however, we stay happily in our chosen pairings.

MacFarlane, that ghost of the past, lurks around the grounds still, lending a hand when needed, attempting to spy through windows and keyholes if he thinks he'll catch someone in action. He is not often disappointed. He does nobody any harm. I have forgiven him his betrayal of Benoit and so, I think, has Benoit himself – although he remains silent on the subject.

Lebecque and I go from strength to strength; I love him now as much as I believe he loves me. For a long time I have concealed from him the nature of the adventures I had on the road, until his questions became too much to bear and I decided to end his nagging once and for all by writing out my confession for him to read. I can only assume that this confession, which I will give to him tomorrow morning, will continue to keep the home fires burning through the long winter nights ahead.